The Thief who Sang Storms

SOPHIE ANDERSON

ILLUSTRATED BY JOANNA LISOWIEC

USBORNE

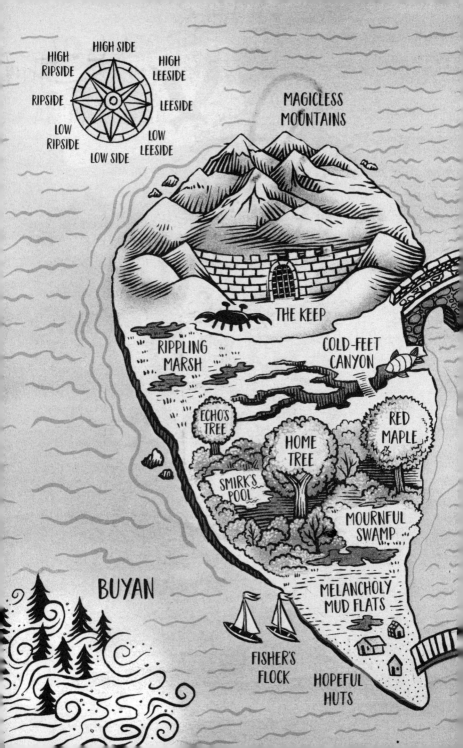

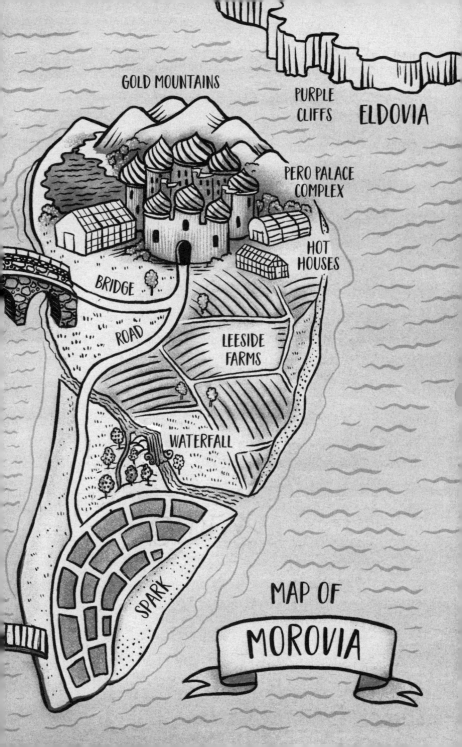

PROLOGUE

The Island of Morovia is shaped like a broken heart. The humans live on the calmer lee side of the island, and the alkonosts – the bird-people – live on the stormier rip side. But it wasn't always this way.

Until three years ago, alkonosts and humans lived together, all over Morovia. My parents and I had a home in Spark – the lee-side town by the shifting, sparkling sea. We loved sitting on our balcony, gazing at the soft sands and salted waves. The view was ever-changing, because our island, Morovia, is one of the Three Floating Islands. Morovia, Eldovia and Buyan all drift across the world's oceans, moving towards and away from each other, and the Fixed Land, in an endlessly varied dance.

Sometimes Eldovia would drift so close to us that we could spot seabirds wheeling around nests on the purple cliffs. Buyan always floated further away, hidden in the mist that clings to it, but occasionally the mist would thin and we'd get tantalizing glimpses of something golden, glistening. We loved searching for new sights and imagining what might lie on the other Floating Islands and the Fixed Land, but we never talked of leaving to find out, because we were happy on Morovia.

My mother sang every day on our balcony, her voice high and bright as the moon, and her wings would open, blue as the sea and yellow as sunshine... My family are alkonosts, which means we're descended from the ancient bird-people of our island.

Most alkonosts look similar to humans, although we're smaller and lighter, and have feathers, while humans have hair. Only a few of us have bird features as prominent as my mother's – whose arms were so covered with long blue and yellow feathers that when she held them outstretched they became wings.

The biggest difference between alkonosts and humans though, and the one that has led to all the trouble on Morovia, is something that can't be seen.

Nearly all alkonosts, by the time we're ten years old, develop the ability to sing magic. There are many kinds of singing magic. I know alkonosts whose songs can make flowers bloom, flames burn brighter, or lightning strike the ground. And there are legends of ancient alkonosts who could change the shape of mountains and the course of rivers, and communicate with the island itself.

My father, Nightingale, can mesmerize people with his magic, and my mother could call butterflies with her songs. I remember them fluttering down to land on her feathers as she folded her wings around me, soft and warm as a summer's day.

It was a summer's day, three years ago, when the ship *Joy* sank. The sea was calm and the sky was clear. *Joy* was taking a short voyage around the island to celebrate a holiday we call the Day of Union, when a tidal wave came out of nowhere.

The two queens of Morovia – the alkonost queen and the human queen – went down with the ship, along with fifty royal courtiers, fifty guests, an orchestra of fifty musicians and one singer: my mother, Halcyon.

As well as sinking the ship, the tidal wave flooded the low-rip side of the island – which is the flatter, lower lying part of the island's rip side. And when the waters receded, a swamp sat stewing, dark and damp and dreary, where pretty dunes and charming woods had stood before. The landscape of the island, and our lives, changed for ever.

Some humans must always have been suspicious of singing magic, because whispers began immediately after the tragedy, saying the tidal wave was so powerful that it must have been caused by magic. Many of the whispers grew into angry shouts. But with both Queens of Morovia gone, and the only heir – Crown Heir Vasha – too young to rule, nobody knew what to do.

Then Captain Ilya appeared. He was the leader of a small group of royal guards called bogatyrs, whose role was to keep the royal families and the island safe. Captain Ilya spoke loudly and with authority. He said he had proof that singing magic had caused the tidal wave, and that it must be controlled for the safety of us all. The humans who were already wary of magic agreed with him, and Captain Ilya spoke so persuasively that soon many others agreed with him too.

Things on the island changed fast. Captain Ilya increased the number of bogatyrs every day, until they seemed to be everywhere. Alkonosts were banned from singing. Then banned from public spaces. Then we were pushed further and further into the swamp.

For the last three years, Nightingale and I have lived

here. We named it the Mournful Swamp because the air is filled with songs of sorrow – for my mother, and for our island. The swamp echoes our songs with its whole being. Willows weep over muddy waters. Sluggish streams murmur with melancholy. Crickets chirp cheerlessly and mosquitoes drone dismally. Even my toad friend, Lumpy, croaks the sound of a breaking heart.

My other friend, Whiskers the swamp-rat, smiles, although that's only because a giant mud crab pinched her lip when she was a pup, scarring one side of her mouth into an upwards curve. She often sighs and scratches her chin with an air of despair, and her brown fur smells funky enough to bring tears to a skunk's eyes.

But in these years that I've lived in the swamp, I've learned that sorrow doesn't always have to be sad. When the glow-worms glow through the gloomy nights and the bluegill fish burp the blues, Nightingale plays his grief on a tin guitar and something in my soul ignites like swamp-gas popping into flame.

My father says that feeling is nostalgia – a yearning for the happiness of the past. And I guess it's impossible to be truly sad when I'm thinking of a happy time – when my mother was still with us, and we lived surrounded by our alkonost and human friends. I think it's more than that though, too. The swamp is our home now and it's beautiful in its own way; a shifting world of sucking muds and dappled waters that provides us with all the food and shelter we need.

Thousands of alkonosts live here, although we rarely see each other. In the early days after *Joy* sank, we lived together in a community. But then Captain Ilya offered rewards to anyone who reported the use of singing magic and a few alkonosts began spying for him in exchange for small luxuries. So now we're scattered like twigs from a nest flung by the wind, and suspicion thorns the space between us. But there is hope here too.

There is a Unity Movement that fights for change. I know that one day soon I will help it succeed, because my name, Linnet, is a kind of a prophecy, given to me through an ancient tradition of using singing magic to glimpse a child's future.

Linnets are small but loud songbirds, whose numbers bloomed on Morovia when alkonosts and humans worked together to create the lee-side farms. My name tells me that my magic will be more powerful than any rules to stop me singing, and that I will somehow use it to bring people together.

It's been three years since my tenth birthday – when my magic should have arrived and yet didn't. But I know when it does come, I will sing a storm that will change the landscape of our lives once more.

My song will send Captain Ilya far away from this island, and unite alkonosts and humans for good. We'll get our old homes and something of our old lives back, and see our friends again. Then my father will smile, like he did years ago, when we lived by the shifting, sparkling sea.

CHAPTER 1

SNAILS
AND TUBERS

I'm knee-deep in mud, wiggling my toes in the warm gloop, searching for snails and tubers for tonight's dinner. Nightingale is perched almost directly above me, on a thick branch of the red maple tree that overhangs the dirt road.

It's a late afternoon in early spring, but it's hotter than a midsummer day. The sun's rays are thrumming down, baking my neck and making my head feathers lift in futile hope of finding a breeze. The air is thick and heavy. If only the temperature would dip slightly, I feel sure a rainstorm would come. We need rain to bring the swamp edges back to life.

Nightingale and I come here, to the lee-side edge of the swamp, at least once a moon. I forage for food with Whiskers and Lumpy, while Nightingale watches the road from the branch above us, waiting for a cart loaded with treasures to come past.

The last time we were here there was a grassy hummock to sit on, and a narrow creek filled with clear, flowing waters. I fished three fat trout from it using a bone hook on a milkweed line, while a gentle rain made everything glisten.

But for the last moon there has been a heatwave, and now the hummock is bare earth, cracked and dry. The reeds around me are brittle and yellowed, and the creek contains only a shallow, stagnant, mud-filled pool.

I blow upwards, trying to cool the sweat-damp skin on my forehead, then I push my right foot cautiously forwards, deeper into the mud. So far, I've found twelve large snails and eight arrowhead tubers – fat, round, edible roots – which is enough for a couple of good meals. But if I can find a few more tubers, I'll be able to make flour from them tomorrow, by pulping them in water and then drying them in the sun's heat.

My toe hits something and I lean down and push my hand gently into the mud, alert for the movement of anything that might bite or sting. My fingers close around another tuber and I smile as I pull it out and carry it over to Lumpy. He's proudly guarding our little mound of food, which is tucked between two exposed roots of the maple tree. He croaks in approval as I place the tuber with the others, then uses his sword-leg to push a slowly escaping snail back onto the mound.

When I found Lumpy and Whiskers, two years ago, they were being attacked by a giant mud crab. Lumpy, who is about as big as my fist, was trying to defend Whiskers, who was only a palm-sized swamp-rat pup back then. Neither of them stood a chance against the crab, who was wider than my arm is long. I scared the crab away by waving and banging a couple of sticks together, but both Whiskers and Lumpy had already been injured.

Lumpy had lost his front right limb in the attack. I kept him safe and caught beetles and crickets for him while he healed, and watched in amazement as a long, thin rod of cartilage with a spiked tip grew in place of his missing limb. This is what I call his sword-leg, and with it Lumpy can crawl as well as any toad, and he catches his own crickets now too. But he chooses to stay with me, even though he could leave any time he likes.

Lumpy glances up at me and winks one of his protruding, round eyes, then waves his sword-leg at the snail he pushed back, as if warning it not to attempt escape again. I give Lumpy a nod of thanks, then lean down to scratch Whiskers's head.

Usually, Whiskers would be foraging with me, but she's collapsed, belly to the ground, dozing in the heat. Whiskers is fully grown now, and as big as a large, fat cat. Her webbed back feet are splayed out behind her and her white snout is resting on her brown front paws. White whiskers droop either side of her snout like a long moustache and her eyes are half-closed against the dazzle of sunlight, making her look calmer than I know she is.

Whiskers has always had a nervous disposition, perhaps because of the crab attack when she was a pup. Like Lumpy, Whiskers is independent and free to leave, but she never wanders far from my side. And Lumpy and Whiskers never wander far from each other, either. They have a special bond and their own way of communicating. Lumpy taps Whiskers with his sword-leg and Whiskers grunts back at him. I have my own way of communicating with them both too, and I usually know what they're feeling from their posture and gestures.

Whiskers grunts without looking up and I know she's longing to go back to our home-tree, in the cooler central swamp. We've been here by the red maple for

at least an hour, but not a single cart has come past. Nightingale, unmoving on the branch above us, is still staring intently at the road though, showing no sign of giving up.

"Shouldn't be long now, Whiskers," I whisper hopefully, scratching her head again before I walk back to the muddy pool. As soon as I step into it, something unseen in the mud grabs my little toe and pinches so hard I clench my teeth to stop from crying out.

I pull my foot up and frown at the mud crab dangling from my toe. It releases its grip and scuttles away. It's only a small one, about as wide as my outstretched hand, but still Whiskers squeals and scrambles backwards into a hollow beneath the maple's roots, her eyes rolling in panic.

"It's all right." I try to soothe Whiskers, while wiggling my pinched toe in an effort to make the ache go away.

Nightingale makes a cooing sound from the branch above, like a pigeon, then holds out his left hand, palm down, which is his signal to be quiet and hide. I creep closer to Whiskers, putting my finger to my lips to ask her to be silent, then duck down amongst the roots and reeds.

I'm well camouflaged in the swamp. In the years we've lived here, it seems like the swamp has crept over me. My head feathers, which are short and fluffy, used to be red and white, but during my last few moults – which is when old feathers shed and new ones grow – my feathers have become the mud-brown and algae-green of the swamp. And my skin, which used to be uniformly pinkish-white, is now freckled in shades of brown and green, like the dappled waters of a birch-shaded pool. Alkonost skin often changes colour during moults, like our feathers, to satisfy the need to blend in or stand out.

Sometimes I feel like the swamp has seeped into my body too. I sense its tidal surges deep inside. It's hard to explain, but it's as if I can breathe easier when the tide rolls in and the water level rises, and I feel tension building in me when the tide rolls some of the swamp water away. Maybe that's why I feel on edge here, on the drier, far reaches of the swamp. Or maybe I feel on edge because of what Nightingale and I do here, when a cart loaded with treasures comes past.

I hold my breath when I hear the clip-clop of shod hooves, along with the churning of wooden wheels on dry dirt. Nightingale's hand is still held out, palm down.

Stay down. I lift my head just slightly to study the approaching horse and cart.

It's travelling from the direction of Spark, which is about an hour's walk away on the low-lee-side coast. Two humans sit proudly on the shiny, well-oiled cart, and a smile grows on my face because they're the richest of pigeons – which is what Nightingale calls the royal courtiers who live in Pero Palace Complex.

The courtiers are men; tall and broad, and dressed in the luxurious blue silks and gold jewellery that only the most powerful members of the royal court wear. Their cart is loaded with parcels, bags and boxes. It's easy to work out they've spent the day shopping at the market in Spark and are now heading back to their homes in the palace complex, which is almost a day's walk from here, on the high-lee side of the island – which is the mountainous part of the lee side.

Nightingale begins to sing and I stare up at him in wonder. He's beautiful, my father. His voice is sweeter than any sound on Earth, finer and more delicate than music from any instrument or any alkonost or human throat. Sweeter even than birdsong.

The feathers on his head are reddish-brown, like the rich mud of a cranberry bog, and are so long they trail past his shoulders. When we lived in Spark, my father's feathers had a bright iridescence that is now almost gone – but that's just as well, because here he needs to sit in the shadows, unseen. His russet skin has become rough and lined from living outdoors, and his eyes are huge dark pools that ebb and flow with all the sorrow and pain of being an alkonost, banished to the swamp. His beauty tells his story.

Nightingale's song flows out like the maple scent steaming off the tree he's hunched in. He's curved over like a vulture, his clawed feet gripping the branch tight. I've never seen another alkonost with feet like my father's.

When we lived in Spark, I remember people – alkonosts and humans – admiring both my father's feet and my mother's wings. Bird features used to be considered a precious gift from our ancestors. But these days all of us with feathers hide, from humans and from each other, because anyone might be a spy for Captain Ilya.

Bogatyrs often patrol the swamp, and any alkonost even suspected of singing magic is captured and taken to The Keep – which is a heavily fortified, densely guarded enclosure with towering stone walls. It sprang up in the Magicless Mountains not long after Captain Ilya took charge of Morovia, and anyone sent there is never seen again.

So when Nightingale and I cross paths with a bogatyr or anyone else in the swamp, we've perfected the art of slipping away unseen, dipping in and out of the muddy waters, or climbing silently through the trees. Occasionally, if the bogatyrs aren't wearing their magic-proof iron helmets, Nightingale might use his singing magic to conceal us, like he's doing now.

Nightingale's magic is to mesmerize and hypnotize with his songs. It only affects those who he looks directly at, which is why it's not affecting me right now. Before *Joy* sank, Nightingale worked in the hospital in Spark, soothing patients who were in pain, or calming those who were upset. I know Nightingale misses his old job and the opportunity to use his magic for something other than what we're about to do.

His slow, sweet song has entranced both the horse and the courtiers. Their eyes glaze over and they come to a stop right beneath the maple tree. Nightingale, still singing, turns his hand so it is palm up. *Time to move.* Time to be a thief.

CHAPTER 2

COINS AND JEWELS

I hold up a hand to signal Whiskers and Lumpy to stay where they are, then I slip out of my hiding spot amongst the roots and reeds and creep silently up to the dirt road. The courtiers on their cart don't see or hear me, so deeply lost are they in Nightingale's song.

I'm not particularly small or light – I'm almost as big as a human my age – but I've learned to be stealthy in the swamp, to move smoothly like the waters. I glide round to the back of the cart and let my gaze roam over all the parcels and boxes.

Nightingale has taught me to be selective about what I steal. I'm looking for a few small valuable items that will be easy to carry to Echo, the leader of the Unity Movement that seeks to make all our lives better.

Echo will exchange the treasures I steal for important things that are hard to find in the swamp –

medicines, tools, blankets – then she'll give them to the alkonosts who need them most.

The treasures I steal also fund secret missions. I don't understand them fully – because they're secret – but I know they aim to remove Captain Ilya from power and build unity between alkonosts and humans, so that we can work towards living happier lives together.

In the last three years, these missions have achieved nothing. But perhaps the next one will be successful. And if not, when I get my singing magic, *I* will lead a mission that will change everything. The prophecy of my name makes me sure of this: my magic will be powerful and far-reaching, like the song of a linnet, and it will bring alkonosts and humans together. But until my magic comes, all I can do to support the movement is steal treasures at the swamp edge.

My gaze lands on a palm-sized parcel stamped with the mark of the jeweller, Turquoise. Perfect! I reach over and take it. It's heavy for something so small and my smile widens as I wonder what valuables might lie inside it.

I leave everything else. Nightingale says if we only take a little, and only from the richest courtiers, they might not even miss it. And if they do, they'll often think they mislaid it, or at worst got pickpocketed in the market. It's important they don't think they got robbed on this road, because that would lead to more patrols by bogatyrs, which would make stealing more difficult for us, and everything more difficult for the Unity Movement.

I should retreat to the roots of the maple tree now, but I can't resist circling round the cart to the courtiers. They're wearing the soft smiles of Nightingale's enchantment and one of them has a ring with a shining jewel on it, as big as a dewberry.

Though I know Nightingale will disapprove, I slip the ring off the courtier's finger. Then, almost without thinking, I dip my hand into the shoulder bag the other courtier is carrying and lift out a small coin purse. These courtiers have so much, I'm sure they won't miss a few more things, and we need as much help as we can get. The coins in this purse and the jewel on this ring will help alkonosts in the swamp survive our banishment, and maybe even fund a mission that finally allows us to return to our homes.

Memories of my life in Spark flow through my mind. Sitting with my parents on our balcony. The green curtains, delicate as dragonfly wings, swaying in the slightest breeze. The sweet fragrance of sea-kale flowers drifting from the shingles further along the shore. And my mother, singing.

Everything about my mother was as bright as sunshine. My pulse races when I think of her, as if I'm on my own secret mission in my mind. I can't let Nightingale see when I'm remembering her, because it might push him further into his grief. So I take out my memories in private and polish them like cherished jewels.

I remember all of us visiting our closest family friends – Fleur, Clay and Silver – and my mother and Fleur laughing together so much that they made the room shake. And I remember my parents sitting together on Spark beach, their arms cradling each other's backs, while I played kickball with Dunnock, Brambling and my other friends from school, or built sandcastles with my once-best-friend, Hero. I smile at these memories, and at the thought that the treasures I'm stealing now might help Nightingale and me reclaim some of that happiness.

Satisfied with my thefts, I creep back down into the reeds where Whiskers and Lumpy are waiting for me, their expressions anxious. Nightingale changes his

27

song to a livelier tune. The eyes of the horse and the courtiers remain glazed, but the horse trots on towards the palace complex. Neither the horse nor the courtiers will come out of their trance until they're further away, and they won't remember any of this.

Nightingale swings down from the branch and walks towards me with his jerky, birdlike movements. Nightingale has always been tall and thin, but he used to seem more solid somehow. After *Joy* sank, he curved like marram grass in the wind, aged a thousand years in a day and lost his perpetual smile. He's frowning now – a frown of worry. I know it's because I took the ring and the coin purse, but I also know Nightingale won't say anything here. He'll wait until we're near the relative safety of home-tree.

Nightingale signals that we should leave with a tilt of his head, then moves swiftly into the shade beneath the maple. I go to its exposed roots, where Whiskers and Lumpy have sat up attentively. I pick up my bag, which I wove from nettle fibres last year, and place the coin purse and the parcel I stole inside it. I'm about to put the ring away too, but it's so pretty I decide to slide it onto my thumb instead, so I can admire it as we walk.

Lumpy watches me pack away the snails and tubers,

croaks in approval, then crawls up onto Whiskers. He always rides on Whiskers's head, sat between her small round ears, when we walk longer distances through the swamp.

I follow Nightingale, with Whiskers trotting at my heels and Lumpy keeping an eye on the path ahead. I keep glancing at the ring I stole. It's gold, with one large, multi-faceted jewel. The jewel is clear, but bright streaks of colours flit across its surface like tiny rainbows.

"Is this a diamond?" I whisper. My heart flutters at the thought. I've never stolen anything as valuable as a diamond before.

Nightingale turns and looks down at the ring. One of his dark feather-eyebrows arches as he slides it from my thumb and examines it. "I think it is, Linnet. A colourful one, highly prized." His feather-eyebrow falls again. "This will be missed. I've told you before about stealing from courtiers' hands. They'll suspect singing magic. Bogatyr patrols will increase and more of us will be sent to The Keep. The Unity Movement has lost so many already. What if the bogatyrs take Echo? Or me?"

Cold fear grips me at the thought of Nightingale being captured. "I wouldn't let them," I say firmly.

Nightingale looks at me silently, his eyes troubled.

I know he's thinking that I couldn't do anything to stop the bogatyrs, and he's worried what would happen to me if I were left alone in the swamp. I silently wish, for the millionth time, that my singing magic would come. Then I wouldn't feel so powerless and vulnerable.

Guilt for taking the ring falls over me, and I try to shrug it off. "If the ring is so valuable, think how much it could help the movement."

Nightingale opens his mouth as if he's about to say something, but then he passes the ring back to me, turns away and continues walking.

"Think how much it could help the Unity Movement," I repeat, jogging to catch up with him. It frustrates me when Nightingale doesn't share his thoughts. He doesn't talk enough about anything, and that makes our troubles grow bigger, like a warning cry swelling in a frog's throat.

When Nightingale doesn't talk, it means I don't get to talk either. So his silence silences me. If only he would open up, it would help both of us – especially with our grief.

Nightingale's grief is so enormous that it engulfs my own, like the morning mist swallows the swamp. It sits heavy and is hard to see through – so when Nightingale is lost in his grief, he doesn't see me or mine. He only stares into the past, alone, not realizing that I would visit the past with him if he let me.

I find those times difficult. I wish I had singing magic to sing away his pain, or sing him back to me. But all I can do is get on with the foraging and the cooking, tell stories to Whiskers and Lumpy, and wait for Nightingale to come back to the present.

I reach out and touch Nightingale's arm. "Perhaps this ring will fund a mission that will get us home again, to Spark," I whisper. "You could go back to work, and I could go back to school. We could see our friends again. And in the evenings, we could sit on our balcony, watching seabirds and searching for glimpses of the other Floating Islands."

Nightingale turns to me. Salt tears glisten at the edge of his eyes and I panic, thinking I've made his grief swell. I shouldn't have mentioned our balcony, where my mother used to sing. But Nightingale looks at me with attentiveness. Relief washes over me, because he's still here – not lost in his memories.

"The Unity Movement isn't going well, Linnet," Nightingale says gently. "The last time I visited Echo, she said things are hopeless."

I frown. I want to say that Nightingale should have told me this before – it's been nearly a moon since he last visited Echo – but I swallow back the words. Nightingale doesn't tell me what he and Echo talk about because he thinks it might put me in danger. I hold up the ring again instead. "Well then it's good that we have this. Something so valuable is sure to help."

Nightingale shakes his head. "You don't understand, Linnet. Too many people who worked with the movement have been sent to The Keep – both alkonosts and our human allies. Now almost everyone is too scared to help. There is nothing we can do."

"That's not true." I stuff the ring into my bag with trembling fingers. "There's always something we can do." I lift my chin and try to sound confident, despite the doubts wavering inside me. "We must keep fighting for unity." My eyes widen as I realize something. "A part of you must think so too, or why else would we be here, stealing treasures?"

"We weren't stealing for the Unity Movement today, Linnet. I have another idea." Nightingale looks down at his long, clawed feet and furrows his brow. His expression makes me feel like I'm sinking into deep, sucking mud.

"What?" I ask nervously.

"I'm going to suggest something," Nightingale says quietly, "and I don't want you to respond straight away. I want you to think about it, all the way to home-tree, then we'll talk after we've eaten."

My brow furrows like Nightingale's.

"I'm serious, Linnet." Nightingale lifts his face. "I know what your first reaction will be, but I want you to give the idea some thought. Because considering how the movement has come to a halt, and how your magic hasn't come—"

"Yet," I interrupt. "How my magic hasn't come yet."

"...And how you deserve a proper childhood—" Nightingale continues.

"Just tell me!" I blurt out.

"We could exchange that ring for a boat, Linnet. A sailing boat with a cabin, like the ones the sea-fishers use. They gather on the mudflats at Fisher's Flock, and I'm sure one of them would be happy with a trade like that."

"We don't need a sailing boat." My frown deepens.

"We could leave Morovia and make a fresh start on one of the other Floating Islands. Buyan drifts far away, but Eldovia is often close enough to sail to." Nightingale turns and walks away before I can respond.

33

He was right, my first reaction is to say no, for a thousand reasons. We know very little about Eldovia, and even less about Buyan. Few people have been to either, and those who have return with conflicting stories. Some say there are alkonosts on Eldovia who live in harmony with lizard-people. Others say that the lizard-people are dangerous, or that they don't exist at all. And there are so many bizarre tales about Buyan that nobody knows what to believe.

Anyway, Morovia is our home and always has been. All my memories of my mother are here. And all our friends are here – alkonosts hiding in the swamp like me and Nightingale, and humans separated from us on the lee side of the island. I want to see them all again.

I want my old life back, not a new one somewhere else. Leaving Morovia would take away everything that I've dreamed of for these last years.

If the Unity Movement can't unite our island, then I will when I get my magic. I've been working hard to make it come. I practise singing every day, using exercises my mother taught me to improve the power, control and range of my voice. I hum and chant, sing scales and songs, and even play with noises like buzzes and clicks, desperately trying to feel some magic in my throat or in the air around me. My magic will come soon. It *must*.

I follow Nightingale, my movements almost as jerky as his with anger. Whiskers glances up at me with a look of confused concern, and Lumpy lets out an indignant *"Phoot"* as Whiskers's movement makes him wobble.

"It's fine," I murmur to myself as much as them. "Nightingale just made a thoughtless suggestion." Looking at Whiskers and Lumpy, I realize they're yet another reason we can't leave. They're part of our family now, and they need to live here in the swamp, not on a sailing boat or on an island we know nothing about.

When we get our old home back in Spark, at least I could visit Lumpy and Whiskers in the swamp, but if we leave Morovia I'll never see them again. Or see any of my friends again. I'll never walk home from school with Silver again, or play kickball with Dunnock and Brambling, or hear our elderly downstairs neighbour Lark talking softly to his pet angelfish.

That Nightingale would even suggest we abandon our island, our friends and our neighbours is unbelievable. We have to stay and fix our problems, not run away from them.

With every step I become more resolute. I can't let Nightingale take us away. So I need to think of a way to convince him that we must stay, and I need to do it before we get to home-tree because that's when we're going to talk about this.

I can't tell Nightingale I want to stay because of the memories of my mother here – that would only upset him. So I think of my other reasons for wanting to stay – my friends, my home, the places I love.

As often happens when I think of my past and my future, it's thoughts of Hero that rise to the surface. I can't believe this divide between us will last for ever. There must be another way forwards. I miss my once-best-friend so much, and I remember the day we met as clear as if it was yesterday...

The Day I Met Hero

Six years ago, when I was seven years old, on a warm Songsday afternoon in early summer, my mother asked me to go to the market near our home in Spark to fetch some things. Because I was young, I rarely went anywhere on my own and excitement rushed through me at the thought of the freedom and responsibility I was being given.

My fingers worked too fast to buckle my sandals, so my mother crouched down to help. She calmly slid the leather straps through the wooden clips and the long blue and yellow feathers on her arms brushed against my knees as she gave me my instructions.

I was to go to the fruit stall on the ripward side of the market and wait until the seller began giving out the end-of-day bags. These were the large paper bags bursting with a mixture of fruits that needed eating up, so were sold cheap at the end of the day.

My mother gave me a copper coin and told me to keep it safe. Then she kissed my cheek and smiled as she opened the door for me.

I held the coin so tight that I could feel the pattern on it pressing into my palm. All coins on Morovia have the same pattern. On one side is a long feather, a symbol of the kindness of the ancient bird-people of the island. And on the other side is the symbol of unity: an alkonost with fluffy head feathers and a human with plaited hair, holding each other tight.

I stepped through the door and blinked my feather-eyelashes at the dazzling sunshine. Our home was on the first floor of a house that overlooked the beach. The exterior walls were painted bright sunrise orange, and the flat roof was full of potted leafy plants that blew in the wind, as if the house had hair. Our door opened to an outdoor staircase that tumbled onto the sand and, once my eyes had adjusted to the light, I raced down the steps and along the beach, my head feathers tingling in the sea breeze and a huge smile on my face.

I was out of breath by the time I reached the market, which was held in a square beside the far end of the beach. I slowed down and walked between stalls, my eyes widening to take in all the sights. I'd been here with my parents many times, but being on my own made everything feel fresh and new.

There were long, wooden tables stacked with boxes of fish and shellfish laid to rest on melting ice. Alkonost and human sea-fishers and shellfish-gatherers were sitting behind the tables, laughing loudly together. Colourful silks with ancient alkonost symbols streamed from display racks, and traditional human-made jewellery glistened against black velvet backdrops.

I breathed deeply, inhaling the smells of sunflower seeds roasting the traditional alkonost way with pepper and lime, and delicacies made by humans, such as charred spicy flatbreads and hot sugared doughnuts that made my mouth water.

Although alkonosts and humans have their own traditional foods, lots of us like each other's foods too. My favourite alkonost food is seed cakes sweetened with raisins, but I love the sweet breads made by humans too.

Vegetable sellers were holding up their end-of-day bags and shouting, "Mixed greens for a copper, mixed roots for a silver." But when I got to the fruit stall, the lady with pink and blue feathers who worked there was still preparing her bags. So I stood and waited.

The market was busy and I waved to a few people I knew; friends of my parents, and a few of my friends from school. They were with their parents, which made me feel even more grown-up to be on my own.

Then I spotted another girl on her own, who was about my age. She stood tall and proud, had light brown skin and long, shiny black hair tied in a plait that trailed down her back. She was wearing a blue silk tunic, like the ones the courtiers always wore, and deerskin trousers, like the bogatyrs – the royal guards – wore. I watched the girl, curious. She had to be from Pero Palace Complex, but the children who lived there had their own school and rarely came to Spark.

After a few minutes, I decided this girl was the kindest person I'd ever seen. Her strong hands were quick to help anyone and everyone. I watched her carry a bag of tubers to a silver-haired lady's handcart, pass a string of onions to an elderly man with bright orange feathers and return a dropped doll to a toddler who was moulting fluffy down. She noticed what people needed and was there to help before they'd even considered asking.

I was so focused on watching the girl, I didn't hear the people shouting at me to get out of the way. A donkey pulling a cart was bolting through the market, knocking over stalls and braying loudly. Someone grabbed my shoulders and practically lifted me out of the donkey's path, saving me from being trampled at the last moment.

The girl leaped towards the donkey and somehow managed to grab its reins and hold it steady, even when it bucked in panic. A man with dark green feathers, who must have been the donkey's owner, rushed over and thanked the girl, then soothed the donkey with soft words before leading him away. But the market remained in chaos.

Fruits and vegetables, spilled from upturned stalls, were rolling all over the ground and people were trying to gather them up before they were ruined. I leaned down to help and noticed the emptiness of my hands. *My coin.* I must have dropped it. I stopped still, all the warmth draining from my body.

I ducked low and scanned the ground, desperately trying to spot it. My heart began racing as I realized how difficult it was going to be to find. I wanted to ask everyone to stop what they were doing and help me look for it, but they were all busy and I was too ashamed to say anything. My mother had given me this one job and I had messed it up.

I blinked back tears as I walked in circles, searching for the coin while making bargains with Fate in my head: *If I find the coin, I'll clean my room like my mother asked me to*, or *If I find the coin, I'll work extra hard at school*. But it didn't work. I wondered if praying to a deity, like some of the humans did, might work better than bargaining with Fate. But I wasn't sure how to do that anyway.

What if someone else has picked it up and taken it? I suddenly thought and I looked around at everyone nearby until my eyes landed on the girl. She was standing a few paces away, looking back at me with golden-brown eyes and a piercing gaze that made me feel like she could see right into my thoughts.

"You've lost something," she said.

"My coin." I nodded. "A copper coin. It was in my hand, but I must have dropped it."

The girl began looking with me. We walked from the fruit stall down to the beach, then back again. The fruit seller was giving out her end-of-day bags now and they were selling fast.

"It's gone," I said, my heart sinking. I knew my mother wouldn't be cross. She was never cross with me. But I was disappointed that I would have to return empty-handed.

"We'll find it." The girl smiled and nudged my shoulder, and I don't know why but I believed her. So we walked from the stall to the beach again.

"I've found it!" The girl leaned down and rose back up with my coin in her hand.

"Thank you." I beamed as I took it from her.

"Hero," she said, and I must have looked confused because she explained. "My name is Hero."

"I'm Linnet. Quick, come with me." I grabbed

Hero's hand and pulled her towards the fruit stall. "I need to buy one of those bags before they're all sold."

I was so relieved when the fruit seller passed me one of the end-of-day bags, I couldn't stop smiling. "Let's sit on the beach and you can choose any piece of fruit you like," I said to Hero. "As thanks for helping me."

We walked to the sand and sat side by side. Hero looked into the bag thoughtfully. "Would you like to share an orange?" she asked and I nodded. Hero took one, and as she peeled off the skin, she told me that she lived in Pero Palace Complex, where her mother was a courtier and her father was a bogatyr. She said it was frustrating living there because she had no freedom. All the children had to stay with Crown Heir Vasha, who was always kept safe in the palace, away from dangers such as bolting donkeys. "It's so silly," Hero sighed. "Morovia is really very safe."

Hero explained that she had snuck out of her palace home and hidden on a cart to visit Spark market. She said she wanted to be a bogatyr like her father when she was older, so she needed to get to know the island, because as well as guarding the royal family, bogatyrs were often sent on expeditions and quests. Hero told me that bogatyrs watched the seas for signs of storms, and sometimes sailed out to save whales or dolphins trapped in fishing nets. She said bogatyrs explored the mysterious Magicless Mountains, where singing magic failed to work, and they'd built the bridge over Cold-Feet Canyon – a dangerous place where icy mists rose from dark depths, chilling bones and, occasionally, making people disappear.

Hero told me bogatyrs were some of the strongest, kindest and most courageous people on Morovia, who helped and protected others and went on amazing adventures, and that one day soon she would join them. Hero's bravery made me feel brave.

I told Hero about the prophecy of my name and how I wanted to use my magic – when it came – to bring people together in friendship. Hero listened and nodded, and I felt like my wish was more possible than ever before.

We shared the orange as we talked, and I thought it was the most delicious fruit I'd ever tasted – perhaps because it was sweetened with our hopes and dreams. I pointed along the beach to show Hero where my home was, and I told her about my parents and friends. I said if she came to Spark again she should visit, because at this time of year we often ate and played games on the beach.

Our shadows stretched towards the sea as the sun set behind us.

"I have to go." Hero rose to her feet. "My only way home is to sneak onto one of the carts leaving the market for the palace." She gave me a dazzling smile. "But I'll come to see you next Songsday if I can."

I waved as Hero ran back towards the market. Then I picked up my end-of-day bag and carried it carefully home, my cheeks aching from smiling.

Halfway along the beach I spotted something glistening in the sand. It was a copper coin. I leaned down to pick it up and realized it was probably *my* copper coin – the one my mother had given me. I must have dropped it running along the beach on the way to the market, and Hero must have given me a coin of her own when we couldn't find mine.

I looked at the alkonost with fluffy feathers and the human with plaited hair holding each other on the coin, and I knew, right then and there, that Hero and I were going to be best friends. We fitted together in a way I'd never felt before, and our dreams shone brighter for having entwined.

The next seven days were the slowest of my life; Nestday, Liftday, Flightday and Glidesday crawled by; Soarsday and Swoopday felt never-ending. When Songsday finally came, I was so excited that I got up before dawn and sat on the beach, hoping that Hero would come. When I spotted her running across the sand towards me not long after sunrise, my heart leaped.

We spent the whole day together: walking along the shore, picking around the rock pools, swimming in the sea and playing kickball with some of my friends from school. In the afternoon, we helped my parents build a small fire and we baked potatoes stuffed with smoked fish, by wrapping them in cabbage leaves and tucking them in the embers.

After we'd eaten, Hero and I built a sandcastle together. We lay side by side on our bellies, the waves frothing at our feet as we sculpted tower after tower. We placed flower flags on the top of each tower and decorated the castle walls with shells. We dug a moat and strengthened it with smooth, dark pebbles. And we made a seaweed garden that had tiny glassy snails crawling in it.

Hero found a perfect mussel shell still hinged together, glowing blue as a twilight sky, and as we placed it in the biggest tower to create a grand entrance, our cheeks pressed together, warm and soft.

We made up a song about our castle – one verse while it was standing tall, and a second while the tide washed it away – and we giggled as we sang it.

We built a castle on the shore
flower flags and shells for doors
a seaweed garden to explore
in our castle on the shore, on the shore.

The tide rushed in, wave by wave
flooding moat, towers cave
falling shells, a flower grave
as the tide roared in, wave by wave.

Hero and I became best friends, as I'd known we would, and for the next three years she visited me almost every Songsday. I couldn't visit Hero's home, because there were too many rules involved in visiting Pero Palace Complex, and Hero wouldn't be able to explain how she knew me without giving away the fact that she'd been sneaking out, which would get her into trouble.

But the risks and effort we put into our friendship made it feel all the more special.

My parents weren't happy with Hero keeping secrets from her parents, but after a long discussion, and much pleading from Hero and me, they decided all they could do, until Hero was ready to tell her parents herself, was to make sure that Hero got to and from the palace complex safely. So they helped Hero find cart rides with friends who we knew and trusted.

If the weather was warm when Hero visited, we'd play on the beach, and if it was cold we'd stay in my home or go to visit one of my friends from school or wander round the library or shops. Occasionally my mother, who worked in the theatre, would get us tickets for an afternoon show. Hero loved being able to do all the things that she couldn't at the palace, and she said I was the only friend she had who she could truly be herself around.

Sometimes Hero would bring two wooden staffs with her and we'd practise stick-sparring moves she'd learned while watching the bogatyrs train. Once she visited on a huge silver-grey horse who she had "borrowed" from the bogatyrs' stables, and we rode together along the beach and through the shallow waves.

It was such an amazing experience that I dreamed of it every night for moons afterwards, and always woke smiling.

Hero wanted to be a bogatyr more than anything, and as her tenth birthday approached she began planning to tell her parents of her dream. From the age of ten, anyone, alkonost or human, could ask to begin bogatyr training. There were a few selection tests, but nothing that Hero wouldn't soar through.

I didn't know what I wanted to be, but I started to wonder if I should train as a bogatyr too, so that I could spend more time with Hero. I had lots of friends back then, but I loved spending time with Hero more than anyone. She was kind, brave and adventurous, and full of stories and dreams that made my heart race with excitement. We became so close that we knew what each other was thinking without having to say a word.

But then everything changed in the worst possible way. When *Joy* sank I lost my mother, my home and my best friend too. My heart aches when I think of Hero. For three years we were together, and for three years we've been apart. I wonder if she misses me as much as I miss her.

One day soon, I will help Morovia become united, and then Hero and I will be together again. I'll reach across all the time and troubles that have divided us, and I'll pull her into a hug. Because friendships like ours are important. You can't leave them behind.

CHAPTER 3

FIRE AND FOOD

Nightingale and I arrive at home-tree as the sun is disappearing behind the densely packed trees of the central swamp. Finally, the air cools and I can breathe more easily. I feel calmer too, having straightened out what I want to say to Nightingale during the walk home. He said we won't talk about leaving Morovia until after we've eaten, and that's fine with me. My belly aches with hunger and I can't wait to fill it.

The crickets have begun their pulsing, droning evening song and the midges are dancing to it, swirling haphazardly in the last of the pale golden sunbeams that creep through narrow gaps in the foliage. The midges aren't biting at the moment, and if they start I still have some of the birch-bark tar that I made to protect my and Nightingale's skin.

For the last three weeks our home-tree has been a huge cypress, so wide that Nightingale and I couldn't lock arms around it, and so tall that I must strain my eyes to see the top of it. The tree rises from a wide channel of calm water that can be shallow or deep depending on the tide. Pale grey-green trailing moss dangles from the lower branches, dipping into the water below on one side and onto a grassy hummock the other side. Some people might think this is a strange, damp and shadowy place to live, but I think it's beautiful.

Nightingale sweeps a section of the trailing moss aside like a curtain and invites me to walk through first. His face is lowered, but his dark eyes look up at mine with a spark of something that I haven't seen since before *Joy* sank. My brow furrows as I wonder if I'm reading his expression right. Has his plan of leaving Morovia stirred some excitement about the future? I shake the thought away. Once I've explained to Nightingale why we must stay, I'm sure he'll forget his plan and focus on what we can do to unite our island instead.

"I'll gather firewood." Nightingale lets the moss curtain fall back down, enclosing me, Whiskers and Lumpy in this cosy, green space. I listen to Nightingale's footfalls moving away. Nightingale can walk silently if he wants to, but he often makes a small amount of noise on purpose when we're separated, so that I know where he is.

Whiskers sits on the grassy hummock so Lumpy can crawl off her head, then she climbs down the other side to take a drink and a dip in the water. I slip off my bag, which contains the ring and the other treasures I stole, and place it on the ground beside Lumpy, knowing that he'll want to check the snails in it. Then I lift my face and arms into the air and stretch.

My gaze drifts through the soft, feathery spring leaves above, searching for our things, to check all is as we left it. Our sleeping pods are still suspended from a thick branch, high above. The pods are made from deerskin and lined with rabbit fur on the inside. Twisted rope, made from cedar-bark fibres, webs over the outside of the pods and we tucked twigs and moss all over them, for disguise and warmth. Another pod dangles nearby, which contains our cooking equipment, tools and a small amount of stored food. Nothing has been disturbed and I breathe a sigh of relief.

We've had food stolen in the past, although Nightingale says we shouldn't get upset about it. He says that anyone hungry enough to steal is welcome to our food, because there's always more to be found in the swamp.

Our only real concern is that bogatyrs might discover where our home-tree is. Nightingale is on their list of outlaws because when the Unity Movement first formed someone reported him for being a part of it, presumably to get a reward from Captain Ilya. So if bogatyrs find Nightingale, they'll take him to The Keep. And most likely me too. That's why we move around so much. A home-tree is only ever home for a moon or two at the most. And home is never more than these three pods, ready to be carried away at a moment's notice.

Although the swamp is beautiful to me, I long for a more permanent home. I often dream of our old home in Spark, and wake up wondering if it still looks the same and if our belongings are still there – all the things we couldn't bring with us when we were taken from Spark: my mother's songbooks; Nightingale's treasured guitar, which was painted sunset red and had twelve shiny gold strings; the clay bowl I made my parents as a midwinter gift; my favourite drawings and paintings, and the treasures on my old windowsill. They weren't treasures like the coins and jewels I steal on the road, but treasures I collected with my family and friends: pebbles, fossils, shells, seabird feathers and dried flowers.

I can't think of our old home for long though without my chest tightening. When we're able to return, it will be painful, because it won't be the same without my mother. And going there, to a place so full of memories, might push Nightingale even deeper into his grief. But I still want to go back. I want to feel my mother close, with Nightingale by my side. Perhaps then he'll finally talk about his feelings with me.

I crouch down and stare at Lumpy to bring myself back to the here and now. He's guarding the snails again, pushing them into my bag with his sword-leg when they try to escape. "I'll prepare the fire pit, then get a box for them," I say, and Lumpy sighs disappointedly in response. He likes guarding things, but the snails will have to be boxed up for a while before we can eat them, to give any nasty things they've been nibbling a chance to leave their bodies.

I step off the grassy hummock onto a small section of muddy bank. The thick, furrowed base of home-tree's trunk rises out of the water ahead. Its bark is striped with algae where the water level rises and falls in cycles, and knotty buttress roots peep above the water's surface like giant toad heads. A couple of the roots stretch onto this muddy bank, making useful seats, and I sit on one of them now and start digging into the mud with my hands.

We always cover the fire pit with mud to hide it when we leave home-tree, but only a thin layer, so it doesn't take long to reveal the circle of rocks. I can hear Whiskers pulling cattails out of the water a little further along the channel, and crunching the shoots with her long teeth.

Once the fire pit is exposed, I rinse my hands in the water, then walk along the roots to the tree's trunk – barefoot, as always. Nightingale has offered to help me make some simple shoes from deerskin, but I like being able to step into water without worrying about getting shoes wet, and to feel the ground with my feet and the bark when I climb.

I climb home-tree now, pushing my fingers and toes into furrows in the red-brown bark, until I reach our storage pod. I step onto the branch below it, take out the few things I need for cooking, then climb back down to the fire pit.

Nightingale has returned with an armful of sticks and twigs and is already building the fire, so I go to prepare the food. First, I put all the snails into a small cedar box I made and tie it shut with a strip of old leather. Lumpy frowns and crawls away, probably to catch crickets for his own evening meal.

I carry the tubers I collected to a freshwater spring, hidden in foliage on the channel bank. Whiskers follows me, with the slightly lost look she always has when Lumpy isn't with her. She sits beside me as I peel the gooey skin off the tubers, rub the round roots clean, stack them in a bark bowl, then carry them back to the fire pit.

Flames are licking up around the sticks, which are now crackling in the pit. Woodsmoke is curling into the air and sparks are flying. My shoulders tense, because by making a fire we risk being seen by bogatyr patrols, but I remind myself that we're deep in the swamp and the trailing moss around us creates a fairly good hiding place, obscuring the fire from view.

Nightingale has brought our blankets down from our sleeping pods. They came from our old home in Spark and are made of soft, grey felt, worn thin from so much use. He's brought his tin guitar down too, and my heart lifts to see it, because I love it when Nightingale plays.

When we were forced out of our home in Spark, Nightingale left his treasured sunset-red guitar behind, and for almost a year he didn't play or sing at all. But then he built this new guitar. He used an old storage tin that we found washed up on the mudflats, carved the neck and pegs from maple wood, and made the strings from swamp milkweed fibres – the same way we make our fishing lines.

Nightingale wraps his blanket around his shoulders and passes me mine so that I can do the same, to protect myself from the damp air now rolling in off the water. The tunic I'm wearing is worn thin and is too big for me, because it's one of Nightingale's. I grew out of my own clothes years ago. So I'm wearing what used to be Nightingale's trousers too, but I cut them into shorts, because it's easier to wade through water channels and climb trees without damp fabric tangling round my legs. The waist of the trousers is too big, but I use a thin strip of leather to hold them in place.

I sit on a root opposite Nightingale, the fire between us, and place the bark bowl full of tubers on a rock. Whiskers sits on my foot and her eyes light up when she sees Lumpy, with a few spider legs dangling out of his mouth, crawling towards us. Nightingale busies himself feeding the flames with twigs, and I stab two of the tubers with long sharp sticks and begin roasting them over the fire.

"It's a shame we've nothing to eat with these." I watch the pale pink skin of the tubers slowly brown. "I hoped to catch a fish today, but the creek by the red maple was all dried up. Then I meant to gather some wild garlic on the way home, but I forgot."

Nightingale dips his hand into his tunic pocket and pulls out a few long, spiked leaves. "I found some while gathering firewood."

"Yes!" I rise to my feet and lean round the fire, take a leaf from Nightingale and nibble the edge of it. Wild garlic is one of my favourites. It's slightly bitter, but so moreish.

"Do you remember your mother used to flavour bread with it sometimes?" Nightingale's eyes glaze over, as if he's under one of his own enchantments. They always do when he looks into the past.

I nod. "She used to make those little pastries too, with wild garlic and lemon." I lick my lips. Breads and pastries are traditionally human foods, but they're the ones I've missed most since living in the swamp. Sometimes I make flour from dried tubers, then mix some with water and toast twists of the dough on sticks. The twists are nice, but not the same as human-style breads. I wonder if any humans miss alkonost foods. Our closest family friends, Fleur, Clay and Silver, are humans, and they loved the traditional alkonost seed cakes my mother would bake when we all shared a meal every Nestday.

I open my mouth to say something about the seed cakes, but then decide not to when I notice the look of sadness stretching over Nightingale's face like a shadow. I must pull him back to the present, so that we can talk about the future. "Arrowhead roasted over an open fire is pretty special too," I say, passing Nightingale one of the sticks now that the tubers are cooked through. I blow on mine before biting into it. The outside is crispy, the inside soft and fluffy, and it warms me right to my core.

Nightingale eats his tuber while staring into the flames, his eyes still glazed. "We had a nice home, Linnet, back then. I had a good job. And you had friends." He glances up at me. "For these last few years, I've been hoping the Unity Movement would get us home again, but it's failed, Linnet." Nightingale sighs. "I still believe that we can have a proper home, but not here. We can't keep living like this. It's time we left the swamp, and Morovia."

Lumpy, who has crawled up onto Whiskers's head, lets out a loud, indignant *"Phoot"*, and Whiskers looks up at me with concern.

"Morovia is our home," I say firmly. "We're managing fine in the swamp. And one day soon we'll be able to go back to Spark. If the Unity Movement isn't going well, that doesn't mean we should give up. It means we should fight harder or fight differently." I rest my half-eaten tuber in the bark bowl, then lift the tiny leather bag that I wear around my neck over my head. "Do you know what I keep in here?" I ask, opening the bag.

"One of your mother's feathers." Nightingale nods.

"Yes. But there are a couple of other things too." When I push my fingers past the small yellow feather that I found on my mother's pillow after *Joy* sank, my breath quickens and I blink back my tears, because I can't let Nightingale see them. Whiskers rests her face against my leg and Lumpy taps my shin comfortingly with his sword-leg.

For the first year after Halcyon died, I couldn't

even look at the feather without rivers of tears running down my cheeks, but my grief is different now. Most of the time it's like an emptiness in a hidden chamber of my heart. But sometimes, like now, it swells into a chasm that threatens to swallow me up. I've learned to breathe through these moments, knowing now that they do pass. And I've learned that even though touching my mother's feather brings sorrow, it can also bring comfort. So I take a long slow breath and feel the softness and strength of the feather. Then I push my fingers further into the tiny bag and pull out the two small gold necklaces beneath.

I hold up the necklaces and as they twinkle in the firelight my heart aches. But I also fill with hope that when I tell Nightingale why I keep these necklaces, he will abandon his plan to leave Morovia and realize why we need to stay and fight for our home and friends.

CHAPTER 4

TWO HALVES
OF A HEART

Nightingale looks at the necklaces trailing from my fingers like the moss trailing from the tree around us. Each necklace has a charm shaped like half a heart, and they fit together to make a whole.

"They were yours and Hero's," Nightingale says.

I nod and take a deep breath. This is the first time I've told anyone what happened between Hero and me. "Hero bought them for us and we wore them all the time. But then she came to see me the day after *Joy* sank." My stomach twists at the memory. "She said the tragedy was the fault of alkonosts. She was angry and upset, her face hot and covered with tears. She threw her necklace to the floor, then left."

"I'm sorry, Linnet." Nightingale shakes his head sadly. "Hero shouldn't have said those things."

The words I wanted to say fall silently off my tongue.

Even though I felt in my heart that Hero was wrong, it's strange to hear Nightingale say it so simply. I've spent the last three years trying to explain and excuse her actions.

"*Joy* sinking took so much from all of us." Nightingale blinks back tears and my own eyes well up to see his pain. But he takes a breath and his voice is steady when he continues. "Captain Ilya's speeches twisted people's grief into anger and hate. I think many more humans than we ever realized were distrustful of alkonosts. Some people say that Captain Ilya grew up in a small community of humans who lived in the Magicless Mountains because they wanted to live away from singing magic, and the humans he lived with are his new bogatyrs. I don't know if that's true. But since Captain Ilya has been in power, he's definitely nurtured distrust towards alkonosts and made it grow. Morovia has changed, Linnet. Life here will never be the same. I think…" Nightingale's breath rattles in his chest and I know he's thinking about Halcyon again. I frown to hide my own pain as I think of her, gone. "A fresh start, away from Morovia, could be a good thing," Nightingale says. "We could make a new home, I could find a new job, and you could make new friends."

"I don't want new friends," I say stubbornly,

frustrated this conversation isn't going how I planned. I wanted the necklaces to make Nightingale remember our friends – both alkonost and human – and realize that our old lives are worth fighting for. "I want my old friends back," I explain firmly. "And I'm sure most of them want the same thing. Fleur, Clay and Silver will miss us and want to see us again, won't they? And Dunnock and Brambling, and their mother, Robin. And our downstairs neighbour, Lark."

Nightingale sighs and nods. "Yes, but—"

"And Hero will want to see me again," I interrupt, my voice wavering a little because this might be more of a wish than a fact. "Hero wasn't thinking straight when she said those things. She was upset and angry because of *Joy* sinking. I think she must have lost someone she loved too." I frown with the frustration of not knowing for sure. Hero and I never got a chance to talk or comfort each other after that day, because Captain Ilya tore us and the island apart. I take a deep breath before continuing. "But people don't stay upset and angry for ever," I say firmly. "I keep our necklaces because I believe we can be friends again." I pour the necklaces carefully back into the tiny bag. "I believe all alkonosts and humans can be friends, and that Morovia

can be healed. Then we'll be able to stop living in isolation, go home, and see our alkonost friends again too. But if we leave, we'll never get to see that."

"If we stay, we might never get to see it," Nightingale says gently. "The Unity Movement has fallen apart, Linnet."

"But I haven't given up hope that we can make things change." I move around the fire, crouch beside Nightingale and rest my forehead against his, like we used to do when I was little and he tucked me into bed at night. "Please don't give up," I whisper.

Nightingale's eyes fill with tears and I panic, thinking I've upset him again. Desperate to distract him, I leap up.

"The treasures!" I exclaim, to change the subject. I jump over to the grassy hummock and pick up my bag. "Let's see what we've got. There is this fine diamond ring, of course." I pull the ring from my bag.

Lumpy flops off Whiskers's head and crawls to me, croaking eagerly in the way he does when he wants a job to do. "Can you take this to Nightingale, please?" I ask, placing the ring in front of him. Lumpy picks the ring up in his mouth and crawls over to Nightingale.

As well as guarding things, Lumpy loves carrying

things. It started when his sword-leg grew after the crab attack. He used to bring me offerings of beetles and crickets, and I'd say "Take them to Nightingale" as a kind of joke, but he'd actually do it. He soon learned our names and would carry morsels of food, or the small treasures I stole, back and forth for fun.

Lumpy reaches Nightingale, who leans down and holds out his hand so that Lumpy can deposit the ring on his palm. The flames from the fire reflect on the diamond's surfaces, making it look like a tiny, glowing sun.

"Something so valuable must be able to help the fight for unity," I say as I carry the coin purse and the parcel I stole back to the fire. I pass Nightingale the purse before sitting down again. "Can you count the coins while I see what's in here?" I open the small parcel stamped with the name of the jeweller, Turquoise, and frown at the heavy black rock I find inside. "What's this?" I ask, passing it to Nightingale too.

"It's basalt from the Gold Mountains, near Pero Palace Complex. It's not rare or valuable." Nightingale turns the rock over in his hands.

"Why would a jeweller parcel up a worthless rock?" I take the rock and place it with the others around the fire pit. "Well, we have the ring anyway. And how many coins?" I ask.

"Five gold, seven silver, one copper." Nightingale passes the purse back to me. "That should be enough to give us a good start on another island. The last time we visited the mudflats, Eldovia appeared quite large on the horizon, so it must be close."

"I want to stay on Morovia," I say, frustration at having to repeat myself flapping inside me like a hummingbird's wings. "We belong here. What do we even know about Eldovia? It might have as many problems as Morovia."

For a moment I wonder what the other Floating Islands are like, the way my parents and I used to when we all sat on our balcony in Spark. But I push the thought away. I don't want to leave for another island. I want to sit on our balcony again, where my mother sang songs, because when we return there, I'll hear them on the breeze. And I'll walk to where my mother and I sat on the beach on our last day together, and I'll feel her wings around me. These places are special, because they hold my memories of her. We can't just leave.

"We could ask the sea-fishers about Eldovia tomorrow morning," Nightingale suggests. "Some of them are always on the mudflats at Fisher's Flock before dawn, and I've heard a few of them sailed to Eldovia recently with thoughts of finding a new home. I'm not the only one thinking about leaving Morovia, Linnet. The alkonost fishers have really struggled since Captain Ilya banned them from working with humans. Perhaps they'll be able to tell us more about what Eldovia is like, and that will help us decide."

"Let's fix *our* island, not abandon it for somewhere else." My whole heart pleads for Nightingale to understand how I feel. "I want to see our friends again, and I want to go back to our old home in Spark. Halcyon's songbooks are still there..." My words get stuck in my throat. I take a slow breath in while silently chastising myself for letting my grief slip out. I take the ring from Nightingale and put it in the coin purse. "Let's take these treasures to Echo tomorrow instead, and talk about how we might use them to save the Unity Movement. Please. Let's try, just one more time."

"And if the treasures can't save the movement?" Nightingale raises one feather-eyebrow.

"They will. They *must*." I reinforce my voice with all my strength. "And if they don't," I continue when Nightingale sighs, "then when I get my singing magic,

I will fix everything. My magic will bring everyone together, like the prophecy of my name says."

"Linnet, you're thirteen," Nightingale says gently. "I've wished your magic would come and that you could use it to unite Morovia. I know how much you've wanted that, and how much you've practised your singing. But name prophecies can be interpreted in many different ways, you know that. And alkonosts who don't get their magic by the time they're ten rarely do. I think it's time to accept—"

"My magic will come," I interrupt quickly, angry that Nightingale has not only given up hope for unity, but hope that I will get singing magic too. I can't accept that. All the alkonosts I know have singing magic; my mother did, my father does, and Dunnock, Brambling and all my other alkonost friends... Without magic, what kind of alkonost would I be? And if I'm wrong about my name prophecy, then how can I change anything on Morovia? It's Nightingale who is wrong. I know my day will come. I turn away from him and stare into the flames, the same way he does when he doesn't want to talk.

We sit in silence for a while, but I soon start fidgeting as I try to think of something else to say to make

Nightingale change his mind. I'm not like him – I can't sit comfortably while unresolved troubles waft through the air like the smell of a torn skunk-cabbage leaf.

Whiskers, who is lying on my foot again, also can't sit comfortably in the tense atmosphere. She retreats towards the burrow she dug under the grassy hummock. Lumpy taps her head goodnight, flops off her, then crawls into his leafy, rooty nook, which is beside Whiskers's burrow. I watch them both settle into their cosy nests and it calms me a little.

The twilight has been swallowed by the shadows of night and a chorus of frogs and crickets is jingling softly through the trees. Across the water, fireflies are flashing and a couple of raccoons are chittering as they forage on the bank.

Finally, Nightingale breaks our silence by picking up his tin guitar and strumming a tune I've not heard before. Nightingale often improvises when he plays, expressing his feelings with music. Most often it's grief, played out through slow, deep melodies, with discords of pain and anguish. But tonight, he plays a smooth, thoughtful tune, with ripples of hope and the occasional thrum of excitement. The spark I saw earlier flashes in his eyes, and I realize how much I've missed it. More than anything I want Nightingale to be happy, but I wish that didn't mean leaving Morovia... I sigh, wishing I could make him *want* to stay.

"*Linnet...Linnet...*" Nightingale sings my name and a laugh springs from my mouth. He hasn't sung with such liveliness in years. His head feathers lift, and the way they reflect the firelight reminds me of the way they'd shine in the sunshine when we'd walk along the beach in Spark. "*Linnet... Please, tomorrow... Before dawn breaks the night... Let's go to the sea... Let's look at the waves and dream at the sight...*" He glances up at me, a small smile on his face, and I laugh even louder at the sight of it. His fingers dance over the guitar strings and his tune lifts my heart up to the stars twinkling beyond the lacy canopy. "*Let's talk to the fishers about faraway lands... And as the sun rises high... Let's think... Of new beginnings... Hand in hand...*"

I rise to my feet as Nightingale's song drifts into the swampy green darkness. "All right," I say, as I gather up our things into my bag. "We'll go to the sea before dawn. *Just to think*," I stress. "And *maybe* talk to the sea-fishers about Eldovia. But I'm not promising anything."

I lean down and say goodnight to Whiskers and Lumpy, sliding my hand into Whiskers's burrow to stroke her, and peeping into Lumpy's nook to wink at him. Then I move to Nightingale and kiss him goodnight.

He smiles again. "Thank you, Linnet. I know how difficult it is for you to think about leaving Morovia. I wouldn't ask unless I truly thought that it was the only way forwards." He reaches up and gently rests his hand on the back of my head and his forehead against my own. This time it's my eyes that fill with tears, as I think about leaving everything that we've ever known. "We could do it," Nightingale whispers. "We could be happy somewhere else, together."

I blink back my tears, give Nightingale a little nod, then turn, climb up home-tree and curl into my sleeping pod. It's warm and cosy, and I begin humming some musical scales, trying to feel some magic in the notes, but I can't concentrate.

What if, when we're on the mudflats tomorrow morning, talking to a sea-fisher, Nightingale persuades me to swap the diamond ring for a boat? What if his smile and the spark in his eyes leads me away from everything else my heart desires?

I know Nightingale would never use his magic on me, but his smile is just as powerful, because I want him to be happy. But I don't see how *I* can be happy if we leave, not when so much of my heart is here.

I pull the coin purse from my bag and feel the ring inside it. *A diamond ring.* A tiny thing with the power to take us away from here. Or maybe with the power to fix everything.

An idea nibbles into my mind, slightly bitter but moreish, like the wild garlic leaves we ate tonight. I could take the treasures to Echo – the leader of the Unity Movement – myself, once Nightingale is asleep. I could ask her if there's any way we could use the ring to revive the movement. And I could ask if there's anything I could do to make my singing magic arrive, and my name prophecy come true, because it feels more important now than ever.

I haven't seen Echo in almost three years, but I know her. She was taken away from Spark at the same time as Nightingale and I, and we lived on the mudflats together for a few moons. Echo gave me singing lessons back then, to try and help my magic come. They didn't work, but maybe she can show me something new to try.

The more I think about it, the more it makes sense. I can't leave Morovia until I know for sure whether there's anything I could do to help bring unity. And the only way for me to find that out is to talk to Echo myself.

Echo's hideout is less than an hour's walk away. I could go and talk to her and return before Nightingale wakes in the morning. My stomach churns with guilt and worry at the thought of sneaking away from Nightingale in the night, but this is my only chance to do anything before he takes me to Fisher's Flock to begin his plan of leaving here.

I peer out of my sleeping pod. The night is calm and still, and its misty breath clings to the trees. I can't see the moon, but I can see its silver light reflecting on the dark water. The swamp is beautiful and inviting: warm and damp, black-green in the shadows, with glow-worm stars and firefly meteors.

The excitement of a secret night-time mission flutters in my chest, and the thought of seeing Echo again brings a smile to my face. During the moons we lived on the mudflats together, Echo was the strongest person in my life. I watched her create a community from nothing but mud, driftwood and broken hearts. But then bogatyrs drove us into the swamp, and I haven't seen her since.

Nightingale has always said it's too dangerous for me to visit Echo because, as leader of the Unity Movement, Captain Ilya's bogatyrs are always looking for her. My stomach churns again with this thought, but right now Echo is my only hope of finding a way to stay on Morovia. So I take a deep breath and, as I wait for Nightingale to fall asleep, I focus on my memories of Echo, starting with the day we met...

The Day I Met Echo

Three years ago, about one moon after *Joy* sank, bogatyrs came to our home in Spark. Nightingale was sitting on our balcony, staring out to sea. It was all he'd done since the day of the tragedy. So it was me who opened the door.

The bogatyrs burst in so fast they nearly knocked me over. They were wearing strange metal armour over their deerskins that I'd never seen before, and helmets with thin, rectangular eyeholes. Four bogatyrs clanged around our home, while one bogatyr unrolled a piece of paper and began reading. But his face was hidden behind his helmet and I couldn't make out his words.

I asked if he would please remove his helmet, but he ignored me. I couldn't think why bogatyrs would be here, treating us like this. My father and I had done nothing wrong. And we were in mourning, like everyone else on Morovia.

Since the tragedy, almost everything on the island had been closed: the school, the market, the library. I think the hospital had been open, but Nightingale hadn't been going to work. It had been a time of quiet emptiness, of words dwindling into silence and a feeling of not knowing what to do. But now these bogatyrs had arrived with noise and purpose. Something was happening, but I didn't understand what.

Two bogatyrs lifted Nightingale to his feet. Nightingale stared at them, wide-eyed and trembling, as disorientated as if he was being lifted to the moon. I rushed over and told the bogatyrs to leave him alone. I explained my mother had been on *Joy*. Then I babbled something about how Nightingale was wearing his grief like a cloak pulled tight against him, and that he couldn't see out and no one could see in. It was something a lady had told me to explain why Nightingale hadn't spoken since the tidal wave.

Finally, one of the bogatyrs removed their helmet

and told the others to stop. Nightingale collapsed into his chair and began crying. The bogatyr was a young boy with dark hair, weary eyes and a flushed face marked with pressure lines from his helmet. "You have five minutes to pack," he said. "Then you and your father must come with us."

"Where?" I asked, but the bogatyr put his helmet back on without answering. Coldness crept over me and questions rang in my ears. I knew Captain Ilya had been making speeches, blaming alkonosts for the tragedy and saying singing magic was dangerous. Was that why we were being taken away?

Anger and fear rushed through me, but I pushed them back. We only had five minutes to pack, and I knew Nightingale couldn't help. I rushed around, putting things into the big straw bag that we usually used for picnics on the beach. Some instinct must have taken over, because without thinking, I packed essentials: blankets, clothes, a cooking pot, fire flints and some food.

I picked up my mother's yellow feather and Hero's necklace, which matched the one around my neck. Then I paused beside our bookshelf. My fingers ran over the spines of my mother's songbooks, but it was impossible to choose one to take. They all held memories of her.

Then a bogatyr said it was time to leave and led Nightingale through the door. I told myself we'd be home soon, pulled my fingers away from the songbooks and followed.

Outside, the sky was grey, the sea wind cold and the gulls screaming. On the sand below our home were more bogatyrs and three long wagons with barred sides and roofs, harnessed to horses. Our alkonost neighbours were being herded from their homes along the beach and into the wagons. My mouth opened in disbelief. This didn't look or feel like anything that should be happening.

Neither of the other Floating Islands were visible on the horizon. I wondered if they'd deserted us because they didn't want to be even a distant observer of what was happening here.

Nightingale and I were pushed into one of the wagons and we sat side by side at the back. There were at least ten other alkonosts in it, their brightly coloured feathers jaded, their faces downcast. I recognized most of them. Our elderly downstairs neighbour, Lark, his skin and feathers white as bleached bone, was clutching a bowl with his pet angelfish in it. Dunnock and Brambling, two of my friends from school, were huddled against their mother, Robin, in a ruffle of red and brown feathers. Everyone had wide, scared eyes.

"What's going on?" I asked the lady next to me as the wagon rolled along the beach. She was small, with fluffy grey-brown feathers on her head, neck and arms, and beige, softly wrinkled skin, like the pages of a well-read book. She wasn't elderly, but she was older than Nightingale, and had a calmness about her that made me feel comforted.

"Singing magic has been outlawed," the lady replied. "And anyone whose job involved using it is being rehomed."

I frowned, trying to work out what that meant for us. Surely Captain Ilya and his bogatyrs couldn't force us out of our homes. Why wasn't everyone on the island here to stop this? Where were our human friends?

Hero sprang into my mind, saying the tragedy was the fault of alkonosts, and my frown deepened. I had hoped she said those things unthinkingly, because she was racked with grief. But now I wondered if she really meant them. Did all humans blame us? Did they want us to go?

I thought about Fleur, Clay and Silver, and I knew in my heart they wouldn't want this. My mother and father were so close to Fleur and Clay that I often called Fleur "Aunty" and Clay "Uncle". And Silver was like a cousin to me – we used to hold hands when we were little and paddled together in the waves on Spark beach. The wagon passed the empty market, and through the bars I saw bogatyrs standing on street corners. I wondered if they were stopping our friends from helping us.

The wagon continued along the beach, towards the low-rip side of the island, and confusion swirled inside me. I knew there were only mudflats there, and dense woods that had been flooded by the tidal wave. "Where are we being rehomed?" I asked.

"I don't know." The lady shook her head. "My name is Swiftlet." She gave me a small, reassuring smile. "But everyone calls me Echo, because of my magic – I can make my thoughts echo into the air." Echo dipped her hand into the bag on her lap and pulled out a sea-green, swirly moon-snail shell. She held it to her mouth, quietly sang a few lines into it, then passed it to me.

The moment I touched the shell I felt Echo's magic flowing into me like the warmth of a hot drink, and an image appeared in my mind of the Three Floating Islands, but as I had never seen them before. I was flying high above them, and I could feel wind over and under my wings. Spray filled the air from waves crashing far below. There was a storm, and the islands were huddled so close together that someone could have stepped from one to another.

"What is this?" I asked curiously.

"It's a memory." Echo smiled. "Not mine of course – I can't fly. This memory has been passed down over generations, through magic like my own. It's the last time the Floating Islands came together, to weather a storm that lasted many moons."

The image in my mind changed. The storm ebbed away, the islands moved into calmer seas, then drifted apart. Sheet clouds cracked open and beams of sunlight lit up the islands, making them glow like a string of jewels. Then the images faded as Echo's magic fell away.

"I've never seen magic like that, and I never knew the islands could drift so close together." I smiled as I passed the shell back to Echo, then realized it was the first time that I'd smiled since *Joy* sank. I felt strangely disloyal. Not disloyal to my mother – I knew she would want me to smile at Echo, because she always encouraged me to be polite. But I felt disloyal to Nightingale somehow. He was sitting beside me, but his mind was far away. I feared my smile might widen the space between us, as it rooted me in the here and now, while Nightingale remained distant and hidden. I was worried that beneath his cloak of grief, Nightingale might be permanently broken and slipping away. But I didn't know how to pull him to me, and I needed to be present, with Echo, to figure out where we were being taken and what we could do about it.

"I'm Linnet and this is my father, Nightingale," I said. The salt sea air blew through my feathers and I took a deep breath to steady myself. "My mother was on *Joy*," I added.

"My brother, Tern, was on *Joy* too." Echo's eyes dampened.

I put my hand over Echo's, too choked with emotion to say anything else.

The wagon slowed and we crossed a small log bridge over a tidal inlet. Then we rolled to a stop, but I felt like the earth was still moving as I looked around.

To our left, a muddy beach stretched to the ocean. And to our right lay the flooded woods – the swamp – lush and green and draped in a fog like blown breath.

I stared at it and a strange longing to explore it – to escape into it away from everything that was happening – swelled inside me.

The bogatyrs released us from the wagon and one of them read from another roll of paper, but like the bogatyr in our home, his helmet made him difficult to understand. I caught the words *enemies to safety, outlawed magic*, and *until Spark can be made safe*.

"Why are the bogatyrs wearing helmets?" I asked Echo in frustration.

"They're made from iron extracted from the rocks in the Magicless Mountains," Echo replied. "They protect them from singing magic."

I looked around at the alkonosts on the mudflats with me, wondering why anyone would need protecting from us. About thirty of us had been brought here in the three wagons, and everyone looked small and scared. I scowled at the bogatyr, then gathered my and Nightingale's belongings and helped the other alkonosts with theirs.

The wagons rolled back towards Spark, surrounded by clattering, armoured bogatyrs.

"What do we do now?" I whispered to Echo.

Echo took a deep breath, then clapped her hands together and spoke loudly enough for everyone to hear.

"We'll work together to build shelters. Then we'll make a meal. Then we'll decide, together, what to do next."

Without Echo, the following moons would have been impossible, especially for me. Echo was the only one who could reach Nightingale. She gave him simple, clear instructions and, to my amazement, he followed them. His thoughts were still elsewhere, but if Echo told him to collect driftwood or cut logs or help with the building of shelters, then he'd do it.

I helped Nightingale with whatever he was working on, and that made me feel like the distance between us wasn't so vast. Having something to do helped me fight my own waves of grief too, as I blinked back tears and focused on what needed to be done.

Sometimes the waves of grief were too powerful though, and I'd crouch on the muddy sand and bury my face in my knees. Echo always noticed and would appear at my side and wrap her arms around me, her fluffy feathers warm against my skin. When my breathing calmed, Echo would pull me up and find me another job.

Wooden huts sprang up in a long line between the

muddy beach and the swamp. More alkonosts arrived almost every day, brought in the wagon-cages, along with news of rules Captain Ilya had made to separate the people of Morovia. We worked together to make sure everyone had food, water and somewhere warm to sleep.

I learned that Echo was a kind of historian, a keeper of the old ways. Part of her job had been teaching ancient forms of singing magic, and I persuaded her to give me lessons. I hoped they might make my magic come.

More importantly though, Echo knew how the ancient bird-people of Morovia had lived. She taught us how to make fishing lines from plant fibres, and traps to catch rabbits and squirrels. We collected shellfish from the mudflats, and roots, tubers, berries, nuts and seeds from the swamp. We cooked and ate together, and sang together in the evenings, our voices drifting over the tidal inlet and far out to sea. They were mostly sad songs of loss and mourning, but they made us feel less alone.

Nightingale didn't sing. But he was slowly healing. I liked that he was busy doing things, instead of staring out to sea. He built us a beautiful little hut with a window that faced the water, and made us driftwood beds and a stone oven, and he put a rope ladder and swing on an alder tree behind our hut.

My friends often sat by the tree with me and we'd play on the ladder and swing. There was Dunnock and Brambling, more friends from school, and new friends, like Teal and Whimbrel, who had lived in Pero Palace Complex. They said that all alkonosts had been sent away from the palace and were no longer allowed to be courtiers or bogatyrs. Alkonosts were being sent away from the lee-side farms too, and all of us were building new homes on the mudflats.

I decorated our hut with mobiles made of seabird feathers and shells that I collected from the muddy beach, and Nightingale helped me carve toy animals from pieces of driftwood. I loved exploring the mudflats and the swamp, and I enjoyed spending time with my alkonost friends. But I missed my mother, and our human friends, especially Fleur, Clay and Silver. And I missed Hero, even though I was angry with her for saying that *Joy* sinking was the fault of alkonosts.

I wondered what Hero was doing now; whether she knew what had happened to me and other alkonosts, and whether she cared. But there was always so much to do, foraging and building, that there was little time to dwell on these thoughts.

Echo held meetings in the evenings. We named the huts the Hopeful Huts and talked about organizing a movement to stop what Captain Ilya was doing and bring unity to Morovia.

Occasionally, alkonosts and humans snuck between the mudflats and Spark. We learned many humans didn't support Captain Ilya, but that anyone who opposed him was accused of being an *enemy to safety* and was sent to The Keep.

I sat in Echo's meetings, trying to figure out how I could help. But the older alkonosts would talk for hours, and sometimes Echo would shoo me and the younger alkonosts away to collect crabs or play kickball.

Nightingale stayed in the meetings though, and it was during them that he began to listen and talk in full sentences again. He joined in conversations about petitioning to speak to Crown Heir Vasha, who could remove Captain Ilya from power. No one had seen Vasha since the tragedy, and Echo was worried this was part of Captain Ilya's plan to keep control of the island.

Despite the problems the new Unity Movement faced, I believed it would succeed. I imagined what

Hero and I would say to each other when we were reunited. Hero would apologize for the things she'd said and for throwing her necklace on the floor.

I'd thought about that day so much, and how Hero's face had been hot and wet with tears. I became sure that Hero must have lost someone when *Joy* sank too. So I would forgive her and say that I understood her painful words were said in anger. I began wearing our necklaces in a tiny leather bag around my neck, and I ached to see Hero running along the beach towards me. I wanted to move on from that awful day and make our friendship perfect again, like the tide made the mudflats all smooth after we'd ruffled them up digging for shellfish.

Some nights I couldn't sleep for thinking about Hero, and it was on one of those nights that Echo came to our hut, her feather-eyebrows low and her gaze urgent. "We must leave, now. Bogatyrs are coming to take us to The Keep."

"Why?" I asked sleepily, as confused as the day bogatyrs took us from Spark.

"Someone here told Captain Ilya about the Unity Movement and gave him a list of names," Echo said. "We're accused of being enemies to the safety of Morovia."

"But…" My voice trailed off. This didn't make sense. We weren't enemies to anyone.

"Hurry!" Echo urged, pulling me from my bed. "Pack only what you need." She talked to Nightingale as I packed essentials, just as I had in Spark: blankets, clothes and a few things for cooking.

I heard Echo tell Nightingale about a meeting that was to be held at the next new moon. She said the Unity Movement would continue in secret, and we'd have to be wary of who we trusted now.

Echo hugged me before she left, and whispered that I should keep Nightingale busy and talk to him even when he was silent. Less than five minutes later, Nightingale and I slipped into the night-darkness of the swamp. Many others did too, and we all drifted away from each other without a word.

Since then it's been just Nightingale and me, living day-to-day, tree-to-tree; stealing to fund the Unity Movement and making bargains with Fate in the hope of change to come.

The years have flowed by, slow as swamp water, and still we hide. I often think about our friends, the swing on the alder tree, and the driftwood animals that Nightingale and I carved. I wonder if they're still there.

We've never gone back, because nobody lives in the huts any more.

All the alkonosts are in the swamp, yet we are all alone. It's been like this for too long. I must do something to change Morovia before Nightingale makes us leave. And right now, finding Echo and asking for her help is my only hope.

CHAPTER 5

NIGHT SONG

It's deep in the night when I finally hear Nightingale's gentle snores drifting from his sleeping pod. I tie the coin purse with the diamond ring inside to the strip of leather I wear around my waist like a belt, then hold my breath as I step silently out of my pod onto the branch below.

My heart flutters with nervousness as I climb down the furrowed trunk of home-tree, but when I step onto the roots at its base, excitement rushes through me. I'm going to find Echo and, with her help, I'm going to figure out a new plan to bring unity to Morovia so that we don't have to leave.

Nightingale has always taken the treasures we steal to Echo alone, because he believes the further I'm kept from the activities of the Unity Movement, the safer I'll be. But almost every time he's journeyed to Echo's hideout, I've followed him, hiding in the trees.

For years, I thought I was so silent and stealthy that he didn't know. Then, about a year ago, he turned around while I was following him, looked straight at me and winked. I felt like bursting out laughing. I think he knew all along. We never talked about it afterwards and I carried on following him, wondering why he let me.

I think perhaps he felt comforted knowing where I was, but a part of me also hoped that he secretly *wanted* me to know where Echo's hideout was, because he knew that I could be useful to the Unity Movement one day. I smile, thinking that day has finally come.

Whiskers pokes her head out of her burrow, her half-smile widens, and I hear her tail flicking back and forth against the leaf-lined walls behind her. "All right," I whisper, scooting along the roots until I step onto the muddy bank beside her. "You can come too, but we must be quiet." I lean down to peer into Lumpy's nook and he peers back at me. "Can you stay and guard Nightingale?" I ask, not wanting to leave my father completely alone. If bogatyrs came in the night, at least Lumpy could warn him with one of his high-pitched alarm calls and give him a chance to escape. Lumpy croaks firmly in response, crawls a little way out of his nook and holds his sword-leg out in front of him in his guarding pose. "Thanks, Lumpy." I smile and hop onto the grassy hummock as Whiskers leans down to say farewell. I know she doesn't like leaving Lumpy, but the way she glances up at Nightingale's sleeping pod makes me think that she understands the importance of not leaving my father alone. Whiskers lowers her snout to Lumpy and grunts softly, and Lumpy responds by affectionately patting her cheek with his sword-leg.

We've had so many different home-trees over the last few years that I now have a good map of the swamp in my head. I quickly decide the best way to reach Echo's hideout in the dark of night, pull back the trailing moss curtain, then begin walking high-ripward along the deer trail that runs beside the water. The canopy is thinner over the water, letting through just enough moonlight for me to see by.

Whiskers walks at my heels, her webbed back feet leaving deep prints in the soft mud, and her tail leaving a line as it trails behind her. The water to our left is flowing slowly, with a shimmering, silver surface. Glow-worms shine like eerie blue stars in the thick dark foliage to our right, and birds rustle in the leaves above. Occasionally I spot the moon peeping out from behind branches. It's a fat, waxing, almost egg-shaped orb.

When we reach the confluence of the water channel with another that flows from the high side of the island, I lean down and scratch Whiskers's cheek. "I'll climb over through the trees and you swim across." I tilt my head to where I plan to meet Whiskers on the opposite bank. She lifts her snout up to my nose and makes a few gentle grunting sounds before turning and slipping into the water.

I climb the nearest tree, a huge white oak, my hands gripping each branch tight and my bare, muddy feet pressed onto the rough bark. I walk along a thick horizontal branch that overhangs the water, until it tangles into a willow tree the other side. I feel like a spider must feel in her web: at home and safe. I rarely fear anything in the swamp. It's only people – alkonosts and humans – that I'm wary of, in case they spy or work for Captain Ilya, but I can usually hear them from far away. I glance down and see Whiskers smoothly swimming across the water below me. She must sense me looking, because she glances up and twitches her snout.

The swamp is quiet. Perhaps too quiet, I think, and my feathers start to tingle. The only noise is the barely audible splash of Whiskers swimming. But then a voice, singing, rises from somewhere ahead and I stop still. It's an alkonost, singing magic. I frown as I try to work out the best thing to do. Should I retreat and take a different route to Echo's, or try to sneak past the alkonost?

Whiskers's tail splashes in the water and I look down and watch in horror as she turns and starts swimming away from me, towards the singing. I make a few of the grunting sounds that I use to call her, but she ignores me and swims faster and further away.

I crouch down, grab the branch I'm standing on, then dangle from it by my hands and slip into the water. It has the same warmth as the air and feels soft and slimy against my skin. I kick my legs like a frog and swim smoothly after Whiskers as fast as I can, my mind muttering regrets for bringing her with me. Although I know that if I had told Whiskers to stay in her burrow, she would have followed me anyway.

Whiskers swims further away from me, dipping in and out of sight as she glides through the shadows of overhanging trees. I struggle to keep up, but finally she turns and climbs onto the bank. I'm relieved only for the tiniest of moments, because then she disappears into undergrowth.

I make more grunting sounds, trying to call her back

as I swim to the bank. The singing is louder now. The alkonost is nearby and my heart pounds as I realize Whiskers is moving towards them. I rise out of the water and wade through ferns that reach almost to my shoulders, desperately trying to spot Whiskers.

The song changes from a slow, gentle tune to a faster, more urgent hum, and I hear Whiskers crashing through the ferns ahead. She's speeding away from me and I race after her, not caring now how much noise I make. This is a bad decision, because I soon lose track of Whiskers again as her noise is drowned out by my own.

I stop, hold my breath and listen again. I can't hear Whiskers now, but I can still hear the singing, twenty or thirty paces ahead. I peer into the darkness. The vegetation is so thick here, it's difficult to see anything, but finally I make out a small clearing lit by faint moonlight.

There's a young boy in the clearing, with long feathers trailing down his back, humming a song as he leans towards the ground. He lifts something with both hands and panic flares through me as I see it's Whiskers. Then my panic turns to horror as I spot a spear shining in one of the boy's hands, and realize he's using his magic to hunt for swamp-rats.

CHAPTER 6

CAPTURED

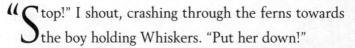

"Stop!" I shout, crashing through the ferns towards the boy holding Whiskers. "Put her down!"

The boy looks up at me in shock, but keeps his grip on Whiskers, who is lying perfectly still in his arms, her eyes glazed over.

"Please put her down," I say, quieter, as I draw closer. The boy is small and thin and younger than me – maybe eight or nine years old. His head feathers are long, striped blue and white, and his light blue skin is silvered by moonlight falling from between the leaves above.

"I caught her." The boy pulls Whiskers closer to his chest. "So I'm keeping her."

"No, you can't." I step forwards and reach for Whiskers, but flinch back in shock when another boy jumps down from a tree branch above and lands between me and the boy holding Whiskers. This second boy is older – maybe eleven or twelve years old, with mottled orange-brown feathers and skin, a longer face and more serious expression. He's at least a hand's-breadth shorter than me, but he straightens his spine and opens his arms, blocking my path to Whiskers. "Leave my brother alone," he says firmly.

"I will as soon as he gives me Whiskers," I reply just as firmly.

The younger boy peers around his brother to look at me. "There's plenty of meat on her. We could share." His eyes light up at the suggestion and he smiles, revealing a gap where one of his front teeth is missing.

"You can't eat Whiskers! We've been friends since she was a pup." I hold out my hands, hoping the boys will give her back to me now. "Please," I add. "You can't eat my friend."

The boy holding Whiskers sighs sadly. "I suppose not." He glances at his brother and his brother nods reluctantly before stepping aside so that I can lift Whiskers free.

"Thank you." I smile with relief as I cradle Whiskers, who is still in an enchanted sleep. I glance around, thinking that I should leave now. These boys might be the sort of alkonosts who trade information to Captain Ilya's bogatyrs in exchange for cocoa beans from the palace hothouses, or blankets made from the wool of mountain sheep. But I hesitate.

It's so rare that I get to talk to anyone other than Nightingale, and there is something about the boys that is making my heart ache. They're both too thin, all sharp bones and hollows, like they haven't eaten properly in moons. No wonder they wanted to catch Whiskers.

"I'm Jay." The younger boy smiles. "And this is my brother, Kestrel."

"I'm…" I hesitate again as my thoughts branch in two directions. I'd like to give the boys my name, but I'm still not sure whether they can be trusted. Whiskers wriggles as Jay's magic falls off her, and I lower her to the ground. "Whiskers and I should really be going."

"Have you got any food?" Jay asks suddenly.

"No. But there's plenty here." I glance at the ferns around us. "Some of these are edible."

Kestrel's eyes widen. "Which ones?"

I lean down and peer into the ferns. I should move on and get to Echo's, but it will only take a moment to show Kestrel and Jay something they can eat. I find a few young shoots of ostrich fern, snap two off and pass one to each of the boys. "You can eat these, raw or cooked."

Jay takes a bite and hums with satisfaction. Kestrel studies his shoot closely and looks down into the ferns, trying to find more.

I snap off another shoot for Jay. "I don't understand why you're so hungry. You were using your singing magic to lure Whiskers, weren't you?"

Jay nods as he looks round for more shoots.

"Well, if you can use your singing magic to hunt, why isn't your belly full of rabbit and squirrel, fish and crab?" I ask. At the word *crab*, Whiskers whines and moves closer to my leg.

"My magic doesn't always work." Jay crunches through another shoot. "It hardly ever works, to be honest. And sometimes it has completely the opposite effect, especially on crabs – they always run away when I sing."

"What about all the shellfish, snails, plants and tubers in the swamp?" I ask, leaning down to give Whiskers a comforting stroke. "You don't need magic to forage for food."

"We're not sure what's edible and what's poisonous," Kestrel says. He's gathered a handful of fern shoots now and he holds them out to me questioningly. "Are all of these safe?"

I nod. "Isn't there anyone to help you?" I ask, wondering if Jay and Kestrel have any family or friends in the swamp.

"Our parents were captured by bogatyrs about three moons ago," Kestrel explains. "I've been taking care of Jay as best as I can, but I wish I'd paid more attention to the foods my parents collected. I didn't think they'd..." Kestrel's voice trails off and he sniffs. "Anyway, thanks for the ferns. These will help. And once you and Whiskers have left, Jay can try to sing for another swamp-rat. No. A rabbit," he corrects, glancing at Whiskers apologetically.

I nod, but I don't move. It doesn't feel right leaving Jay and Kestrel here alone. Anger at the bogatyrs who took their parents is prickling my skin, and I feel that I should do something to help the boys. I wonder whether to ask if they want to come to Echo's with me, or back to my and Nightingale's home-tree.

There's still a shadow of suspicion in my mind, but I don't want to let it sweep coldness over me. I want to make sure Jay and Kestrel are safe and have some food and shelter – the same way the alkonosts on the mudflats cared for each other when we were first taken away from our homes.

"We'll be fine," Kestrel says, as if he knows what I'm thinking. "We've been managing on our own, and we're getting better at it every day."

"All right." I nod thoughtfully. "There's something I need to do now anyway, and my father and I are going to the mudflats in the morning. But why don't you come to our home-tree later on tomorrow and we'll share a meal?" My words rush out before I can change my mind. "It would be nice to have some company," I add with a small smile.

Jay smiles back at me with his missing-tooth grin. "It would be nice. Where's your home-tree?"

I hesitate again for a fraction of a second. "Do you know the big cypress in the wide channel, low-lee side of here? It's far taller than any of the others around it."

Kestrel nods. "I know the one. Won't your father mind us coming?"

"I think he might enjoy the company," I say hopefully. "And we have some stored food. Are you sure you'll be all right tonight?"

"We'll be fine. I think Jay would like another go at singing for some food anyway." Kestrel glances at Jay.

"Definitely. I'm getting better at it." Jay nods.

"Your magic certainly worked on Whiskers," I agree, a shudder running through me as I think how close Whiskers came to being a meal. I give her another stroke and decide that I need to keep a closer eye on her from now on.

"The song I use to call rabbits is different to the song I use to call swamp-rats," Jay explains in a reassuring voice.

Jealousy nips into me because Jay already has his magic even though he's years younger than me. It might not always work, but at least he has something to practise with. I try to shake the jealousy away. Maybe tomorrow, when we all eat together, Jay and Kestrel could give me some tips for singing magic.

"My name is Linnet," I say, remembering I haven't introduced myself yet, "and my father is called Nightingale. I look forward to seeing you both tomorrow." I raise my hand in a farewell, then turn and walk back towards the water with Whiskers at my side, my doubts now replaced with excitement for their visit.

A smile widens on my face as another thought occurs to me – whatever happens on the mudflats with Nightingale in the morning, we can't leave Morovia when I've invited people for a meal in the afternoon.

Whiskers and I reach the channel and look around until I spot a twisted black willow that looks familiar and I figure out where we are. The air is already lightening from green-black to green-grey. Dawn must be less than an hour away. I let out a sigh, because I don't have enough time now to find Echo and return to home-tree before morning.

Going back will take longer than it took to get here, because when I swam after Whiskers the current helped me, but now I'd have to swim against it. I decide to walk along the channel bank instead, until I can find some trees to use as a bridge to cross the water. I'm too scared to let Whiskers swim alone now so I'll have to carry her across too, but I've done that before.

"Come on." I stroke Whiskers's head, then we walk back towards home-tree, while I try to figure out the best way to explain to Nightingale why I left in the night and why two boys are now coming to share a meal with us. I'm disappointed that my plan to see Echo has failed, but I'm glad that I met Jay and Kestrel and now have something to look forward to that doesn't involve leaving Morovia.

I don't spot home-tree until the morning chorus has begun and the sun's first rays are making shining diamonds of the night dew speckling the plants of the swamp. A thin stream of smoke is rising from our fire pit and I pick up my pace as I realize Nightingale must be awake already – which means he'll have noticed I'm not in my sleeping pod and will be worried about me.

When I draw closer my feathers tighten against my scalp. Something is wrong. The smoke from the fire is too thick and too acrid, like wool burning. And there are noises that make my heart pound with fear: the high-pitched alarm call of a toad; rough, human voices and the clang of iron – the sound of armoured bogatyrs.

I tell Whiskers to hide in the foliage and climb into the nearest tree, like Nightingale and I always do when we hear bogatyrs in the swamp. I carry on climbing through the branches, closer to home-tree, until finally I see Nightingale on the muddy bank.

He's flanked by two enormous bogatyrs, who make him look tiny as a child. They're wearing full iron helmets that protect them from singing magic. I stifle a yell and rush towards Nightingale through the trees, but he looks up, straight at me, and without lifting his hand from his side he holds it out, palm down. *Stay down.*

Lumpy lets out another alarm call from his nook

and I crouch behind a leafy branch and watch, smoke and anger burning my eyes. Nightingale's sleeping pod is crumpled on the muddy ground and his blanket is smouldering on the fire, along with one of our birch-bark bowls.

A third bogatyr is up in our home-tree, rifling through our storage pod and throwing things down. Nightingale's spare tunic flutters through the air, lands in the water and begins floating away. The one cooking pot we have, which I brought from our home in Spark, crashes down and dents on a rock of the fire pit.

Then Nightingale's guitar falls and lands in the mud. One of the bogatyrs beside Nightingale steps onto it, crushing its tin body and breaking its maple neck. "Where is the ring?" he growls at Nightingale, but Nightingale only stares silently at him in response. My stomach twists painfully. *The bogatyrs are looking for the ring I stole.* This is all my fault.

My muscles shake. I want to rush down and tell them it was me who stole the ring, and give it to them. But Nightingale's hand is still palm down, and I know he wouldn't want me to.

A splash sounds in the river and I turn to the noise in panic. *Whiskers!* She's swimming towards Nightingale and the bogatyrs. I open my mouth to call her back, but then I have a thought, a wish, a desire that burns in every fibre of my being: to sing magic, to sing a storm to blow the bogatyrs far away from here. *Maybe this time my magic will come...*

The bogatyrs are still wearing their iron helmets, but I think if my magic was powerful enough, it wouldn't matter. If I could sing a wind that grew into a hurricane, then no helmets could protect them.

Some of the most powerful singing magic often sounds like birdsong, so I close my eyes and begin whistling the slow, flute-like tune of a blackbird. But I don't feel anything. I try the low cooing of a pigeon, the rambling warble of a swallow, the melodic ripple of a chiffchaff, the dreamy song of a mistle thrush, the screech of a barn owl...

"What is that?" A helmet-muffled shout from one of the bogatyrs echoes through the trees. I stop singing and open my eyes. One of the bogatyrs is staring straight in my direction and my heart thumps so hard I think it might break my ribs.

The bogatyr who was rifling through our storage pod has moved onto my sleeping pod, and he throws my bag down – the one I wove from nettle fibres last year.

"Check this," he shouts, and the bogatyr who was looking in my direction leans down to pick it up.

Nightingale's fingers twitch urgently. He wants me to leave. But I can't let the bogatyrs wreck this tiny piece of home we have and take my father away. I close my eyes again and try singing the song of a nightingale bird, desperately trying to feel some tingle of magic. I sing three fast whistles three times, then the *trill* that vibrates in my throat. A tiny breeze makes the leaves around me shiver and my heart soars...is this it? Am I singing magic? Could I sing a storm?

I open my eyes and the breeze falls away. My heart sinks as I realize there's no magic in the air. It was only wishful thinking. *I have no singing magic.*

With a sudden splash, Whiskers rises out of the water and charges onto the bank, grunting angrily. One of the bogatyrs kicks her back into the water. My chest folds in on itself as she squeals in distress. Lumpy crawls out of his nook, waving his sword-leg at the bogatyrs, and almost gets squashed beneath a boot. I'm so angry I feel like my skin is aflame.

I take a slow, deep breath, then sing a single note, as high and bright as the moon, like my mother used to do when she sang magic. It wasn't only butterflies my mother could call with her songs, but bees and other pollinators. If I could sing magic like her, then I could make insects swarm around the bogatyrs and drive them away.

But no insects come. And the bogatyrs continue destroying everything of mine and Nightingale's while Whiskers cowers in the water and Lumpy retreats reluctantly into his nook. Then one of the bogatyrs binds Nightingale's hands behind his back. My single-note song fades into a whispered whimper and my eyes blur with tears. I feel so dizzy, I hug the branch tighter to stop myself from crashing down.

The bogatyrs pull Nightingale away from home-tree, and I gaze after him. Guilt and regret for stealing the ring twists my stomach into a small, hard knot, and my muscles freeze with fear of whatever might come next.

Nightingale's left hand, even though it's bound, remains held out awkwardly, palm down – *stay down*. But I must do something. I can't let the bogatyrs take Nightingale away. I'd be lost without him, and he'd be lost without me. We need each other. Suddenly I feel more alone than I've ever felt before. I clench my teeth and frown. I must think of a way to free him.

Chapter 7

Bogatyrs

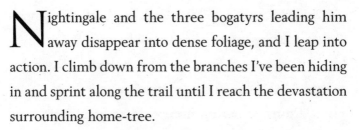

Nightingale and the three bogatyrs leading him away disappear into dense foliage, and I leap into action. I climb down from the branches I've been hiding in and sprint along the trail until I reach the devastation surrounding home-tree.

I don't care about our sleeping pods or bowls, or the bag I made, or our cooking pot and blankets from our home in Spark. My gaze even slides over Nightingale's tin guitar, crumpled and broken. All I want is my father back.

The bogatyrs will be taking Nightingale to the road that skirts the lee-side edge of the swamp, and from there he'll be taken to The Keep. Nightingale told me never to follow him if this happens, but it feels like there's a vine connecting us and that's all I can do. Maybe there will be an opportunity for him to escape before he's taken away from the swamp, in which case I want to be nearby so that we can find each other.

I crouch beside Lumpy and call Whiskers with a few short grunts. There are huge red ants all over the ground and I frown at them in confusion, because I've never seen ants like them before. They're swarming all over what's left of my and Nightingale's belongings. Lumpy's long tongue flicks out, grabs one of the ants and pulls it back into his mouth. He swallows it, then looks up at me and croaks miserably.

"You shouldn't have tried to attack the bogatyrs, Lumpy." I shake my head, remembering how he waved his sword-leg at them. "You could have got hurt. And the same applies to you, Whiskers." I rub Whiskers's cheeks when she appears at my side. "Are you all right?" I scan her body, looking for signs of injury, but thankfully she appears fine. She even does a little wriggle to show me that she's not hurt. "Come on, let's get Nightingale back," I say, determination surging through me.

Lumpy crawls up onto Whiskers's head and we set off in the direction the bogatyrs went. The swamp is too dense for horses and wagons, so the bogatyrs will have left their transport on the road and be travelling on foot. Humans always walk loudly in the swamp, and these bogatyrs are making so much noise that I could hear them from the mudflats.

As well as their clumsy footfalls and clanging armour, they're talking and laughing. How can they laugh when they're taking my father away to The Keep, a place where people are locked up and never seen again?

Anger towards the bogatyrs swells inside me, along with anger towards Captain Ilya and all the humans who help him. Captain Ilya has hundreds of bogatyrs enforcing his rules now, and there must be hundreds more humans who support him in other ways – by following his orders, or simply by doing nothing and ignoring what is happening to alkonosts.

I don't understand why so many humans are willing to see Morovia divided and see alkonosts pushed into the swamp and sent to The Keep. No wonder Echo and Nightingale have given up hope. While humans are allowing such cruelty to happen, how can unity between us be possible?

All of a sudden, I feel foolish for ever thinking that I could have fixed anything on Morovia. I should have listened to Nightingale and left this island with him the moment he suggested it. I must think of a way to free him now, then we can leave, together, like he wanted.

There's a long thicket of tangled redwood trees between here and the road, and I decide to climb up and through them so that I can get closer to Nightingale and the bogatyrs without being seen. "Stay out of sight," I whisper to Whiskers and Lumpy, before grabbing a branch and swinging myself up into the trees.

I can often move faster along branches than over the muddy, stream-split ground of the swamp. Over the years I've learned which branches can take my weight, which ones will wobble or creak, and which ones will snap. The clusters of leaves keep me hidden and, after a few minutes, I'm climbing right above the bogatyrs. There's one walking either side of Nightingale and the third walking behind him. They're all complaining about how today, Nestday, should have been their day off, and how they wanted to spend it in Spark tavern, not the damp and gloomy swamp.

Several of Nightingale's fingers twitch. He knows I'm here and he's signalling me to fall back. But I carry on following, desperately trying to think of what I could do to rescue him. I quietly try singing some of my mother's songs, some of Nightingale's songs, and some of the songs of all the other alkonosts I've ever heard.

I even sing some of Jay's song that he used to lure Whiskers last night. But nothing works.

I try birdsong again: the trill of a crossbill, the chirping of a tree sparrow, the liquid tremolo of a skylark. And though I've tried a million times before, I sing the undulating twitter of a linnet. *Nothing.* I swallow back a groan of frustration and my throat feels sore from trying. Tears well in my eyes, but I can't give up. There must be something I can do…

My mother once told me that singing magic is just one way of turning thoughts, feelings and wishes into action, and that often it's not the best way. She said even when my magic came, I should always pause to consider all the different ways I could achieve something.

So even though I still feel that I'm missing what would be the most powerful part of me, I stop trying to sing magic and try to come up with another plan.

We're nearly at the road. Through the trees I see a wagon-cage, like the one that took Nightingale and me away from Spark. My head spins and my blood rushes ice-cold. The wagon is hitched to a horse, and another horse is nearby. Surrounding the wagon are at least ten young bogatyrs. They're wearing deerskins and small iron helmets that cover their ears, but not their faces. They all look about my age or a few years older, so must be bogatyrs in training.

Then I notice a tall, broad man, wearing plates of armour over his deerskins and a much larger helmet, plumed with a long, golden feather. It's not a real feather, beautiful and soft, but a feather carved from hard, unmoving metal.

Captain Ilya. The head of the bogatyrs and the cause of all the division on Morovia. I've seen him before, patrolling the swamp edges, and Nightingale has told me who he is. I feel an anger rising inside me so fast that my skin prickles with heat.

Nightingale always told me not to hate, because hate can shadow the goodness inside us and be used by people like Captain Ilya to cause conflict. But staring at Captain Ilya now, it's hard not to feel something like hate churning in my stomach and bitter on my tongue. It's because of him that Nightingale and I, and all alkonosts, have lost our homes, our lives and our friends, and it's because of him that we live alone in the swamp, suspicious of everyone. I feel slightly relieved as I realize I don't truly hate Captain Ilya though. It's outrage that I feel, for all the injustice and suffering that he's caused.

The bogatyrs lead my father up to Captain Ilya, and he looks down at Nightingale with a contemptuous sneer. Captain Ilya's helmet falls low over his forehead and has a wide nose plate that reaches down to his mouth. There's also a band of chain mail that drapes from either side of his helmet, covering his neck. The small amount of Captain Ilya's skin that I can see is sunburned red as crayfish claws. His eyes are iron-grey, like his armour, and his gaze is sharp with anger.

"Put him in the wagon," Captain Ilya growls, pushing Nightingale roughly towards the young bogatyrs.

Nightingale stumbles awkwardly and falls onto the dirt road, because his hands are still bound behind his back. I clench my jaw to stop from crying out. Several of the young bogatyrs laugh and I burn with anger towards them. Once again I think how foolish I was for believing there could be unity, when so many humans are so cruel.

But then one of the young bogatyrs crouches down and gently lifts Nightingale back onto his feet. My heart stops, then swells and thumps louder until it fills my chest with heat and noise.

I recognize the young bogatyr.

It's been three years since I've seen her, and she's

grown taller and broader, but she holds herself the same way she always did – upright and proud, with her strong hands poised to help anyone in need. Her hair is still long and shiny and tied in a plait that trails down her back. And she has the same piercing gaze that makes you feel that she can see everything going on around you, and right into your thoughts too.

Hero.

My best friend. Or my ex-best-friend, depending how I think about it.

I stare at Hero, open-mouthed, shock and anger and longing all battling inside me. I've dreamed of this moment, of seeing her again, but never like this. Hero is gently helping Nightingale walk, but to a wagon-cage that will take him to The Keep.

How could she do this? She must remember Nightingale – how we all ate together on the beach and sang together in my home.

Nightingale is holding one of his feet strangely, not putting any weight on it, and I scowl at the thought that's he's been injured. Alkonost bones are light as driftwood and could be easily broken by a human as big and rough as Captain Ilya. How could Hero work for someone so brutal?

Disappointment falls over me. Then desperation makes my heartbeat fast and bumpy, as I realize there's nothing I can do to stop this from happening. Hero helps Nightingale into the wagon and another bogatyr locks him in.

"Take him to The Keep," Captain Ilya orders, swinging himself up onto the horse nearby. "Put him in a holding cell until the trials on Glidesday." Captain Ilya trots away on his horse ahead of the others.

One of the bogatyrs who captured Nightingale climbs up onto the front of the wagon and flicks the reins, and the horse walks slowly highward. As the wagon wheels roll and scour into the dirt road, I feel as if they're crushing me.

The other two bogatyrs who captured Nightingale and the group of younger bogatyrs, including Hero, all follow the wagon on foot. I stare at Nightingale sitting in the cage, my heart hammering against my chest like it wants to break free and follow him.

Nightingale doesn't look in my direction but his hand is still palm down – he knows that I'm watching and he wants me to stay hidden.

But I find myself creeping further along the branch, away from the cover of the leaves, so that I can keep my father in sight. My thoughts are panicked; I'm still desperately trying to think of something I could do to free him. My mother was wrong – singing magic is the *only* way that I could stop this from happening, and I don't have any.

All of a sudden, Hero turns and looks straight at me with her sharp, piercing gaze. It takes my breath away. I stare back at her, feeling like I know everything and nothing about her. I wonder if she's going to tell the other bogatyrs where I am, and fear tightens around me, like the time I got tangled in eelgrass when swimming. I won't be able to help Nightingale if I'm captured too.

Hero's expression is stiff and unreadable. But then she nods almost imperceptibly, dips her hand into her pocket and pulls out something small and shiny. She throws it into the air and it catches the light as it spins. It's a copper coin, like the one that started our friendship six years ago. Hero catches the coin, turns and walks away.

I breathe again. *Hero saw me.* She didn't tell the other bogatyrs where I was, and she showed me a copper coin. Does this mean she still feels the bond of our friendship? I wonder if she's only working for

Captain Ilya because she has no other choice. Then my mind leaps to a desperate, impossible thought – I wonder if she could somehow help me free Nightingale.

Doubts and confusion swirl in my head, but my heart races with hope – not only that Hero might be able to help me free my father, but that perhaps there is hope for unity between alkonosts and humans after all. Because if there's a chance my and Hero's friendship can be healed, then maybe Morovia can be healed too.

I think of the copper coin, spinning in the air. Captain Ilya has made many changes on Morovia, but he hasn't changed the coins. They all still have the symbol of unity on them: the alkonost and the human, holding each other tight.

I remember our life as it was – all our alkonost and human friends and the kindness between us – and I know in my heart that's more powerful than the cruelty being shown by Captain Ilya and those who support him. Perhaps a few of my other human friends would help me now, besides Hero. Friends who I've known and trusted all my life. My thoughts turn to Fleur, Clay and Silver.

All the time we lived in Spark, it felt like we were one big family, bonded by love rather than blood. I have thousands of happy memories of us spending time together, but one bobs to the surface above all the others: the day that Silver took me to Uncle Clay's workshop and I learned about different kinds of magic...

The Day I Visited
Uncle Clay's Workshop

Four years ago, when I was nine years old, on a cold afternoon in early winter, there was a chimney fire in my school. No one was hurt, but we were asked to go home while the fire was put out and the chimney checked.

Nightingale was at work in the hospital and my mother was in a performance at the theatre. So I walked to Silver's house with him, as I had been told to do if there was ever an emergency.

Silver, Fleur and Clay lived a short walk from my school, near the centre of Spark. The front room of their home was Fleur's apothecary shop, where she sold natural remedies that she made from the plants she grew on their roof.

I was feeling down that day and I stared at my shoes as I walked alongside Silver. I hadn't done well on a spelling test, even though I'd practised the evening before. I hadn't got the part I wanted in the midwinter play and, worst of all, three alkonosts in my class had turned up with their brand-new singing magic, while mine still hadn't arrived.

I was now the only alkonost in my class with no magic, even though I practised singing more than anyone and wanted my magic to come more than anything. Without magic, I felt incomplete and somehow lesser.

Silver must have noticed that I was glum, but he didn't say anything. Silver never said much. He always preferred to do things rather than talk. When our parents visited each other, Silver and I would play together, and he'd always bring a small wooden box full of tiny tools and broken watches. We'd sit in silence, trying to fix them. I enjoyed taking the watches to pieces, but I never had the skill or patience to put them back together again. Silver didn't mind though, and whatever I pulled apart would be reassembled the next time I saw the box.

When we were a street away from Silver's home, he stopped walking and looked at me thoughtfully. "Would you like to come and see my father's workshop?" he asked.

I glanced up at him. Even though Silver was human and two years older, he wasn't much taller than me, and he often held his head low, which made him look even shorter. His light brown skin had a tinge of pink that made him look perpetually flushed with shyness. His eyes were big, his smile nervous, and his curly, ash-brown hair lifted and swayed around his head with even the slightest of movements.

"Okay," I replied, thinking that Uncle Clay's workshop might distract me from my gloomy thoughts. I knew Clay was a potter, but I'd never seen him at work before.

It's not unusual on Morovia to meet humans whose names suit their professions, as many humans also follow the ancient tradition of naming their babies using singing magic. There are alkonosts you can visit who can use their songs to glimpse into a child's future and suggest a felicitous name. So it made sense that Fleur worked with plants, Clay with clay, and I imagined that one day Silver would become a watchmaker crafting the finest silver watches.

Originally the tradition was alkonost, of course, used to give alkonost babies a fitting bird-related name. Fate does not give perfect visions of a child's future though, only clues of what might be, in the form of simple images such as a type of bird or flower. This means name prophecies can be interpreted in different ways. When I was named Linnet, my mother said that perhaps it was because I would grow to have a song much more powerful than my size, or perhaps I would work with fabrics, because linnets love flax seeds and linen is made from flax.

It was Nightingale who suggested I might help people work together, because the numbers of linnets bloomed on the island when alkonosts and humans worked together to create the lee-side farms. And I've always felt, in my heart, that this is the true prophecy of my name. But on this day, all I could think about was how I wouldn't be able to have a powerful song, or do anything important, until I got my singing magic.

Silver led the way to a large wooden shed on the rip-side edge of Spark. Inside, it was warm and smelled of baked clay and acorn coffee. Uncle Clay was sitting in a corner on a high stool in front of a large spinning disc. One of his feet was moving back and forth, pushing a bar of wood that made the disc spin. On the spinning disc was a lump of clay, and beneath Clay's hands it was slowly growing into a smooth, cylindrical tower.

Clay was leaning over the tower, deep in concentration. His white face was streaked with dried grey clay, and his hair was a matching grey, haloing his head like dandelion seeds. His large round glasses, perched on the end of his nose, made him look slightly owlish.

I watched, mesmerized, as the clay tower grew taller, and then Clay put his thumb into the top of it and, still spinning, the tower opened out like a flower. A kind of goblet was forming in his hands, and it was beautiful.

Silver walked to another corner of the room where he began heating water over a small stove and arranging lovely round, cauldron-like cups all in a row. I sat on a stool opposite Clay and watched him work, amazed by how the tiniest of his movements was causing such big changes in the shape of the clay.

Finally, the wheel stopped spinning and the goblet stood proud and finished. Clay looked at me and smiled. "Little Linnet," he said. "To what do I owe this pleasure?"

"There was a chimney fire at school, so they sent us home." I sighed, remembering all the other heart-sinking things that had happened that morning.

"And this fire has made you sad?" Uncle Clay raised his eyebrows, which made him look even more owlish, and I smiled.

"No. All the other alkonosts in my class now have their singing magic, but mine still hasn't come." I sighed again, expecting the same response from Clay that I always got from my parents whenever I complained about my lack of singing magic. *"Your magic will come. You're only nine. Be patient."* But Clay didn't say any of those things. He just nodded thoughtfully, then rose to his feet.

"Here." Clay gestured to the high stool that he'd been sitting on. "Try a different kind of magic."

"Really?" Excitement rushed through me at the thought of using the wonderful spinning wheel to make clay take shape beneath my own hands.

Clay nodded, took off his apron, draped it over me and tied it at my back. Then he showed me how to get the wheel spinning and throw a lump of wet clay onto it. Within moments my lack of singing magic, along with every other disappointment of the day, was forgotten, and I was focused entirely on the clay.

At first the clay wouldn't behave the way I wanted it to. It started to form a nice tower, but then it wobbled out of shape and collapsed. I didn't mind though. It felt so smooth in my hands, and the more I played, the more I learned to control it.

Clay gave me pieces of advice, and Silver walked over with steaming mugs of acorn coffee and watched as a small tower turned into a wide, low bowl in my hands. When I was happy with my bowl, I stopped and admired it. It was perfectly symmetrical and as smooth as silk.

"Can I keep it?" I asked. "Can I paint it? I'd love to give it to my parents as a midwinter gift."

"You can do all of those things, but it will take time," Clay replied. "First, your bowl must dry for at least a week. Then it must be baked in the kiln – that big oven over there – which takes another day." Clay nodded to a large dome-shaped oven at the back of the room, which had a lovely orange glow emanating from a small, curved opening at its base. "Once your bowl

has cooled, you can glaze it in different colours, but then you'll have to bake it again too."

My shoulders slumped a little at the thought of all the waiting, but I also smiled at the thought of coming back to Clay's workshop to complete all the tasks, especially the glazing in different colours.

I drank my acorn coffee while looking at all the wonderful things Clay had created in his workshop. There were cups, bowls, jugs and other practical items, but also beautiful ornaments, like vases being hugged by octopus tentacles, and pencil holders shaped like fish.

Uncle Clay was mostly a quiet person, like Silver, so we didn't talk much, but occasionally he'd pass me something to look at or point out a clever feature of a design, like the teapots with gravity-defying lids and built-in gates to filter out tea leaves.

Once our coffee was finished, we walked together to Silver and Clay's home. We arrived as Aunty Fleur was closing her apothecary shop and she bustled us inside and pulled us into a warm hug.

Fleur was a short lady – not much taller than me even when I was nine – with dark brown skin and long black hair, most often plaited into scores of braids and tied up on her head with a thick band of fabric. Today the fabric was orange and blue and matched her long dress, which was in one of the traditional human styles.

We sat around the big table in the small kitchen behind the shop, drinking chamomile tea and eating toast with honey while we talked about our days. Even though Clay and Silver were usually very quiet, Fleur had a way of making everyone talk. Silver showed us some sketches of a watch he'd designed at school while he was supposed to be studying history, then he pulled out his wooden box of broken watches and began dismantling some of them to build something new from the parts.

Clay talked about the goblets that he'd been making, which turned out to be for a large order from Pero Palace Complex, and I talked about the bowl that I'd made in Clay's workshop. Fleur told us about a detoxifying remedy she'd been brewing from dandelion roots, then her eyes lit up as she told us about the uses of other parts of dandelions and how she thought it was amazing that such a common plant had so many incredible properties.

Time flew by and soon it was dusk, when my father would return from his work at the hospital. Aunty Fleur wrapped her shawl around both of us and we walked arm in arm to my home while she continued telling me facts about dandelions.

As Fleur and I snuggled close together to shield each other from the cold evening air, I remember thinking about Silver's watches, and Clay's pottery wheel, and Fleur's remedies. I thought how Clay was right: that there are different kinds of magic.

And now, as Nightingale is being taken away from me, I realize that I will need a different kind of magic to free him.

CHAPTER 8

SPARK

I watch as Nightingale disappears around a bend in the road, trapped in the wagon and guarded by all the bogatyrs, including Hero. I feel wobbly and my thoughts are swirling haphazardly, like midges in a sunbeam.

I must follow my father and find a way to free him. But on my own, against all those bogatyrs, I have little hope. Even if Hero helped, which I'm not entirely sure she would, it would still not be enough.

I climb down from the tree I've been hiding in, my stomach twisted with guilt for stealing the ring and churning with worry for Nightingale. I need to think quickly to save him. The thought of my father being locked up behind the towering stone walls of The Keep and never seeing him again makes my feathers tighten with fear.

My feet hit the ground and I crouch down beside

Whiskers. She's sitting amongst the tree's roots, whining mournfully as she stares in the direction Nightingale was taken. Lumpy, perched high on her head, is squeaking with distress and waving his sword-leg frantically.

"It's all right, I'm going to get him back." I rub Whiskers's cheeks and nod to Lumpy. My gaze drifts in the direction of Spark. Fleur, Clay and Silver are still in my thoughts, and I think asking for their help might be my best chance.

Alkonosts are not allowed in Spark any more and are sent to The Keep if caught there. That's why neither Nightingale nor I have returned since we were forced out. But I could be careful. I've become good at moving silently and hiding in shadows. Still, my blood runs cold at the thought of being captured. I won't be able to free Nightingale if I'm sent to The Keep too.

I look back into the relative safety of the swamp and frown. I could go to Echo's hideout and ask for her help as I'd planned instead, but the Unity Movement – even before it fell apart – never freed anyone from The Keep. And the thought of going back into the swamp alone makes me feel nauseous. I've had enough of hiding there.

To free Nightingale, I must think differently and act differently. It's time I reached out beyond the swamp and risked asking for the help of our human friends. I rise to my feet and try to gather enough courage to walk away from Nightingale, towards Spark.

My head is fuzzy from not sleeping all night and I take a deep breath to push back my tiredness. The sun has only been up for an hour, but already its rays are burning hot and I'm thirsty and hungry. But Spark is just an hour's walk away.

I wonder how much the town has changed, and a worry that Fleur, Clay and Silver might not even be there any more sprouts inside me. But the only way to find out is to go and see for myself. I look down at Whiskers and Lumpy and bite my lip.

"I'm going that way, to Spark." I nod my head in the direction of the town. Whiskers and Lumpy stare at me expectantly. "You two should stay in the swamp—"

Lumpy interrupts me with a loud *"Phoot!"* and Whiskers moves closer to my legs. I sigh. I'd rather they stayed safe in the swamp, but I know they won't leave me, especially now that Nightingale is gone. "All right, but we must be quiet and stay out of sight."

In an effort to make myself look more human in

case I'm spotted, I untie the triangle of nettle fabric that I've been wearing to protect my neck from sunburn, place it over my head and tie it at the back. The fabric covers my head feathers, but the fact that I'm so muddy, dressed in worn-thin, ill-fitting clothes, and accompanied by a toad riding on a swamp-rat, makes it pretty obvious that I'm an alkonost from the swamp. It's the best I can do though. I take another deep breath and set off.

I check the dirt road carefully and strain my ears listening for carts before crossing it. Then I clamber down into a ditch beside the road, so that we can walk out of sight. As we move towards Spark, I draw all my memories of it to the front of my mind: the layout of the streets and alleyways, the positions of the shops and tavern, the busier areas and the quieter ones. And slowly, I work out the safest way to approach Fleur, Clay and Silver's home.

They live on a busy street near the centre of Spark, but the back of their house is quite sheltered. I could loop around the town and sneak in that way. And as it's Nestday, most of the streets should be fairly empty.

My stomach rumbles with hunger and my thoughts turn to Nightingale, caged in the wagon. He won't have had breakfast either, and I wonder if the bogatyrs will give him anything to eat or drink during the journey to The Keep, which will take most of the day.

My worries churn into anger as I question how the bogatyrs knew where to find Nightingale. I'm angry with myself, because suspicions about the boys I met last night are squirming inside me. I told Jay and Kestrel where my and Nightingale's home-tree was. Is it possible that as soon as I left them, the boys ran off and told bogatyrs where to find Nightingale in exchange for some food? I don't want to think these thoughts, but I can't help it.

I sift through my mind, trying to think of another explanation. The bogatyrs knew about the ring I stole, but Jay and Kestrel couldn't have known about that. I breathe a sigh of relief as my suspicions about them fall away. But I still can't work out how the bogatyrs found our home-tree. And now guilt for stealing the ring and causing this trouble is twisting my stomach yet again.

Whiskers nudges my leg and grunts nervously. I look up and my eyes widen at the sight of Spark ahead. It feels like for ever since I've seen this crescent-moon-shaped cluster of brightly coloured square houses, with leafy gardens rising from their flat roofs. The town hugs the curved sweep of soft, golden sand that separates it from the sparkling waters in the bay. Today the waters are pale blue and almost as still as a lake. Morovia must be drifting across one of the shallow, tropical seas of the world. The gulls that usually spend their days screeching and diving are now calm dots on the sand, probably preening in the sunshine.

Something swells in my throat. Perhaps it's the nostalgia Nightingale talks about – the yearning for the happiness of the past. My life in Spark was carefree. I had my parents, our friends, Hero, and long days spent playing on the sand and splashing in the waves. I swallow back the lump in my throat and push my memories away. Right now, to stand a chance of reclaiming any of that, I need to focus on getting into Spark unseen and finding help.

I continue walking, making silent bargains with Fate in my head: *If I get Nightingale back, I won't steal from a courtier's hands ever again, or abandon my father in the night.*

My gaze shifts to the purple cliffs of Eldovia, which is floating closer than I've seen for years. My chest tightens with the thought that if I'd gone straight to sleep last night, and Nightingale and I had left for

Fisher's Flock before dawn, then he would never have been captured. To make everything right, I must find a way to free him. Then we can decide what to do next, together.

"Stay close." I tap my leg as Whiskers falls behind. She skips to catch up with me and we continue walking in the ditch until we get to the town's edge. Several bogatyrs are guarding the road, and I frown at them from the shadows. When I lived in Spark, the road was never guarded.

I creep silently away from the ditch and onto a dusty, hedge-lined track that circles around the back of the town. Bright green fields lie beyond the hedge to our left and I'm so hungry I think about sneaking into one of the fields and stealing a few leaves of cabbage or one of the spring onions whose scent fills the air. But farm workers might be in the fields and I can't risk being caught, so I stay hidden behind the hedges until we reach the shaded backstreets of the town's high-side edge.

There are more bogatyrs here, guarding street corners. The sight of them makes my heart pound with fear and fills my thoughts with confusion. I'm not sure why Captain Ilya keeps Spark so well guarded. All the alkonosts are too scared to leave the swamp, let alone come here.

I avoid the bogatyrs by slipping through the shadows of the quieter alleyways, but I sense their presence even when they're out of sight. Spark feels dangerous and unwelcoming, as buzzing and barbed as a cloud of hornets. It's nothing like the friendly atmosphere that I remember.

The place itself is familiar though, but like a long-ago dream that I'd accepted had drifted away: the bumpy feel of the cobblestones, the dry earth smell of the clay house bricks, and the sweet smell of flowers growing in baskets dangling from walls and in pots on the roof gardens.

Apart from the bogatyrs the streets are empty, which is strange. Even though it's Nestday, I thought a few people would be out; visiting friends, sitting in the sunshine in their backyards or gossiping by their gates. But the humans must all be indoors.

I duck past windows and hide behind the low walls that separate backyards, until finally I reach Fleur, Clay and Silver's home. It's halfway along a row of about twenty terraced houses, each one of them a small sunshine-yellow square joined to the next, like a line of toad spawn. My heart aches as I think how it must be nice to still be living with neighbours so close.

I push the gate to their backyard gently, hoping it's not locked. It creaks open. I dash inside with Whiskers and Lumpy, then close the gate, crouch behind it and breathe a sigh of relief.

The scent of the herbs Fleur grows on her roof fills the yard, both sweet and bitter. I remember playing up there with Silver, and Fleur explaining which plants she used to make different remedies. My heart quickens at the thought of how close I might be to my friends after all this time apart.

I creep closer to the kitchen window and peer in cautiously. There's no sign of anyone and desperation swells inside me. I *need* my friends to be here. I've risked capture by coming to find them…

Coldness sweeps over me as I suddenly realize what else I've risked. Fleur, Clay and Silver could all get in trouble if I'm found here. They could be accused of being enemies to safety, or of working with the Unity Movement, just for talking to me. They could be sent to The Keep too.

I've been so focused on asking for their help to free Nightingale, I didn't think enough about *their* safety.

They might not want to see me or help me because of the danger it would put them in. I stifle a groan. I shouldn't have come here. Even though I need help to free Nightingale, I don't want to put my friends at risk to do it. My shoulders fall and I shake my head sadly. "Come on, Whiskers, Lumpy," I whisper, creeping back towards the gate. But then the kitchen door swings open and footsteps rush towards me.

CHAPTER 9

FLEUR

I turn just in time for Aunty Fleur to engulf me in a hug. She almost lifts me off the floor and presses me so tight against her that I can't speak. "Linnet, what's hap—" Fleur stops herself, pulls away from me and looks up and down the row of terraced houses nervously. "Come inside." She grabs my hand and leads me into the cool shade of the kitchen.

Whiskers and Lumpy follow close at my heels and once we're all through the door, Fleur shuts and bolts it, then draws the curtains. "It's so good to see you!" she exclaims. Her words are ordinary, yet they feel strange as I've not heard anything like them in years. And her voice is familiar but also wavering, and the tears sparkling in her eyes remind me how wrong it is that we haven't seen each other in so long.

"It's good to see you too, Aunty Fleur." I smile,

blinking back my own tears. Fleur looks just as I remember. Her long braids are tied up on her head with a band of dark green fabric that matches her long green dress. I glance down at my muddy clothes and suddenly feel completely out of place inside her clean home. I slide the triangle of nettle fabric off my head self-consciously.

The stone floor beneath my bare feet feels cold and smooth, unlike anything in the swamp, and the walls around me make me feel a little trapped and breathless. "I shouldn't have come here though." I shift uncomfortably. "I don't want you, Uncle Clay and Silver to get in trouble."

Fleur nods. "I understand. But I don't think you would have come here unless you really needed to, and I can see your father isn't with you…" Fleur takes a deep breath and dabs her eyes with trembling fingers. "Sit down, Linnet. You're here and we're safe, for now. I'll make some tea and you can tell me what's happened. Can I get anything for these two?" Fleur glances down at Whiskers and Lumpy.

Whiskers is pressed so tight against my leg that her coarse brown fur is scratching my skin. She shifts from paw to paw, her eyes roll as she tries to make sense of the kitchen and a quiet, high-pitched whine rises from her half-smile. Lumpy, sat on Whiskers's head, waves his sword-leg at Fleur, his bulging eyes narrowed.

"I'll hold them for now, until they get used to being indoors." I bend down and scoop Whiskers, with Lumpy still on her head, into my arms. "But they might like some water once they've calmed down a little, please." I sit on the nearest chair. Like the floor, the chair feels too flat and too smooth, and the sound of it scraping against the stone floor seems too loud. "This is Whiskers." I stroke Whiskers's cheek gently. "She's a coypu – a swamp-rat. She's been with me since she was a pup. And this is Lumpy." I wink at Lumpy. "They're very close. We all are."

"I'll find something to put water in." Fleur turns and begins rummaging in a cupboard full of bowls.

"I came here because Nightingale…" My words stick in my throat as I picture the bogatyrs leading my father away.

"Has he been captured?" Fleur puts two small bowls of water on the table for Whiskers and Lumpy, but Whiskers remains pressed tight against me and Lumpy stays firmly rooted on Whiskers's head, staring at everything suspiciously.

I nod. "I wasn't sure what to do. I thought maybe you could help, but now that I'm here it seems like a foolish idea that could get you into trouble. I should go back to the swamp and look for help there."

Fleur turns away from the kettle she's set to warm on the stove and sits opposite me. "You were brave coming here, Linnet. And I'm glad you did. You've reminded me how brave we all need to be. Especially now, with the Unity Movement collapsing."

"You know about the Unity Movement?" I ask.

Fleur nods. "Silver and I often work for the movement. We do all we can to help get supplies into the swamp and fight for change."

My eyes sting. I should have known that Fleur would be trying to help.

"But so many of us have been captured these last few moons, people are now too scared to do anything." Fleur shakes her head sadly. "It's becoming impossible."

The hopelessness I feel must show on my face, because Fleur pauses and tries to smile reassuringly. "Try not to worry, Linnet. Together, we'll figure out the best thing to do." The kettle whistles. Fleur stands again and pours water into three cups. The smell of chamomile, sweet and herby, rises into the air and I feel a little calmer. Fleur places a cup in front of me and sits again with one of the others.

"Silver is asleep upstairs," Fleur explains when she sees me looking at the third cup, still sitting near the kettle. "He was up working late – he's an apprentice at Circadian, the watchmaker's, now – and he often brings his work home. But he'll be down soon."

"What about Uncle Clay?" I ask. "Is he in his workshop?"

"Clay died two years ago," Fleur says. She looks down into her cup, inhales slowly, then looks back up at me with tears spilling from her eyes. "He was caught working for the Unity Movement, sent to The Keep, and he died there shortly afterwards."

Fleur's words hit my heart like stones and a suffocating fog falls over me. I shake my head in disbelief as I try to catch my breath and focus.

Fleur leans forwards and puts her hand on my arm. "I'm sorry, Linnet. This must be a shock for you."

"I…" I stare at Fleur, not knowing what to say or do. Something inside me has collapsed and swallowed my voice. Images of Clay race through my mind. I see him working at his potter's wheel, deep in concentration, his face streaked with clay, his round glasses perched at the end of his nose. "He can't be," I say firmly. "It must be a mistake."

"Have you heard about the quarry in The Keep?" Fleur asks and I shake my head. "Everyone sent to The Keep works in a quarry, digging iron ore out of chalk cliffs. They use the ore to make the magic-proof armour the bogatyrs wear. Captain Ilya wants to quarry enough of it to make huge areas of the island magic-proof." Fleur pauses and takes a sip of tea. "About one moon after Clay was sent to The Keep, there was an accident in the quarry." Tears stream down her cheeks and the room spins around me. The buzzing, barbed feeling that I had on the way into Spark returns, with even more power. Everything is so much worse than I thought. I can't believe Clay is gone. I need to get Nightingale away from The Keep right now.

"Aunty Fleur, I'm so sorry." I finally find my voice, although it doesn't sound like my own. I hold Whiskers tight and blink back my tears. "I didn't know...did Nightingale?" I ask.

Fleur shakes her head. "It's difficult and dangerous to send messages between here and the swamp. Captain Ilya's rules limit the movement of humans as much as alkonosts. Anyone who leaves Spark without permission risks being sent to The Keep."

I frown. I assumed the bogatyrs guarding Spark were to stop alkonosts coming here, not to stop humans from leaving.

"Things are bleak at the moment." Fleur takes another sip of tea. "But I still have faith change will come. Even more so, now I see you here. I've missed you, Linnet, and all alkonosts. And the vast majority of Spark has missed you too."

"Really?" I ask doubtfully. "For Captain Ilya to have remained in power for so long, and to be doing all this, he must have many supporters."

Fleur sighs and looks at me sadly. "I'm sorry, Linnet. I still think of you as a young child, but you're not, and I shouldn't try to protect you from the awful truth. You're right that there are many humans who support Captain Ilya, and who want singing magic to be controlled. And the speeches Captain Ilya gives have made this worse."

My frown deepens so much that my head starts to ache and I move a hand from Whiskers to rub my forehead. Lumpy looks up at me and croaks mournfully.

"But", Fleur continues, "there are also many humans

who believe, whether singing magic caused the tragedy or not, that blaming every alkonost is wrong. Many of us miss our alkonost friends and are desperate for unity. Also..." Fleur leans forwards with a small sparkle in her eyes. "I believe more humans are starting to doubt Captain Ilya. As the years have gone by, even those people who were suspicious of alkonosts have seen how much more difficult our lives are without you all, and without singing magic."

"What do you mean?" I ask.

Fleur nods to the window, where bright sunlight is forcing its way through the narrow gap between the curtains. "This heatwave, for example. Usually, a group of alkonosts with weather magic would sing wind or rain to cool the island. Alkonosts have always kept Morovia's climate stable, pushed back harsh weather and regulated the seasons, no matter where the island drifts. And then there's the crops and seafood. Traditionally humans have always been the stronger farmers and fishers, and ensured everyone on the island has plenty to eat. But singing magic was used to boost the harvests on the lee-side farms and help fishers find the richest waters. Illnesses here are better cured using a mixture of medicine and magic, and the wildlife of

the island thrives more when it's protected by us all…"
Fleur's voice trails away and she takes another sip of
tea before continuing. "Morovia needs humans and
alkonosts working together, sharing their strengths
and skills to make things better for us all, and I believe
many humans who supported Captain Ilya at first are
starting to realize that. But right now they're too scared
to oppose him."

"If people are too scared to oppose him, then
nothing will change." I shake my head in frustration.
"Morovia won't be united until alkonosts and humans
work together to remove Captain Ilya from power."

"I agree." Fleur nods. "And if we don't, then we'll
end up living in fear for ever. So…" Fleur raises her
eyebrows. "Let's start with Nightingale. Tell me what
happened. When was he captured?"

"This morning." I hug Whiskers closer as it all floods
back into my mind. "Bogatyrs are taking him to The
Keep right now. What can we do to free him?" My mind
races desperately at the thought of Nightingale in such
danger and I suddenly remember the coin purse at my
waist. "I have treasures! Could they help?" I fumble
under Whiskers and manage to untie the purse, even
though Lumpy tries to prod my arm away with his

sword-leg and croaks at me in annoyance. "There's a few coins in here and the biggest diamond ring I've ever seen." I place the purse on the table in front of Fleur. "They're stolen," I add quietly, heat rising into my cheeks, even though I'm sure Fleur guessed this already.

"They might help." Fleur nods. "There are several courtiers and bogatyrs who have been known to help the movement in exchange for coins or valuables. It will be extremely dangerous asking for anyone's help though."

My heart races with panic. Our chance of saving Nightingale feels as fragile and vulnerable as a sea urchin shell on a rocky beach.

Fleur puts her hand on my shoulder. "I'll do everything I can to keep all of us safe, Linnet, including Nightingale. I just want to make sure you understand the risks."

"I do." I nod. "But I need Nightingale. We need each other. So I must try to free him. But if you or Silver got captured because of me—"

"That's our risk to take," Fleur interrupts quickly. She looks at me, all the tears in her eyes now replaced with determination. "Seeing you again has made me realize where we get the courage from to take risks, and why we need to do it."

I look at Fleur in confusion, but then my eyes widen as I understand what she's talking about. "Love," I say. "That's what gave me the courage I needed to come here – love for Nightingale, and for you and Uncle Clay and Silver."

Fleur smiles, and in this moment I feel I have enough love in my heart to give me all the courage I need to free my father, and maybe even enough to free all of Morovia too. But having courage is not enough. I need a plan – a plan to outfox Captain Ilya and hundreds of armoured bogatyrs guarding a fortified Keep. And right now, I have no idea how to do that.

CHAPTER 10

SILVER

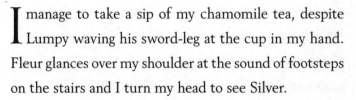

I manage to take a sip of my chamomile tea, despite Lumpy waving his sword-leg at the cup in my hand. Fleur glances over my shoulder at the sound of footsteps on the stairs and I turn my head to see Silver.

He's grown so much, he's taller and broader than many adult humans now. His hair is longer too and styled in thick twists that fall to his chin. But he still has his soft, childlike features, his big eyes and shy smile.

"Hello, Silver." I smile to see him again, but sadness is welling inside me. My heart aches that since I last saw Silver he's lost his father, and it also aches for everything else that we've missed in each other's lives too. Seeing both Silver and Hero today has made me realize how much they've grown up without me. And I guess I've grown up without them too.

I look down at myself. I'm bigger, stronger, a great deal muddier, with brown and green freckles, and my feathers are now brown and green too. On the inside I feel like a whole different person. I used to worry about spelling tests and enjoy playing kickball and building sandcastles on the beach. But my life since then has been focused on finding enough food to survive, stealing for the Unity Movement and avoiding being captured by bogatyrs.

"Linnet." Silver's voice is deeper than I remember. "I can't believe you're here." He leans down and gives me a hug that is awkward because Whiskers and Lumpy are still in my arms. Silver draws away quickly when Whiskers grunts defensively and Lumpy lunges at him with an angry scowl.

"Silver is a friend," I whisper to Lumpy and Whiskers, then look up at Silver. "Sorry, they're just nervous to be inside a house."

"Where's Nightingale?" Silver's eyebrows draw together with concern.

"He's been captured." Anger rises in me as I say the words.

"Oh no." Silver pales as he glances over to Fleur. "We must do something," he says urgently.

Fleur swigs the last of her tea, then picks up the coin purse and fishes the ring out of it. The diamond catches the light and both Fleur's and Silver's eyes widen in the same expression of awe. "Linnet brought this and I'm going to trade it for coins. Then we'll bribe some bogatyrs or courtiers to help us." Fleur stands, lifts a small leather satchel from the back of her chair and loops it over her shoulder.

"Be careful," Silver says, worry lining his face.

"Always." Fleur nods.

"The bogatyrs were looking for that ring when they captured Nightingale," I warn.

"I'm taking it to someone I trust." Fleur squeezes my shoulder, then puts the coin purse back on the table. "Stay with Linnet?" Fleur asks Silver, and he nods again.

Fleur rises onto her toes to kiss him. "There's tea on the side for you." She leans down to drop a kiss onto my forehead too. "I'll be back in an hour or two." Fleur sweeps out of the kitchen through a bead curtain made from hundreds of tiny shells, which separates the shop from the rest of the house.

Silver follows and I hear him bolting the door after Fleur's gone. He picks up his tea when he returns and screws up his face. "Ugh. Chamomile. Do you want some cocoa instead?"

"Yes please." I gently shift Whiskers a little so that I can tie the coin purse back to my belt.

"It's good to see you again, Linnet." Silver smiles his familiar shy smile. "I'm so sorry about everything that's happened. After you and Nightingale were taken from Spark, my parents and I and lots of other humans tried to stop Captain Ilya and his bogatyrs. But they had armour and weapons, and they sent anyone who opposed them to The Keep. These last few years have been awful."

Silver opens a wooden bread bin and lifts a huge brown loaf onto the table, and my stomach rumbles at the sight of it. "I've missed bread so much," I say without thinking.

"I'm sorry." Silver's cheeks flush. "I'm going on about how awful it's been here, but at least we've had food and been allowed to stay in our homes." He finishes making the cocoa and places two mugfuls on the table, along with a jar of honey. Then he begins to slice the bread. "What's it like in the swamp?" he asks.

"Wet and muddy." Now that she's calmed a little, I offer Whiskers the bowl of water Fleur put on the table, and she laps some of it up with her small pink tongue. Then she leans back, her now wet whiskers dripping over me. I rub her cheeks and smile. "The swamp is lush and beautiful too though. I love it in many ways, but I miss Spark, and my old friends..." I look at Silver and once again can't believe how much he's grown. While Nightingale and I have been living day to day, years have drifted by.

"I've missed you too." Silver passes me a thick slice of bread dripping with honey. It's on a pretty plate, with yellow flowers painted around its edge. My heart aches, because I recognize it as something that Uncle Clay made.

"Silver, I'm so sorry about your father. Aunty Fleur told me," I whisper. "I still can't believe it."

Silver nods and his mouth draws into a tense line. Despite his size, he looks very young and vulnerable all of a sudden.

I rub tears from my eyes with the back of my hand. "You know, last night Nightingale suggested we talk to the sea-fishers about leaving Morovia. But I didn't want to, so I snuck off. If I'd listened to him and we'd gone to Fisher's Flock this morning, then he wouldn't have been captured."

"Don't blame yourself, Linnet." Silver shakes his head. "All of this is Captain Ilya's fault, not yours. Morovia is everyone's home and none of us should have to think about leaving."

"I don't want to," I admit. "But I should have talked to Nightingale about it more. I left him alone…" I frown at the memory and my voice trails off as I start making bargains with Fate in my head again. The cocoa has made me feel sleepy and my eyelids are drooping, my feather-eyelashes creating a pattern over my vision like the trailing moss around home-tree.

Silver glances down at Whiskers, who is now asleep on my lap, occasionally grunting and twitching in her dreams. "Would you like me to make a bed for…"

"Whiskers." I nod. "She'd like that. And if you have a small box for Lumpy, he might settle down and sleep too." I glance at Lumpy, who is still frowning and waving his sword-leg at the room in general.

Silver makes a nest of old blankets for Whiskers and brings a box filled with leaves for Lumpy to make a nook in. Then we sit and wait for Fleur to return, our fear for her making time move as slowly as a snail stuck in dry sand. Silver talks a little about his apprenticeship at Circadian: how he's learning about watches, clocks and locks too. He says watches are still his favourite though, and that his dream, once Morovia is united, is to open his own watchmaker's.

I must fall asleep at some point while Silver is talking, and Silver must move me, because I wake on a bigger, more comfortable chair beside Whiskers's nest. Through the small gap between the curtains I see dusk blooming, thick and deep blue-grey.

"Where's Fleur?" I frown in confusion as I look at Silver. He's standing by the bead curtain, staring into the shop and the street beyond.

"She's not back." Silver turns to me, his face lined with worry.

I rise to my feet and move towards Silver, my feathers drawing against my scalp. Aunty Fleur should be back by now. The thought that something must have happened to her is making me feel sick. "What can we do? Do you know where she went?" I ask.

We both fall silent as the slow clip-clopping of hooves echoes along the street towards us. The horse comes to a halt outside the shop, voices mumble, then both Silver and I jump as three loud bangs shake the front door. Whiskers leaps up in fright and Lumpy lets out a loud *"Phoot"*.

I back away from the bead curtain as Silver peers between the rows of tiny shells. "There are three bogatyrs," he whispers. "Young ones. But a wagon is behind them and I can't see if there are more bogatyrs there."

"I must hide," I whisper, my heart racing as I look around the small kitchen for the best place. If I'm caught here I'll be sent straight to The Keep – and most likely Silver too, for sheltering an alkonost. Whiskers rushes over to me with Lumpy precariously clinging onto one of her back legs.

Silver opens the largest cupboard and drags a sack of flour out of it. I try to squeeze into the space he makes and flinch at another bang, even louder than the first three. The front door cracks and I hear it swing open and smash against a wall. Heavy footsteps storm into the shop and before Silver or I have a chance to close the cupboard door, the bead curtain is pulled down. Tiny shells tumble and roll all over the stone floor as two bogatyrs, a little older than Silver, barge into the kitchen, cracking the shells beneath their heavy boots. Guilt crashes over me as I see the fear in Silver's eyes – this is all my fault.

The bogatyrs must not have expected to find an alkonost here though, because they're wearing deerskins but no iron armour or helmets. Yet again, I wish I had some singing magic that I could use to blast them out of this kitchen and away from us.

Silver yells in pain as the larger of the bogatyrs grabs both his arms, twists them behind his back, then slams him against the wall. "You're accused of conspiring to sell stolen goods and—"

"No!" I step towards the bogatyr without thinking. Whiskers stays huddled against my leg, and Lumpy – who has made it all the way to Whiskers's head now – squeaks angrily at the bogatyrs. "Silver hasn't done anything wrong!" I shout.

The other bogatyr lunges towards me, swinging a long wooden staff as if he's going to hit me with it. I'm trapped between the wall, the chair and two bogatyrs, and I can hear a third bogatyr approaching through the shop. I have nowhere to run and the staff is hurtling towards me. All I can do is crouch lower, close my eyes and hold up my hands to shield myself from the incoming blow.

Time slows and the only thought that fills my mind is that I wish, with my whole being, I could sing some kind of magic to get Silver and me out of here. Because if we're sent to The Keep, then there will be nobody to save Nightingale, and nobody to save us.

CHAPTER 11

HERO

I feel the wall against my back and Whiskers's fur against my ankles. My eyes are shut tight and I'm expecting the wooden staff to land at any moment. But a blow doesn't come.

"What are you doing?" the bogatyr in front of me yells and I peep my eyes open to see the staff being wrenched from his hands by the bogatyr behind him. My eyes widen as I look up into her face and see a familiar piercing gaze.

"Hero," I whisper, as, with one swift movement, she sweeps the staff under the bogatyr's legs and he crashes to the floor. *Hero is defending me.* Relief and gratitude rush over me like a cool tide.

The bogatyr holding Silver releases him and brandishes his staff at Hero instead. Hero spins around, whipping another staff from behind her back against his legs and he crashes to the floor too, smashing a box filled with some of Fleur's remedies. Glass vials wrapped in webs of protective straw spill out and roll across the floor. The label on one of them catches my eye: *Sleepbane*.

"Wait!" I call to Hero, who is now standing over the two fallen bogatyrs, a staff in each of her hands, poised to attack. I lean down, grab the vial and open it. Then, covering my mouth with one hand, I reach out and drip a drop of the light blue-green potion underneath each bogatyr's nose.

The bogatyrs' eyes widen for a moment, then close, and their bodies go limp. I sigh with relief. "How long will the sleepbane last?" I ask Silver.

"An hour or so," Silver replies. "We need to decide what to do quickly."

Hero looks at the vial in my hands. "Can I use it? There's another bogatyr outside, guarding the wagon. I'll send him to sleep while you and Silver get your things, and Fleur's things too." Hero glances over at Silver. "Your mother was captured with stolen goods and is in the wagon outside. I can help you all escape to the swamp, but we must leave now. Bring only what you need and assume you won't be returning." Hero

169

leaves the kitchen and I turn to Silver, all the warmth draining from my body.

I open my mouth to apologize for bringing this trouble, but then I spot a couple of duffel bags dangling from a hook on the wall and realize it's more important to pack. I grab the bags and pass one to Silver. "Get blankets and clothes. Quick."

Silver runs upstairs and I move around the kitchen, cramming food into a bag along with a cooking pot and some utensils. Sadness closes around me with the all-too-familiar action of packing up things in a rush, along with the knowledge that my plan has crumbled and I'm returning to the swamp without Nightingale. How will I free him now? I try to comfort myself with the thought that at least I have Silver, Fleur and Hero helping me, but I'm also worried that I'm just putting more people I care about in danger.

I lean down and pick up the blankets Whiskers was using as a nest. She's huddled close to my legs, grunting nervously as she eyes the bogatyrs asleep on the floor. Lumpy is perched high between her ears, frowning furiously at the bogatyrs.

Silver returns with his bag full to bursting, just as Hero shuffles back into the shop, dragging a huge unconscious bogatyr behind her. "Help me!" she urges, struggling to move the bogatyr across the floor. Silver and I rush over, grab the bogatyr's arms, and help drag him into the kitchen, where we abandon him beside the others.

I look up at Hero, a smile on my face despite the danger buzzing in the air. "Hero," I say, my cheeks flushing with heat. "It's good to see you again."

"There's no time to talk." Hero's face is stiff and serious. "We must leave Spark as quickly as possible. You two will have to get into the caged part of the wagon with Fleur, so that we don't look suspicious, and I'll free you all when we get to the swamp."

"Why are you helping us?" Silver asks. "You're going to get into so much trouble for this, aren't you?"

"We can talk later," Hero says. "If you want my help to escape, come now."

Silver turns to me. "Ready?"

I lift the bag I packed and check Whiskers and Lumpy are still at my side. "I'm sorry, Silver," I whisper as we walk through the shop part of his home.

Silver puts his hand on my arm. "All of this is Captain Ilya's fault, not yours."

I nod, burning with anger as I think how no one and

nowhere on Morovia is safe under his rule. Anyone – alkonost or human, in the swamp or in Spark – might have to flee their home-tree or house at a moment's notice.

We step past the smashed door of Fleur and Silver's home and onto the dark street. Night has swallowed dusk now and the buildings of the town hide the moon and nearly all the stars. Hero beckons us to the wagon and opens the barred cage. Fleur is inside, and her eyes well with emotion when she sees us. Silver rushes in and hugs her. "We're being helped," he whispers.

I pick up Whiskers and Lumpy and force myself to climb in too, though I feel sick at just the sight of the bars trapping us in.

"You should sit in silence," Hero whispers as she closes the cage. She slides a padlock through the hasp but doesn't lock it. Then she walks round to the front of the wagon, climbs up, flicks the reins, and the horse sets off slowly, pulling us behind.

My eyes sting with tears. I know Silver said this is Captain Ilya's fault, but it still feels like mine. Because I came here, Fleur and Silver have lost their home. And Hero has put herself in danger by betraying the bogatyrs. The diamond ring is gone, and I'm rolling back towards the swamp with no idea how to free Nightingale.

The wagon slows to a stop not far from the red maple tree where Nightingale and I lie in wait on the days we look for treasures to steal. Hero climbs down from the wagon as Silver opens the barred door and we step onto the dusty road. The sky is bright with stars and the waxing moon shines low over the swamp, bathing everything in a soft pearly light.

Fleur pulls Hero into a hug. "Thank you. As an old friend of Linnet's, I knew you must have a kind heart somewhere beneath those bogatyr deerskins. But helping us tonight was truly brave. What will you do now?"

Hero looks up at the starry sky, then back to us all. "I don't know," she says simply. "I can't go back to the bogatyrs now."

"Come with us into the swamp," I suggest. "At least until you decide what you want to do next. I'm going to try to free Nightingale. But I could show you some places where you could make camp fairly safely."

"I could help you free Nightingale," Hero says. "I know The Keep well. It would be difficult, but if we worked together then I think we could do it."

173

"Really?" My eyes widen and excitement rushes through me.

Hero walks to the front of the wagon and picks up her staff and a bag that I recognize as Fleur's leather satchel. Then Hero flicks the horse's reins so that it starts trotting away on its own. "So the bogatyrs don't know exactly where we escaped into the swamp," Hero explains as she walks back to us and passes Fleur her satchel.

Silver swings one of the duffel bags we packed onto his back and gives the other to Hero. "You've been a bogatyr working for Captain Ilya for the last three years. Why turn against him now?"

I look at Hero, a cold shadow of suspicion creeping over me. But then I remember the warmth of our past friendship: the sandcastles we built, the song we made up together, the hopes and dreams we shared, and the way we knew each other's thoughts without having to say a word. "Friendship," I whisper. "Hero is doing this for friendship."

Hero looks at me and, though her face is solemn, I see a glimmer of a smile at the corners of her mouth. "For friendship." She gives me a small nod and hoists the duffel bag onto her back. "And because I want what is best for Morovia."

I feel a smile curving my own lips as I look from Hero to Fleur and Silver. "Let's get off this road. Captain Ilya's bogatyrs will be looking for us by now." I decide to lead the way to home-tree first, to collect what is left of my and Nightingale's things. When my bare feet step into the almost knee-deep muddy water that fills the ditch at the side of the road, I look at my friends' shoes and frown. "It's probably best if you take those off and walk barefoot. I'm going to lead us through shallow water channels so that we don't leave tracks."

Fleur nods and slips off her shoes, and Hero and Silver lean down to unlace their boots. I take a deep breath and feel, deep inside, that the tide is out. *Thank Fate*, I think, because low tide means more of the swamp channels will be shallow enough to wade through. Fleur puts her shoes inside one of the duffel bags, then ties all the boots to the other bag by their laces. Then we set off into the dark night-shadows of the swamp.

Whiskers skips at my side, happy to be home, and Lumpy is almost smiling as he sits high between Whiskers's ears, looking ahead. Silver, Fleur and Hero follow so close behind I can feel their warmth.

It's strange to be with humans again, but it's a good

feeling. Hope bubbles inside me with every step – not only that we can free Nightingale, but also that maybe, if *we* can work together, then perhaps *more* alkonosts and humans could work together too.

I almost dare not think the thought fluttering at the edge of my mind: that this is the first step to not only freeing Nightingale, but to bringing unity to all of Morovia.

Happy memories flood my thoughts – of alkonosts and humans talking together, playing together… Then a bittersweet memory rises of the last time I heard alkonosts and humans singing together…

The Last Time Alkonosts and Humans Sang Together

Three years ago, I woke to a beautiful morning. Summer sunshine poured through my window and the sweet smell of sea-kale flowers drifted from our balcony. It was the Day of Union, the biggest holiday on Morovia, and I knew it was going to be a wonderful day of celebrations, as it was every year.

My mother had left before dawn, as she always did on the Day of Union, to sing with the royal orchestra. I like to think that she crept into my room and kissed my cheek before she went.

The two queens of Morovia always circled the island in the ship *Joy* as part of the celebrations, with their orchestra of alkonosts and humans playing music, and my mother singing. It was a tradition that symbolized surrounding the island with a protective circle of friendship and song. *Joy* would return in the afternoon, then everyone on board would either join the celebrations in Pero Palace or on Spark beach.

Hero always celebrated in Pero Palace with her family, and I always celebrated on the beach with mine. But we had promised each other that one year we would find a way to celebrate together.

I jumped out of bed and put on my new red silk dress that matched my red head feathers perfectly, then I went to find Nightingale. He was standing on our balcony, gazing out at the sparkling sea with a smile on his face and his long, reddish-brown head feathers iridescent in the light. He leaned down, put his forehead against mine and told me that I looked beautiful. Then we raced to the beach to join in with the celebrations.

Even though it was still early, hundreds of people were already gathered on the sand. Alkonosts and humans were side by side and arm in arm, talking and laughing with each other, even dancing together, despite the fact the musicians dotted along the beach were only tuning their instruments or playing warm-up songs that clashed with each other like the gulls wailing above.

People were wearing their finest clothes. Humans had combed and styled their hair in hundreds of beautiful ways, and alkonosts' feathers had been washed and preened and glowed a thousand different colours. But it was the smiles on people's faces that were the most glorious things of all.

The excitement on the beach was so intense it made the sky brighter, the sea more sparkly and the sand more golden. Nightingale and I found Fleur, Clay and Silver, and we walked together along the beach, greeting everyone, stopping to talk with friends and accepting the foods and drinks we were offered from the huge picnics that everyone had contributed to. There was fresh fruit and seed cakes, smoked fish and sweet breads, iced berry drinks and summer salads.

After eating a little of everything, Silver and I ran off to play a huge game of kickball with almost everyone from school. We ran from one end of the beach to the other, chasing the ball until we were completely out of breath. Then we found our families again and sat on the sand to listen to the speeches.

There were always speeches on the Day of Union, followed by a performance from some of the children, then songs that everyone on the beach joined in with. This year, the first speech was by an elderly person called Sandpiper, who had speckled brown and cream feathers and matching skin. They talked about the fine weather of the year, the bountiful crops, the shellfish harvest from the mudflats, and the building of the new farming and fishing museum on the outskirts of Spark. I listened, but my gaze kept being pulled out to sea in hope of spotting the ship *Joy*, and I was daydreaming about what my mother might be doing at that moment.

I'd never been on *Joy*. It was reserved for the royal families, their courtiers and special guests. I usually imagined it being full of rich, elegant Morovians draped in fine silks and glittering jewels, talking quietly while daintily nibbling shining fruits from the palace hothouses. But that day I thought the Morovians on the ship probably weren't much different to the Morovians on the beach. I imagined them smiling and laughing together, like us.

A lady called Violet gave the next speech. She had dyed her hair to match her name and painted tiny violet flowers onto her face too. Violet called person after person up onto the stage – which was really a bank of sand that had been built up for the celebrations. Soon there were nearly thirty people – alkonosts and humans – squashed onto the stage, smiling and blushing.

I always loved this part of the day, but it was extra special this year. The people called to the stage had all been anonymously nominated to receive a seabird feather dipped in gold, as thanks and recognition of an act of kindness they had performed. And Nightingale was onstage, because I'd nominated him for something he'd done.

Violet gave out the golden feathers and described each act of kindness. Some of them were small, simple acts, like carrying a friend's shopping home from the market, bringing a hot drink to a stranger with cold hands, or dropping off a cooked meal to a neighbour having a difficult day. Other acts were generous gifts of money, supplies or voluntary work to people or places that needed them.

Some of the most moving kindnesses were from people who simply stopped to talk to someone who looked lonely, or offered a hug to someone who looked upset, because it was these seemingly small acts that often had the biggest impact.

When Nightingale was given his feather, I welled with pride as Violet described how he'd used his singing magic to soothe a newborn baby in the hospital with stomach ache, then visited the baby on the other side of Spark every evening for five moons, because his songs were the only thing that would soothe the baby to sleep.

After the presentation of the golden feathers was the children's performance. This year it was by some of the youngest children from my school, but it was the same story as always: the story of the Day of Union, which describes how humans came to Morovia.

In the beginning, there were only ancient bird-people on Morovia. The island drifted across the oceans along with the other two Floating Islands, unseen by the humans who dwelled on Fixed Land.

No one is sure why the Floating Islands float, separate from the Fixed Land of the world. There is an ancient alkonost tale that says the islands are giant turtles – three sisters – searching for their mother. Many people today believe the islands' roots are made of a rare floating rock that exploded from deep in the belly of Earth. But that doesn't explain why the islands usually stay together like a family and dance around each other, even against the currents, or why they drape themselves in mist when Fixed Land is close. Whatever the truth, the ancient bird-people trusted Fate had made Morovia the way it was for a reason, and they were self-sufficient and content.

But one summer's day, thousands of years ago, a ship was wrecked on the shores of Morovia. It was the first and only time that humans came to the island. Usually the island would swerve to avoid passing ships, so many of the ancient bird-people believed that Fate must have brought the humans to Morovia for a reason.

Some of the humans didn't survive the shipwreck, and those who did were weak. The ancient bird-people gathered the humans up in their feathers, arms and wings and nursed them back to health.

Some of the ancient bird-people were unsettled and wanted the humans to leave, and some of the humans were wary of the bird-people too. But Gamayun sang a song that changed their minds – the Song of Unity.

Gamayun is said to have been the most birdlike alkonost ever to have lived. She's described as a beautiful bird with blue-black and fiery gold feathers, and a kind and wise face. Her singing magic is legendary, and she is said to have been able to communicate with the island itself and prophesy the future.

Gamayun sang of a future where alkonosts and humans lived in unity; where they helped and protected each other and were each other's friends and family. Gamayun sang that we would make each other's lives richer and bring great joy to Morovia. In some versions of the tale, Gamayun also sang of stormy times, but of how love and kindness would build bridges to bring us together, and form rafts to ride the roughest waves.

After hearing Gamayun's song, the alkonosts agreed to offer the humans an invitation to remain on Morovia, and when the humans were fully recovered they accepted. The captain of the ship, a lady called Danu, moved into Pero Palace where Gamayun lived. Danu's crew, who were explorers from all over the Fixed Land, moved into both Pero Palace Complex and Spark, creating a beautiful mosaic of cultures and beliefs across the island.

The alkonosts and humans lived together and worked together; shared their knowledge, strengths and skills, and singing magic was used for the benefit of all. Exactly one hundred years after the shipwreck, Morovia was full of joy and everyone's lives were richer, as Gamayun had prophesied.

Two queens were crowned to mark the occasion, and in the centuries that followed Morovia was always ruled by an alkonost queen and a human queen together

– in honour of Gamayun and Danu, who first created a united Morovia. And every year, on the anniversary of the day humans came to Morovia, everyone celebrated the Day of Union.

The children's performance re-enacted the story with brightly coloured costumes. The alkonosts wore traditional shell-beaded silks, and the humans wore deerskins, torn and tattered by the imagined shipwreck. Painted backdrops, showing scenes from different times in the island's history, were held up by some of the older children, while the youngsters performed. The child who played the part of Gamayun – always the most prized role – wore a beautiful costume made from thousands of bird feathers collected from all over the island.

I once played the part of Gamayun, when I was seven years old, and it was one of the proudest days of my life. Nightingale painted a picture of me wearing the feathered costume, and fixed it to the wall above my bed. Often when I couldn't sleep, I would stare at the painting and sing the words to the Song of Unity, as I did during my performance.

Whoever played the part of Gamayun always ended the performance by leading the Song of Unity, and everyone on the beach – alkonost and human – always linked arms and joined in. Some of the lyrics of the song are believed to have been passed down over the centuries from Gamayun herself, from the very song that prophesied our future together.

Shipwrecked on golden sands
Surf cloaking outstretched hands
Light souls fly over waves
Lift hearts from ocean graves.

Kindness, the bird in flight
The star map in the night
Your hands, my feathers strong
Our futures filled with song.
Hold onto me
We float on salted seas
Swim side by side
Climb into clear blue skies.

Nightingale stood beside me as we sang that day, his arm around my shoulders. And on my other side was Fleur, holding my hand tight and smiling her beautiful smile.

New worlds on ancient lands
New friendships proudly stand
Dual fruits of trees entwined
Two joyful songs combined.

Kindness, the fireside warm
The refuge from the storm
My hands, your feathers strong
Our futures filled with song.

You hold me near
Protect from tides of fear
Stand side by side
Float into vernal skies.

Two hearts sincere
Our voices loud and clear
Singing as one
Beneath a golden sun.

As the final chorus rose into the bright blue sky, I looked around and saw hundreds of alkonosts and humans singing and smiling together, and my heart swelled so much it made my chest ache. I felt part of something special.

Tonight, finally reunited with some of my friends, a little of that feeling has returned. I realize it's love for all Morovians that I feel, and I must use it to give me the strength I need – not just to free Nightingale, but also to bring unity to our island home, so there can be kindness, music and happiness once more.

CHAPTER 12

ANTS

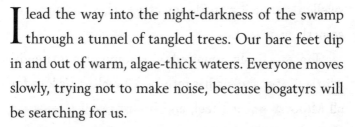

I lead the way into the night-darkness of the swamp through a tunnel of tangled trees. Our bare feet dip in and out of warm, algae-thick waters. Everyone moves slowly, trying not to make noise, because bogatyrs will be searching for us.

The murmurs of the swamp fold around us – a web of a thousand soft sounds that grow louder the more you listen. Water trickles over slimy roots, mud bubbles where buried creatures stir, tiny paws whisper over moss and birds ruffle sleepy feathers.

Whiskers and Lumpy are by my side. At first, they were so excited to be back in the swamp: Whiskers kept splashing up and down the shallow channel while Lumpy repeatedly flopped off Whiskers's head into the water, climbed back up, then flopped off again. But after I asked them to be quiet a few times, they realized the need for silence and stopped.

Fleur and Silver are walking behind me a little unsteadily, but they're gaining confidence as their eyes adjust to the dark and they get used to the slippery channel bottom. Fleur has tied a knot in the side of her long dress to keep it out of the water, and Silver has rolled his trousers up to his knees.

Hero is behind all of us, her trousers also rolled. She moves with confidence and I wonder how many times she's walked through the swamp before, as a bogatyr looking for – and maybe even capturing – alkonosts. The thought is like falling from a tree and being hit by branches all the way down. How could my best friend have worked for Captain Ilya? To stop my anger rising, I focus on how Hero is helping us now. She's covering any tracks we make: smoothing the occasional clump of mud that gets pushed up out of the shallow water by our feet, and readjusting any branches that get knocked by our heads, shoulders or bags.

We pause every few hundred steps to listen for bogatyrs, and when we do my heart pounds so loud I struggle to hear anything but its rhythmic thump in my ears.

Finally, after what could be one hour or several,

I see the tall, branching outline of home-tree rising from the widening channel ahead. The trailing moss that dangles from its lower branches shines in the moonlight, and the tree's shadowy reflection in the dark water is orange-tinged and wavering. I stare at the scene in confusion. Flames are dancing in the fire pit at the base of the tree, and Nightingale's and my sleeping and storage pods – that the bogatyrs threw down – have been fixed up again, although lower than before.

For a moment my heart lifts with the thought that Nightingale might have escaped and returned here, but then I see the silhouettes of two small, thin children huddled together, wrapped in a blanket by the fire. Jay's long blue-and-white head feathers and Kestrel's orange-brown feathers are glowing in the firelight, and I remember that I invited them both here.

"There are a couple of boys in my and Nightingale's camp," I whisper. "Could you wait here while I talk to them?"

Fleur and Silver nod, but Hero steps forward with her staff raised. "I'll come with you," she says.

I shake my head. "I know who they are, and no offence…" I look at Hero's staff and deerskins. "But seeing a bogatyr will scare them."

Hero frowns as if insulted, but nods. I run silently along the roots that snake towards home-tree. "Jay, Kestrel," I whisper as I draw close. They both turn to me and their eyes widen.

Whiskers splashes out of the water, rushes up to Jay like he's an old friend and rolls onto her back, like she does when she wants a belly-rub. Lumpy, clinging to Whiskers's ear, is squashed into the mud and croaks angrily.

"Whiskers!" Jay smiles his big missing-tooth smile as he strokes Whiskers's round belly. "Do you know there's a toad on your ear?"

"He's called Lumpy, they're friends," I whisper. "Bogatyrs might be close so we must be quiet."

Kestrel's orange feather-eyebrows draw together with concern. "Are you and your father all right?" he asks quietly. "We thought you'd been captured—"

"Why did you think that?" I interrupt, suspicion nipping into me again as I wonder if Jay and Kestrel told bogatyrs about my and Nightingale's home-tree after all.

"This place was such a mess when we arrived this afternoon, we knew bogatyrs must have been here," Kestrel explains. "We tidied up and mended what we could, then we waited, hoping you'd return. And when you didn't, we assumed you must have been captured." Kestrel cranes his neck to look behind me. "Are you with your father?"

"No. He was captured," I say, my voice wavering with worry for Nightingale. I look around home-tree. Jay and Kestrel have made it cosy again, and even tried to fix Nightingale's guitar, although it will never be the same. They've built a warm fire, knocked the dent out of our cooking pot and filled it with a snail and arrowhead broth. Sadness aches inside me. Nightingale should be here and we should all be enjoying this meal together.

"I'm so sorry, Linnet," Kestrel says gently.

Jay follows my gaze to the broth. "Would you like some food?"

"It's not safe for any of us to stay here." I glance back along the water channel. "I'm with three friends, and bogatyrs are looking for us. I only came to collect my and Nightingale's things."

Kestrel rises to his feet. "We'll put out the fire and help you pack. Jay and I have a camp not far from here that's never been found by bogatyrs. We could all go there if you like?"

"No one could get past our defences," Jay says proudly. "You should come."

"All right. Thank you." The prospect of getting somewhere safe, to rest and make a plan to free Nightingale, brings a small smile to my face. "But at the first sign of bogatyrs you two must promise to run," I add seriously, not wanting to put anyone else in danger.

"We always do." Kestrel lifts the cooking pot off the fire and Jay stops stroking Whiskers and rises to his feet.

"I'll get my friends. They're human," I say with a wince. Jay and Kestrel both stiffen. "And one of them is a bogatyr," I add, with an even deeper wince. "But she's helping us."

Kestrel nods warily, and I run back along the roots with Whiskers and Lumpy skipping alongside me. By the time I return with my friends, Jay and Kestrel have brought the sleeping and storage pods down from the tree and are dousing the fire with water. "Jay, Kestrel, this is Fleur, Silver and Hero," I whisper.

Fleur smiles warmly and Silver raises a hand in a shy greeting. Hero nods stiffly. Kestrel puts his arm protectively around Jay's shoulder as he pours water on the last of the flames.

The fire sizzles out and darkness falls over us, but in the same instant, brilliant yellow squares – about the size of sea-buckthorn berries – glow dazzlingly up from the ground. They're moving around and are so bright they illuminate our faces as we stare down at them. Lumpy squeaks with delight, flops off Whiskers's head and starts gobbling them up.

"What are they?" Fleur whispers.

"Ants," Kestrel says, as he and Jay push mud over the fire's embers with their feet. "We've not seen them in the swamp before, but they were all over this camp when we arrived. They're red, but a stripe on their backs glows yellow."

I remember the huge red ants I saw all over the ground after Nightingale was captured, and my feathers pull tight against my head. Something doesn't feel right.

"They're tracker ants." Hero peers at the ants, which are clustering around one of the rocks of the fire pit. "The bogatyrs use them to find thieves." Hero glances up at me with an accusing look. "You must have stolen something recently."

"Not since yesterday," I say defensively. My heart races as I look around. All of a sudden, every night-

shadow takes on the shape of a bogatyr, and I see at least three Captain Ilyas staring at me with the same contemptuous sneer that he gave Nightingale.

"I don't understand why you and other alkonosts steal." There's so much hurt in Hero's eyes, it's as if I stole something treasured from her personally.

"How can you not understand why we steal?" I stare at Hero in disbelief. "Captain Ilya and his bogatyrs took *everything* from us! We only steal a tiny amount, and we use it to fund the Unity Movement – to fight to get our lives back and see our friends again."

"Stealing is wrong, whatever your reasons for doing it." Hero looks away from me and peers back down at the ants, as if she's trying to work something out.

"I know it's wrong but..." I frown in annoyance. One of the reasons I loved Hero as a friend was because she always tried to do the right thing, so I shouldn't be surprised by her words. But that doesn't stop them from hurting. "We've been left with nothing," I say bitterly. "So we have no other choice."

Hero continues staring down at the ants and an awkward silence prickles between us. My bitterness swells into anger as I think again of Hero working for Captain Ilya. I breathe out slowly and remind myself that Hero has offered to help free Nightingale, so things are different now.

"How do the ants know Linnet stole something?" Jay asks curiously.

"They're specially bred to follow a scent." Hero leans down and picks up the rock that is most covered in ants, and I frown as I recognize it as the rock that was inside the parcel I stole. Hero carries the rock to the water channel and submerges it. "The last few moons, bogatyrs have been painting rocks with the scent, placing them in parcels that look like they're from jewellers and giving them to courtiers—"

"If the parcels are stolen, the ants lead you to the thieves!" Jay interrupts. He's clearly proud that he's worked it out, but my chest is tightening as I realize bogatyrs found home-tree because of the parcel I stole – and they accused Nightingale of stealing the ring because they knew it was stolen at the same time as the parcel.

Several loud caws cut through the night, along with the beating of large wings, and my heart takes flight. The crows who roost in the bald cypress not far from here have been disturbed. "We need to leave. *Now,*" I whisper urgently, crouching down to knot my and

Nightingale's sleeping and storage pods into a makeshift backpack. Whiskers lowers herself beside Lumpy so he can crawl up onto her head. "Which way to your camp?" I ask Kestrel and Jay. "And can we get there through shallow water channels? I don't want us to leave tracks."

"Ripward along this channel to begin with." Kestrel picks up Nightingale's tin guitar and Jay picks up the cooking pot, which is still full of food, and they step into the water. "Come on, it's not far."

I lift the pods onto my back and urge Silver, Fleur and Hero to follow Jay and Kestrel. Then I step into the water last. Even though it's warm, fear shivers through me. Nightingale has been captured and now my friends are in danger too, all because of me. I must get us to safety. I pause for a moment to listen to the swamp, and I hear what I hoped I wouldn't. My mouth goes dry. It's the faint but unmistakable *clang* of iron armour, and it's coming towards us.

CHAPTER 13

SMIRK

We move quickly and silently through the water channel. I keep pausing to listen for bogatyrs. Whiskers's round ears are pricked up and Lumpy's sword-leg is raised. I can't hear the *clang* of armour any more and I'd like to think that means we're moving away from danger, but I can't relax. Perhaps the bogatyrs following us are moving more quietly now, or perhaps we're heading straight for another patrol.

Kestrel leads us ripward, then we take a narrow stream leeward, then another channel ripward. This channel is wider and deeper – the dark water is up to our knees and is deepening with each step. Up ahead the water spreads out into a large, duckweed-covered pool spiked with horsetails at its edges. Huge oaks line the banks and tangle above us, making a canopy so thick only faint wisps of moon and starlight shine through, so I have to strain my eyes to make sense of the shapes in the darkness.

Silver slips suddenly into waist-deep water and Hero helps him back into the shallows.

"We need to stay at the channel edge," Kestrel whispers. "Parts of this pool are very deep. We're heading to the far side, to that oak with the stork nests." Kestrel points ahead and, as I stare, I slowly make out several huge nests tucked into the branches of one of the largest oaks.

Fleur stops and points at something in the water. "What are they?" she asks nervously. I follow her gaze to what look like bumpy, algae-covered logs floating in the centre of the pool. They're enormous, twice as long as me, and broader than Captain Ilya. I spot more of them on the bank, and my muscles tighten as I realize what they are. Their close-set eyes glint red in the night and their wide smiles are dotted with long, spiked teeth. One of them shifts from the bank and slips into the water.

I lean down and lift Whiskers and Lumpy into my arms. "They're alligators," I whisper, taking a step backwards as fear pumps through me. "Kestrel, why have you brought us to an alligator pool?"

"They're our defences!" Jay beams as he wades boldly forwards into the deeper water.

The alligator that entered the water swims towards Jay, slowly at first, but picking up speed until a wave of water surrounds its snout. I stare in shock, feeling like I should pull Jay back, but he's smiling at the alligator like they're best friends.

"Kestrel, is this safe?" Fleur asks as she grabs Silver's arm and pulls him closer to her. I hold Whiskers tighter and check Lumpy is secure on her head. Hero steps in front of me, her staff raised, as if she's preparing to protect me. A ripple of gratitude runs through me.

"The alligator heading towards Jay is called Smirk and he's almost one hundred years old." Kestrel smiles. "Our father – Plover – can use his singing magic to talk to animals. He made friends with the alligators here and asked them to guard our camp."

"Is Plover here?" Fleur's eyes are locked on Smirk, who is charging towards Jay now. Smirk opens his mouth as he draws closer and Fleur lurches forwards and reaches for Jay. "Jay, come back!" she shouts, her voice panicked.

Smirk stops right in front of Jay, and Jay puts one of his arms around Smirk's thick neck and gives him a hug.

"Plover isn't here." Kestrel takes Fleur's hand and squeezes it. "But I promise the alligators won't hurt us."

Jay has climbed up onto Smirk's back now and they're gliding across the middle of the pool towards the oaks on the far side. Jay is still holding the cooking pot full of broth with one hand and rests his other hand on Smirk's bumpy neck.

"Come on." Kestrel pulls Fleur forwards. "We'll walk around the edge."

Fleur exhales loudly, nods and follows Kestrel, with Silver beside her.

I step towards Hero. Her eyes are wide and her mouth open. "Are you all right?" I ask, nudging her shoulder with my own like I used to do when we were best friends.

Hero looks down at me – she's grown so much she's almost a head taller than me now – and nods slowly. "I think so," she whispers. "Do you really think we're safe from the alligators?"

I look at Jay riding happily on Smirk and I nod. "Yes, I do. And I think the alligators will keep us safe from the bogatyrs. Come on." I grab Hero's hand and pull her after the others.

By the time we reach the far side of the pool, Jay has already climbed the oak and is sitting on a branch beside one of the stork nests, beckoning us up.

"Our camp is in the tree," Kestrel explains. "We made it look like stork nests. I'll show you the best way up." Kestrel guides Fleur and Silver up to where Jay is, and Hero and I follow. It's awkward climbing with Whiskers and Lumpy in one arm, but I've done it before, so I manage.

When we reach Jay, I realize he's actually sitting on a platform made of cut branches, lashed together with vines and balanced in a fork in the tree. He's put the cooking pot in the middle of it, laid out some blankets to sit on and is smiling proudly. "Finally, we can eat together," he says. "I'm starving."

"You could put Whiskers and Lumpy in that nest if you like." Kestrel points to the nest nearest us and I walk along a thick branch to it, one of my arms held out for balance. The nest is lined with ferns and moss and has blankets inside. I lower Whiskers and Lumpy into it, scratch Whiskers's chin and wink at Lumpy. "We'll stay here tonight," I whisper. Lumpy blinks at me and Whiskers grunts her approval before nuzzling into the nearest blanket. When I return to the platform, I find everyone sat around the cooking pot and Silver giving out chunks of bread that he's pulled from the duffel bag I packed in Spark.

The leafy canopy is thick around us, but patches of star-filled sky shine between thinner branches above. Far below, I can make out the alligators floating on the dark pool. "Your defences are amazing." I smile at Jay and Kestrel as I sit beside Hero.

"Yes, thanks for bringing us here." Silver nods as he passes Jay a chunk of bread. "Do you mind me asking where your father – Plover – is?"

"Both our parents were captured by bogatyrs." Kestrel puts his arm around Jay.

"That's awful." Silver frowns. "We should help them escape along with Nightingale." He glances at Hero.

"How long ago were your parents captured?" Hero asks.

"Three moons." Jay's feathers lift with excitement. "You're going to break Nightingale out of The Keep? We must get our parents out too!"

"If your parents have been in The Keep that long, they'll be in the quarry, which is impossible to break into or out of," Hero says solemnly. "The only reason

I think we might be able to free Nightingale is because he'll be in the holding cells until his trial, and they're easier to reach."

Jay's feathers fall back down and Kestrel frowns.

"We haven't made a proper plan yet," I say, dipping the bread Silver has passed me into the pot of broth. "When we do, we'll try our best to think of a way to reach your parents too. If we're breaking into The Keep, I think we should try to free as many people as possible."

"I think so too." Fleur nods, leaning forwards to scoop up some broth.

Hero peers at the broth suspiciously and takes a bite of her bread dry. I have an urge to tease her about not eating the food – the way we used to tease each other gently when we were best friends. But she's sitting so stiff and upright, and her expression is so serious, that I don't say anything.

I thought that when Hero and I were reunited it would be all hugs and laughter, but Hero feels different now. Where she was warm and friendly, she now seems cold and guarded. And although we're sitting close together, it seems like she's on another island, floating far away. I don't understand why Hero's been working for Captain Ilya, and I don't know what she's thinking or feeling now. There are a million questions burning inside me, but one is far more urgent than all the others.

"How will we break into The Keep?" I ask.

"And can we help?" Jay mumbles, his mouth full of bread.

"What skills do you have?" Hero asks, as if she's interviewing bogatyr recruits.

"I have singing magic that draws animals to me," Jay replies. "Although it doesn't always work. In fact, it goes wrong quite often, and then animals run away from me. Crabs especially hate my magic, which is a shame because I love crab cakes."

Whiskers whimpers in her nest at the mention of crabs.

"That could actually be useful." Hero nods thoughtfully.

"How?" Silver lifts his eyebrows.

"There's a moat on the low side of The Keep filled with giant crabs," Hero says and Whiskers whimpers louder. "They're specially bred – like the tracker ants. They defend The Keep."

"I could sing magic to drive them away." Jay nods proudly.

"But singing magic doesn't work in the Magicless Mountains where The Keep is," I say with a frown.

"The moat is at the base of the mountains, away from the iron-filled rocks that stop magic from working," Hero says. "That's why the crabs are in the moat, for extra defence. But Jay's magic should work there. Although once we're inside The Keep, no one's magic will work. The whole place is built on the iron-filled rocks, and the bogatyrs there wear iron armour too."

"My singing magic wouldn't be useful anyway." Kestrel shakes his head. "It makes animals bigger, which is *never* useful to be honest. I can't remember the last time I used it." He shakes his head again and I recognize the look in his eyes. It's a mixture of frustration, disappointment and the same powerlessness that I feel from having no magic.

"My magic wouldn't be useful either." I wince at the half-truth, but I don't want to admit that I don't have any magic at all. Saying it out loud would make me feel even more vulnerable and, right now, I need to feel strong enough to face Captain Ilya and his bogatyrs. "But I can move quickly and quietly," I say. "I'm an excellent climber and I know how to weave ropes and ladders – which we'll need to get over The Keep's high walls."

"I have my tools with me." Silver smiles. "And I can use them to pick any lock on Morovia."

"And I can do more than make remedies." Fleur's eyes twinkle mischievously. "I have some powders in my satchel that I can use to make explosions, which could be a good distraction."

Hero nods. "That's a good start. But it will be difficult and dangerous to break into and out of The Keep. I think it will take more than just the six of us. Is there anyone else we could ask for help?"

"There is Echo," I say without thinking, then regret it immediately, because she's known and wanted by Captain Ilya and must be kept safe.

"I know Echo, though I haven't seen her for years." Fleur yawns and stretches her arms into the air. "She has powerful singing magic, doesn't she? She shared a memory with me once, from one of the ancient bird-people who used plants for healing. I learned more from that memory than from years of study."

I nod, remembering the memory that Echo shared with me on the day we met, of the Three Floating Islands huddled together against a storm. "She does have powerful magic," I whisper, thinking that Echo would be useful in a plan to free Nightingale not only because of her magic, but because, as leader of the Unity Movement, she has the most experience of planning missions too.

"Is she far from here?" Hero asks.

"Well, she's in the swamp, like all alkonosts," I say, feeling suddenly protective of Echo. "Apart from those of us the bogatyrs have sent to The Keep, of course," I add, more accusingly than I intended.

"Why don't you two get some rest?" Fleur suggests. "Then we could go to Echo's at first light and make a proper plan there." She glances at the nests around us. "I guess these are for sleeping in?" she asks Kestrel and Jay.

Kestrel nods and points to a nest above us. "Jay and I will sleep in that one. Linnet can sleep in the nest with Whiskers and Lumpy. Hero can either share with Linnet or take the storage nest next to her. And Fleur and Silver, you can have that one." Kestrel nods to another nest behind Fleur.

"I'll stay on watch for bogatyrs," Hero says.

"There's no need. Smirk will let us know if anyone comes close," Jay says.

"It will be good to sleep for a few hours," I admit, rising to my feet. Making a plan to free Nightingale will definitely be easier when my mind isn't so fuzzy.

"Goodnight, all," I say, my gaze stopping at Hero. Our eyes meet and my heart aches, because she's so familiar and so different at the same time. "Are you coming?" I ask.

Hero replies with a nod and my heart skips a beat. Maybe we'll have a chance to talk alone in the nest, and Hero might soften into the friend I remember.

I turn and walk along the branch to the nest where Whiskers and Lumpy are curled up. Hero follows me, but when I step into the nest she walks on and takes the storage nest instead. She lies down with her back to me, and disappointment falls over me with the thought that Hero isn't going to say anything else.

"Goodnight," I say quietly, as I curl around Whiskers and Lumpy. "Thank you for helping me today. And for offering to help free Nightingale."

Silence swells between us and I wonder what Hero is thinking. I used to feel her thoughts like silent songs in the air, but not any more. Does she miss her bogatyr friends? Does she regret offering to help?

"Linnet," Hero whispers so quietly that I barely hear her.

"Yes?" I lift my head and see Hero's shadowed face looking back at me from her nest. Her eyes are damp pools. "Are you all right?" I ask in concern.

"I want to apologize," Hero whispers. "The last time I saw you, the day after *Joy* sank, I shouldn't have shouted at you. I wasn't thinking straight, and I was so wrapped up in my own pain I didn't even remember your mother was singing on *Joy* until later. I was angry at what had happened and everything hurt so much, because my parents..." Hero stops and swallows back a sob.

"They were on *Joy* too." I finish Hero's sentence for her, my heart aching. "I thought someone you loved must have been, and that was why you were upset. But I didn't know it was both your parents. I'm so sorry, Hero." I reach a hand out to her, but her eyes are closed tight now, and her muscles are so tense they're shivering. My hand drops again as I realize I don't know how to comfort her.

I think of Nightingale and his cloak of grief – how he could only stare out to sea for weeks after *Joy* sank, how he lost his voice for many moons, and how – even now – sometimes his eyes and smile are distant and filled with sadness. Hero's stiffness must be her grief, still locked up tight inside her. "It's so difficult," I say, thinking of my mother now and the yellow feather in the tiny bag around my neck that takes my breath away when I touch it. "But it does get easier," I whisper. "It gets less intense somehow. Like rushing waters seeping into sand and becoming calmer groundwater."

Hero opens her eyes a little and leans further out of her nest. Her face escapes the shadows and shines in the starlight. "I've missed you, Linnet," she whispers.

I wish I could pull Hero into a hug, but she still looks so guarded that I'm not sure she would want me to. "I've missed you too," I say instead. My hand moves to the tiny bag around my neck, where my and Hero's necklaces feel like they're thrumming, eager to be freed.

"It's a shame it had to be like this," Hero says quietly.

My hand falls from the tiny leather bag. "Had to?" I ask in confusion, but Hero has curled up in her nest again and doesn't respond. I frown as worries about Hero creep into my thoughts. What did she mean? I want to trust her, but what if she's hiding something?

I put an arm gently around Whiskers, close my eyes and try to sleep. But despite being tired, I can't. Hero's words won't leave my mind. If she is hiding something then it could jeopardize any plan we make.

I feel like there isn't enough time to figure Hero out though. I must free my father before he's sent to the quarry. After finding out about Clay, I know the quarry is dangerous in the worst possible way. And – according to Hero – it's impenetrable too. But as I look up at the distant stars twinkling through the canopy, I know no matter what Hero or anyone else says, I will do everything I can to have my father safely back with me.

CHAPTER 14

THE SOUND OF ARMOUR

I wake with the morning chorus. Birds are whistling, chirping and chattering all around. Whiskers is snuggled against my chest and Lumpy is tucked beneath my chin. For a moment I wonder where I am, then it all floods back and I sit up quickly. Today, I must find a way to free my father.

I climb out of the nest I slept in, eager to get to Echo's and make a plan. I'm about to wake Hero when I spot Silver sitting on the branch platform, staring out across the swamp. I leave Whiskers and Lumpy sleeping in the nest and go to join him.

"Are you all right, Silver?" I ask as I sit down. Last night, in the dark, I didn't realize how far you could see from up here. But now, in the dawn light, the view is vast and breathtaking. The swamp extends below us, a thick tangle of greenery draped in mist that reaches all the way to the Melancholy Mudflats. The sun is rising on the low-rip side of the island today, making the wet mud shine bright silver.

"I couldn't sleep, so I've been watching the sunrise," Silver says. His face, lit up by the rising sun, looks tired.

"I'm sorry, Silver. You and Aunty Fleur should be waking in Spark, not here. And you should be getting ready for work at Circadian now, not planning to break into The Keep."

"We should all be waking up in Spark," Silver says firmly. "Nobody should be in The Keep. And nobody should be here in the swamp either. Unless they want to be of course." Silver looks out across the treetops and a small smile lifts the corners of his mouth. "You were right about this place," he says.

"Wet and muddy?" I raise my feather-eyebrows.

Silver laughs, glancing down at his tunic and trousers, which are streaked with mud. "Yes, but lush and beautiful too. Oh, look!" He points far out to sea, just ripward of where the sun is rising. "There's Eldovia."

I follow Silver's gaze, and when I spot Eldovia's purple cliffs glinting in the light I think of Nightingale's plan to go there. "Have you ever thought about leaving Morovia?" I ask.

Silver shakes his head. "Despite everything that's happened here, my mother and I have never considered it. Even after my father died." He glances down to the pool below, where huge alligators are slowly drifting amongst the duckweed and horsetails. "Morovia is our home and I love it. Even though it's a small island, there are always new things to discover. The places, the people and the magic here surprise me every day. What I want, more than anything, is to stay and help make our island a place of kindness so that we can all enjoy it. There must be a way." Silver glances at me from behind the twists of hair that have fallen over his face and I see determination gleaming in his eyes. "When we go to The Keep, I want to free your father and everyone else too. Nobody should be locked up in that place, or forced to work in the quarry."

Realizing that Silver is thinking about his father, I pick up his hand and hold it, like we used to when we were little and paddled together in the waves on Spark beach. "You're right. We should try to free everyone. And we should try to help Morovia too. I only wish I knew how. I've always believed my singing magic would bring unity, but it hasn't come yet, so I'm going to have to think of another way to help." I take a deep breath.

"I'll do everything in my power though."

Silver squeezes my hand. "Our power will have to come from togetherness, instead of magic."

I nod and squeeze Silver's hand back.

"Good morning." Fleur sits beside Silver and gives him a kiss on the cheek. Then she leans over and pats my and Silver's hands, which are still entwined together. "It makes my heart sing to see you two together again. I remember you holding hands when you were babies, toddlers, little children..." Fleur laughs. "Then, when you were older, you'd both pore over that box of broken watches and tinker away quietly."

I smile at Silver, thinking how our friendship has always been strong. And how, even though Silver has grown and changed, I still feel that I can trust him. *Unlike Hero.* The strange comment Hero made last night about things having to be like this resurfaces and I frown. "I'm wary about taking Hero to Echo's hideout," I whisper. "Echo is wanted by Captain Ilya and I'm not entirely sure that Hero can be trusted."

"What we're doing is dangerous, so it's natural to be wary." Fleur nods thoughtfully. "And perhaps you're finding it difficult to trust Hero because she's not quite the Hero you remember. But we've all changed with our struggles. Maybe now, more than ever, we need to look for the best in each other."

I bite my lip, thinking how Hero was upset last night talking about her parents, so that comment might have meant nothing. She has helped us already, and we still need her help to break into The Keep. So I could try harder to trust Hero, for Nightingale, and for our friendship too.

Jay and Kestrel climb down from their nest above. "Are you ready to go to Echo's?" Kestrel asks. "I'm sorry, we've nothing to offer you for breakfast."

"There's still some food in the duffel bags, but I spotted some young cattails at the edge of the alligator pool," I say, rising to my feet. "We could eat those on the way. Before we go, can you help me separate the ropes from my and Nightingale's sleeping pods though? We'll need to bring them with us. We could carry some food too, but leave the rest of our things here and travel light." I kneel beside the pods I left at the edge of the platform and begin loosening the ropes webbed over them.

Jay and Kestrel crouch down to help and, with Fleur and Silver helping too, it doesn't take long to untangle the ropes. We loop them into a couple of coils that can be carried over our shoulders. Kestrel takes one and Jay insists on taking the other. Fleur packs some food in her satchel, and we leave everything else in one of the nests. Even Fleur's shoes and Silver's and Hero's boots are abandoned, because it's easier to wade barefoot in the swamp.

By the time we're ready, Hero is awake and Whiskers and Lumpy are sitting up eagerly, waiting to be carried down the tree. We climb down carefully, then Jay rides across the alligator pool on Smirk, while the rest of us wade around the edge. Already it's roasting hot, although the sun is barely up. The air is heavy and all the feathered, furred, scaly and slippery creatures of the swamp are cowering from the heat, hiding in the shadows. I splash water over my face as I gather a few cattails, then show everyone how to use their thumbs to break the shoot and pull out the softer core.

Nervousness gathers inside me when Jay says goodbye to Smirk and we travel further away from the alligators. Whiskers and Lumpy must sense my mood, because Whiskers moves so close to me her coarse fur keeps scratching against my legs, and Lumpy has his sword-leg raised and his wide mouth drawn into a firm line.

"We must be quiet and listen for bogatyrs now," I whisper. "There'll be even more patrols looking for us this morning."

Halfway along the channel I spot a narrow, sandy deer-trail that runs highward, and I suggest we take it. Silver and Fleur walk last, covering our tracks behind us. We follow the trail through tall, tightly packed cedar trees with leafy tops that break the sunlight into shards. The heat is intense. Mossy branches, that should be moist and trickling with water, are dry and crackly. A dove murmurs wearily and a bluebird responds with a lazy warble. Usually, I'd sing something back to them, but I'm straining my ears to listen for bogatyrs.

When the deer-trail meets another, I realize with a jolt of excitement exactly where we are in the swamp. "Echo's hideout isn't far now," I whisper. "We follow that trail to a deep channel and then—" I stop still at Lumpy's high-pitched warning cry, then hear the sound of armour so close that my breath freezes in my throat. Bogatyrs are approaching, and they'll see us within moments.

I look around in panic, trying to come up with a plan. "Everyone, hide in those ferns," I say, pointing to a dense thicket nearby. "I'll lead the bogatyrs away.

Once they've gone, keep going towards the channel. I can't explain this now, but once you step into the water, Echo's magic will hopefully prevent anyone from seeing or hearing you. I'll meet you there soon."

"I'll come with you." Hero steps to my side. I open my mouth to say no, but Hero continues quickly. "I'll help make noise to lead the bogatyrs away, and if you get in trouble I'll defend you." Hero pulls her staff from the pouch on her back and, like when she stood between me and Smirk last night, a ripple of gratitude runs through me. Right now, I feel in my heart I can trust her.

"All right. Stay close. And you two…" I glance down at Whiskers and Lumpy. "Stay close too." Whiskers grunts in response and Lumpy winks. Fleur leads Silver, Jay and Kestrel into the ferns, while Hero and I walk straight towards the sound of armour.

I have a plan to trap these bogatyrs, but fear rises with my every step – because if something goes wrong then we'll end up captured, and I'll lose my one chance of freeing my father.

CHAPTER 15

SUCKING MUD

My heart pounds as Hero and I approach the bogatyrs. Their armour clangs as they walk towards us, then I see the glint of an iron helmet through the trees. "Bogatyrs!" I whisper, loud enough for them to hear, then I rush into the foliage ripward of the path, crashing deliberately into branches so they know which way we're running.

"Keep your feet on roots," I whisper to Hero as the sandy ground softens into mud. Whiskers knows this place, so she's already taking a safe path, dashing along a thick root of a sycamore tree. The ground grows wetter and muddier, the trees thin and the sky appears above us, bright blue with a dazzling sun.

Mid-step, I lean down and scoop Whiskers into my arms. Lumpy, perched high on her head, squeaks as I pull them close. Ahead of us is a bog, full of deep, sucking mud. But I know how to cross it. I scan the ground for the small shoot I'm looking for, then step an arm's length to the side of it. My foot sinks into the gloopy black mud, but when it's ankle-deep I feel the thick root that's buried beneath the surface.

"Put your feet where I step." I glance back to Hero and see the bobbing helmets of bogatyrs weaving towards us. I try to pick up speed but the mud pulls at my feet as if it has fingers of its own, slowing me down. Hero runs close behind me, her feet squelching into the gunge too. When we reach the far side of the sucking mud, I step off the root onto a grassy hummock, fall to the ground and cry out in mock pain. "My ankle!"

Hero collapses beside me, her face twisted with worry, and Whiskers and Lumpy stare at me in confusion. I wink. "My ankle!" I yell again. "I think it's broken!"

Three bogatyrs crash through the trees and one of them laughs as they slow down and stomp towards us. "That's made our job easier," a deep voice echoes from inside one of the helmets.

"I thought there were meant to be three humans with the alkonost," another bogatyr says, pausing to look around. My muscles tense as I think that she isn't going to follow the other bogatyrs across the mud, but after a moment she continues walking and I breathe a sigh of relief. All three bogatyrs start to cross the mud, sinking slowly as they do. They're up to their ankles by the time they notice they're being pulled in, and by then it's too late. The mud has them, and the more they struggle, the deeper they're sucked in – up to their shins, then their knees. The bogatyrs wrestle and groan with effort, but they can't escape.

I rise to my feet, still holding Whiskers and Lumpy. "Let's go." I beckon Hero to follow me back around the pool of mud.

But she's staring at the bogatyrs in horror. "We can't leave them like this," she whispers. "They'll drown in the mud."

"No, they won't." I lean close to her and whisper, "The mud is only as deep as their waists. Once their feet hit the bedrock, they'll be able to walk out. But it will take them hours to wade through – plenty of time for us to get safely to Echo's."

Hero frowns. "Are you sure?"

I look into Hero's eyes, disappointed that she would think I would leave anyone to suffer. "I promise the mud is waist-deep. And they have water pouches and shade, so they'll be fine."

Hero's frown relaxes as we walk for a while, around the wide pool of sucking mud and back to the sandy deer-trail. I lower Whiskers and Lumpy to the ground and we jog towards the channel where I said we'd meet the others.

"How do you know the mud is waist-deep?" Hero asks.

"Nightingale got trapped in it once." My heart races at the memory of the panic I felt when I thought I was going to lose him. I'd slid on my belly across the algae-covered surface, holding onto sharp brambles – because that's all I could find to stop myself sinking in – trying to reach him. I'd watched him getting sucked deeper and deeper into the mud, and I couldn't figure out how to help him. Then his feet hit bedrock and we laughed so much my face and stomach ached for the rest of the day. We were so covered in the clinging sludge it also took the rest of the day to scrape it off us.

"That must have been scary," Hero says and I nod. We've reached the channel now and Hero looks around, worry lining her face. "The others aren't here," she says. "Shall we go back for them?"

"Not yet." I look across the wide channel of water to a thick curtain of trailing moss on the other side.

I've never seen behind it, but I know from following Nightingale that's where Echo's hideout lies. I crouch down and scoop some water from the channel to splash over my face. But really I'm trying to feel Echo's magic.

When she's in her hideout, Echo uses her singing magic to echo out thoughts of stillness and silence to stop anyone from seeing or hearing her. I know in the past she's tried to use this magic to keep everyone in the swamp safe, but it's not strong enough for that and there are limits to how much she can conceal.

My fingers tingle in the water as the familiar warmth of Echo's magic flows into me. She's here, and right now her magic is stretching over this channel. That means Fleur, Silver, Jay and Kestrel might be here too, hidden.

I rise to my feet and look at Hero. She looks back at me with her familiar piercing gaze. "You're wondering if it's safe to take me to Echo's hideout," Hero whispers.

I nod, feeling relieved that Hero has read my thoughts, like she used to when we were friends.

"I've just trusted that you aren't leaving those bogatyrs in danger," Hero says. "And I think you should trust me now. You know all I've ever wanted is to help and protect the people of Morovia. All of them."

I take a deep breath, remembering how, on the day we met, I watched Hero helping both alkonosts and humans. That was always her dream, and she always followed it. And it's the reason why she wanted to become a bogatyr – not because she supports the division Captain Ilya has created.

Hero slides her hand into her pocket and pulls out a copper coin. The symbol of unity – the alkonost and the human holding each other tight – gleams in the light. "Every time I've looked at this coin, I've thought of our friendship, Linnet. And I've wondered how we can build unity." Hero takes my hand and presses the coin into it. "I think we want the same thing, but we've been fighting for it in different ways. Perhaps, if we work together, we could actually make a difference."

I smile and slide the coin into my own pocket, relief and hope making me feel suddenly lighter, but also stronger and surer that together we can succeed. "All right." I nod. "We have to swim across this channel. As soon as we're in the water, nobody on the bank will be able to hear or see us, because Echo uses her singing magic to conceal this place. It's perfectly safe," I add, sensing Hero's nervousness at the mention of magic. I take her hand and step into the water. "Come on."

Hero inhales slowly, pulls her shoulders back and follows me. Whiskers jumps in after us; her whole body dips beneath the surface and Lumpy croaks and splutters angrily on her head. Lumpy doesn't like being in deep water with Whiskers, because Whiskers has a habit of diving down without warning. So when we need to swim across a channel, Lumpy prefers to sit on my head.

"Hold on," I say to Hero, and I crouch beside Whiskers and hold out my hand for Lumpy to crawl onto. I never pick up Lumpy – I could damage his delicate toad skin if I did – so I always let him climb onto my hand and up my arm at his own pace. He reaches my shoulder, climbs up my neck, past my ear, and finally reaches the feathers on the top of my head.

Once Lumpy is settled, we walk deeper into the water and I look around for my friends. They emerge from behind a shimmering mist after a few paces. They're standing close together, almost waist-deep in water. "Linnet!" Fleur puts her hand over her heart. "Oh, I'm so relieved. Are we safe?"

"The bogatyrs are trapped and Echo's magic is keeping us hidden here, for now. Her hideout is on the other side of this channel. Can you all swim?" I glance around and am met with nods.

"I've left my satchel hidden in ferns on the bank,"
Fleur says. "It's important the powders in it don't get
wet."

"We'll come back for it," I say, letting go of Hero's
hand as I lower myself into the water all the way to my
chin. It's calm and silky, with yellow pollen floating on
its green surface, and although it's warm it feels nice
after the blisteringly hot air. Fleur sighs as she lowers
herself in too, and Silver smiles as he dips completely
beneath the surface.

Jay and Kestrel start giggling and splashing each
other as they sink into the water. Whiskers grunts
happily and rushes over to join them, where she plays
in the bubbles they're making – trying to nudge them
with her nose and bat them with her front paws.

Hero walks deeper into the water, side-eyeing
Lumpy on my head. "I've never seen a toad trained as
a pet before," she says.

"He's not a pet. We're friends." The channel bottom
drops away steeply and I start swimming, frog-style,
towards the trailing moss curtain. I turn around in the
water to check on Whiskers, who is still splashing with
Jay and Kestrel. "Come on!" I call and they all start
swimming towards me. But Jay and Kestrel keep

stopping to splash each other and laugh.

Silver bobs back up and swims past Fleur. She watches him with playful eyes, then suddenly sends a wave of water towards him. It splashes over his head and he gasps in shock, then laughs and tries to splash Fleur back, but Fleur dips beneath the surface and Silver ends up splashing Jay instead. Jay laughs, turns and kicks his legs to create a huge wave of water that splashes over Hero's face.

Hero glares at Jay, and Jay stops still, his blue skin paling. "I'm sorry," he says nervously, as Fleur emerges beside Hero and splashes her again.

For a moment Hero looks like she's going to say something stern, but then her face softens and she starts giggling. My heart seems to float up into the sky with Hero's laugh. I splash Fleur back in retaliation for Hero, and within moments everyone is splashing each other and we're surrounded by glistening water droplets as we continue across the channel, to the sounds of Lumpy croaking disapprovingly.

It feels wonderful to have stopped worrying about the bogatyrs capturing us for a moment, and to be having fun together, like we used to in Spark. But it doesn't last long. When we reach the trailing moss, everyone slows, quietens and peers at the curtain with curious, nervous eyes. Long threads of it loop and curl like ancient alkonost symbols as they tumble into the water, obscuring what lies beyond.

"Is Echo's hideout through there?" Silver whispers and I nod, my feathers tingling. Even though I can feel Echo's magic, I have no idea what I'll find behind the moss curtain.

I swim through slowly and carefully, so as not to knock Lumpy off my head, and when I emerge on the other side, I gaze in wonder at the scene before me... Until a huge pelican swoops down, her beak as long as my arm. The bird lunges for Lumpy, who is still perched on my head, and I scream.

CHAPTER 16

ECHO'S HIDEOUT

I dip beneath the surface and shield Lumpy with my arm to protect him from the pelican diving at us. Her beak stabs my hand and I try to bat it away. Someone puts an arm around my chest and pulls me backwards away from the bird.

Jay starts singing a fast, high-pitched song, punctuated with something like an eagle's cry, and the pelican flaps her enormous wings, lifts into the air and flies away from us. Jay turns to me, grinning proudly because his magic has driven the bird away.

"Thanks, Jay." I peer upwards to check Lumpy is all right, and see his sword-leg waving angrily in the direction of the pelican. "And thanks, Hero," I say, glancing back to see it was her who pulled me away.

The pelican flies across the calm, green pool ahead of us. The pool is completely encircled by trailing moss and, right in the middle of it, a tall cylindrical house stands on several long legs. The pelican lands on the very top of the house, opens her beak wide and grunts angrily.

The house has been carved from the remains of a huge, dead willow tree – the legs were once buttress roots, and the house itself was the tree's trunk. It has furrowed bark walls and window-holes knocked through knots. Trailing moss drapes from the leafless branches that rise from the top of the house then curve over it like a fountain. Barely visible behind the moss is a small round door, high above the water.

I'm amazed that Echo has a home like this in the swamp. I guess if you can use singing magic to conceal your house, then you can make it more of a home than the trees Nightingale and I have had to move from every moon or two.

I swim towards the house and am about to call Echo's name when the door opens and she pokes her head out.

"Echo!" I beam to see her again. She's wearing a vest and shorts woven from grey-green swamp fibres, and the fluffy grey-brown feathers that cover her head, neck and arms now have a greenish tinge.

"Linnet!" A smile spreads over her kind, round face,

and she waves before throwing a rope ladder down. "I trust Grunt didn't bother you too much." She points upwards to the pelican, who now has her beak opened so wide the top of her head is upside down, and she's letting out the longest, loudest grunt I've ever heard.

The ladder splashes into the water and I grab it with one hand and pull Whiskers close with the other. Then I wait for my friends to climb up. But Hero is holding back, looking nervous.

"Echo is one of the kindest people I've ever met," I say to her reassuringly. "You can trust her, and her magic."

Hero still looks unsure, but she climbs the ladder.

I raise my feather-eyebrows, trying to glimpse Lumpy on my head, and he flops down my cheek, plops into the water, then clambers up onto Whiskers's head. "Come on, you two. It's time you met Echo." And I climb the ladder with the two of them under one arm.

"It's good to see you again." Echo smiles as she helps me up into a cool, circular room. "Although your friends have told me you're here with awful news."

"Nightingale has been captured." I nod. "But we're planning to free him." I lower Whiskers and Lumpy to the floor.

Echo passes me a blanket to wrap around my

dripping body, then pulls me into a soft, feathery hug. I close my eyes for a moment to enjoy the feel of her warmth.

"Please, have a seat." Echo leads me to a chunky wooden stool and gives me a bark cup filled with mors – the berry drink she always made when we lived on the mudflats. Whiskers follows me and sits on my foot. And Lumpy, on her head, stares around the room with his eyes narrowed suspiciously. My friends are all sitting with blankets around their shoulders and bark cups in their hands too.

"Have you met everyone?" I ask.

"Yes, and I've said that I'll help you all in any way I can." Echo sits on a stool beside me. "But you must know The Keep is extremely well fortified, guarded by at least one hundred bogatyrs and – being in the Magicless Mountains – singing magic doesn't work there. Even at our strongest, the Unity Movement never considered trying to free anyone imprisoned there."

"But we have Hero," I say. "She knows how we can break into The Keep and get Nightingale out."

Echo raises a grey-green feather-eyebrow at Hero. "I'm listening."

"Do you have something I could draw The Keep on?"

Hero asks. "It would help for you all to picture it clearly."

Echo walks to the remains of a small fire on a large flat stone beneath a window, extracts a charcoaled stick and passes it to Hero. "You can draw on the floor, I don't mind."

Hero leans down, draws a small cross and labels it with the four directions of the island: *Hi* for high side, *Le* for lee side, *Lo* for low side, and *Ri* for rip side. Then she begins to draw what looks like a large square. I take a sip of my drink, which is cool and sweet, but with a tart bite that makes me feel instantly alert. Nervous anticipation tingles through me. With each line Hero draws, Nightingale feels closer.

"Is that the quarry?" Silver points at a circle Hero has drawn that fills the high-rip side of the square.

Hero nods. "We must free Nightingale before his trial. It's certain he'll be found guilty and sent to work in the quarry, and there's no way to break him out of there."

"Maybe together we can figure out a way to free everyone imprisoned in the quarry," I say, glancing over to Jay and Kestrel, but Hero looks back at me and shakes her head.

"When is Nightingale's trial?" Echo asks.

"I heard Captain Ilya say it would be on Glidesday. The day after tomorrow," I reply.

"I was trying to find out who will be judging him when I was captured," Fleur explains. "I hoped it might be someone we could bribe."

"I know who the judge will be, and there's no chance of bribing them." Hero glances up from her drawing. "It will be Crown Heir Vasha."

Echo's eyes widen. "The Unity Movement has been trying to reach Vasha for years. But Captain Ilya has been keeping them well guarded and well hidden in Pero Palace. I wonder why they are acting as judge now?"

"The Heir is almost old enough to rule now and has asked to begin some royal duties," Hero explains.

"If only there was a way I could reach them and use my singing magic, then we could do so much more than free Nightingale." Echo sighs.

"What do you mean?" I ask, my feathers lifting with curiosity.

"Vasha could remove Captain Ilya from power," Echo explains. "If I were able to use my singing magic in The Keep, then I could convince them to do that and to start working with us towards uniting this island."

"If there's a chance we could bring unity to Morovia,

then we must try!" I exclaim. My brow furrows as I try to figure out how we could make Echo's singing magic work inside The Keep.

"Even if your singing magic worked there, how could you use it to convince the Heir to do anything?" Hero asks.

"My magic echoes thoughts into the air, so I could send them to Vasha." Echo smiles.

"That's terrible magic!" Hero's eyes widen in horror. "Nobody should control people's minds like that!"

"Oh no, you misunderstand." Echo holds up her hands defensively. "It's a very gentle magic – a way of sharing and communicating thoughts and feelings, not controlling minds. I think if Vasha could experience, for a few short moments, the thoughts and feelings of an alkonost, then they would understand us better and be inspired to help us."

"Why don't you just talk to Vasha?" Hero asks. "You don't need magic to do that."

"Captain Ilya would never let me talk to the Heir." Echo shakes her head. "He's denied every request for an audience with Vasha. But if I could use my singing magic then I could communicate a great deal very quickly – enough to convince the Heir to talk to us, free everyone who has been wrongly imprisoned and start working together."

"Is there any way we could make your magic work in The Keep?" Fleur asks.

"The iron in the rocks of the Magicless Mountains stops magic from travelling through the air." Echo frowns.

"Do you remember the day we met, when we were being taken from Spark?" I ask Echo and she nods. "You sang magic into a moon-snail shell and, when I touched it, I felt your magic flow into me."

"The magic was trapped in the shell, then moved into you." Echo nods thoughtfully. "But magic never stays trapped for long."

"Could you trap it in something long enough to carry it to Vasha?" I ask.

"Possibly." Echo keeps nodding and slowly her eyes light up. "This hideout is still concealed with magic even though I'm not singing now. The more magic I sing, the more it lingers. So if I sing enough magic into an object and keep adding to it until we get to The Keep, then it might just work."

I look around the room, wondering what object we could use. My eyes land on a seabird feather dipped in gold, dangling from a piece of string against the wall.

I spring to my feet, making Whiskers jump and Lumpy *"Phoot"* indignantly. "That's one of the feathers given out on the Day of Union for acts of kindness, isn't it?"

Echo's cheeks flush. "I got it when I was very young and am proud of it, so I brought it with me when we were taken from Spark."

I hesitate, not wanting to ask Echo if we can use the feather when it clearly means so much to her. But Echo rises to her feet and lifts the feather down. "It's a perfect choice, Linnet. The vanes of the feather will trap magic even better than a shell, and these golden feathers symbolize kindness, so if I offered this to Vasha as a gesture of peace, there's a good chance they'd accept it."

"How could you get close enough to Vasha to do that?" Silver asks.

"We'll break into The Keep. Then, after we've freed Nightingale and you've all escaped, I'll surrender to the bogatyrs. And when I'm tried by Vasha, I'll offer the feather."

"But if Vasha doesn't touch the feather, or if the magic doesn't work, you'll be left trapped in The Keep!" I look at Echo, a chill of fear running through me.

"I'm willing to take that risk." Echo twirls the golden feather in her fingers. "A moment ago, Linnet, you said, 'If there's a chance we could bring unity to Morovia, then we must try.' And you were right."

I look at my friends, excitement sparking inside me. Fleur smiles and Silver nods. Jay's and Kestrel's feathers lift with eagerness. Hero looks from the golden feather in Echo's hand to me. There's a line of worry creasing her forehead, but she gives one firm nod before continuing to draw the map of The Keep onto the floor of Echo's home.

My own feathers lift and tingle as I realize what we're about to plan: a secret mission not only to free my father, but to remove Captain Ilya from power, free everyone in The Keep and the quarry and unite all of Morovia. Perhaps, in a few short days, Nightingale and I will be sitting on our balcony back in Spark, gazing at the soft sands, the salted waves and the ever-changing view. Or perhaps, I think with a shudder, if it all goes wrong, we could be locked up in The Keep ourselves before the end of today, with no chance of escape or unity ever again.

I take a deep breath to steady my nerves and remind myself that nothing will change unless we take risks, and that I have enough love in my heart to give me the courage I need to do this.

CHAPTER 17

PERCH

The rest of the day in Echo's hideout passes in a flurry of activity. We pore over Hero's map of The Keep and make a plan of how we can break in to free Nightingale, then break out again. We go over every detail several times. Our plan is dangerous, and there's lots that could go wrong, but there's also a good chance it could work, and that makes hope fizz inside me.

When the sun begins to fall through the sky in the afternoon, Echo says she needs some time alone to concentrate on singing magic into the golden feather. She lends us a small raft made from branches so we can collect Fleur's satchel that she left in the ferns on the other side of the channel.

It's still scorching hot, so all of us slip into the water and swim beside the raft. Jay sings magic to stop Grunt the pelican from attacking Lumpy. We collect the satchel in silence, knowing we're at the edge of Echo's magic, but once we're in the water again, we relax a little.

Back in Echo's hideout, I weave together the ropes we took from Nightingale's and my sleeping pods to make a rope ladder that Hero says will be long enough to climb The Keep walls, while Silver questions Hero about the types of locks in The Keep.

Echo gives Jay some singing lessons to help him understand how to control his magic better, because he must sing the giant crabs away from us when we reach the moat. I try to listen to the advice she's giving. If I could make my magic come, I might be able to offer something more. But I know that my role – to get everyone over The Keep walls – is important too, and that together we have the power to make this plan work.

As the sun sinks low and the day's heat eases, we gather on a small balcony at the back of Echo's home. Our plan is to walk the treacherous route to The Keep through the cool and cover of darkness. Then, after dawn, hide and rest before breaking in tomorrow night. But before we set off, we need to eat. So we dangle bone hooks on fishing lines into the water, until we catch enough perch for everyone.

Kestrel and I carry Echo's flat hearth rock onto the balcony and build a fire, so that we can roast the fish on sticks over open flames, and Echo boils some fleshy green samphire stalks to eat with them.

Hero peers down into the water below the balcony as she nibbles the white flaky meat of her perch. A speckled brown and orange butterfly – a fritillary – dances past and we both stare after it. I wonder if Hero remembers singing with me and my parents, and butterflies that my mother's magic had called fluttering all around us.

The butterfly disappears into evening shadow and Hero turns to me. Her eyes are damp and, like when we were best friends, I feel her thoughts. She's full of grief and sorrow that my mother was on *Joy*, and she wants to say something, but doesn't know how. I give Hero a small smile, hoping that she feels my thoughts too – that I know and I understand.

Echo lifts the golden feather that she's tied around her neck, and quietly hums more magic into it.

"Is it working?" Kestrel asks and Echo nods in response as she sings.

Jay drags a stalk of samphire between his teeth to get the fleshy bit, then sighs as he looks down at the picked-clean bones of his perch. "How do you get your magic to stay in one place?" he asks Echo. "If I could do that, I'd keep all the perch in one part of the swamp, so I could dip my hand in and get one whenever I was hungry."

Echo stops singing and laughs. "I don't think that would be fair on the perch, but if you promise to use your magic responsibly, then I will teach you how to do it. It takes a great deal of concentration and practice, though, to make a song linger like a memory. And you have to keep refreshing the magic or it drifts away – just like talking about memories keeps them alive."

My chest tightens as I think about my mother again. I love remembering her, but I don't often talk about my memories, because I worry they might push Nightingale further into the past when I need him in the present.

I look around at my friends and realize that here I could talk about my mother without that worry. So I take a deep breath and say, as steadily as I can, "I remember every one of my mother's feathers – how soft the short blue ones near her ears were, and how strong the long yellow ones on her arms were. And I remember how warm and safe I felt when she held me."

Speaking the memory out loud feels like something trapped inside me has been let out to fly free. Tears well in my eyes, but I feel my mother close to me and that brings me comfort. All of a sudden, I want to do this with Nightingale. As soon as he's free, I want us to sit and talk about our memories of Halcyon together. Even if it means that he falls into the past, at least we'd be there together.

"I remember my father's hands." Silver looks up from the fish he's been eating. "How the cracks and lines of his skin were nearly always filled with clay, and how he would scrub them clean and pink before a meal. And I remember how he'd get up early in winter to make a fire to warm the house before my mother and I got up. If I heard him, I'd creep out of bed to help and he'd wrap his cardigan around me, so that we were both snug inside it."

Tears spill from Fleur's eyes but she doesn't wipe them away. "I remember Clay peeling apples. I don't know why that memory sticks so much. I guess little details can leave big imprints." Fleur laughs, although tears are still streaming down her cheeks. "He'd use a small knife that was his father's, and all the peel would come off in one long, curly strip. Then he'd cut thick triangular slices and always offer the first one to me."

"I don't have many memories of my parents," Hero

says quietly, staring down into the water. "They were always busy. But that doesn't mean I don't miss them. Sometimes, when I think about them, I miss the things we didn't do – the things I hoped we'd do one day. They promised that one summer we'd hire a house in Spark near the beach." Hero glances over to me. "And that we'd have a proper holiday together. But that will never happen now."

I wonder if I should put my arm around Hero to comfort her, but again she has a stiffness about her that makes me think she might not want me to. It must be grief that has changed her this way, so I lean a little closer to her instead, hoping being nearby will offer some comfort.

"Our home is in Spark." Jay looks over to Hero and smiles. There are a few stalks of bright green samphire sticking out of his teeth. "It's not near the beach, but it's not too far to walk. You could come for a holiday there with my family, once we're together and are allowed home again."

Kestrel nods. "You'd be very welcome. Our parents are really nice."

Hero looks up. "That's kind of you," she says. "Perhaps, one day."

Lumpy, who is sitting near my knee, croaks eagerly. "You want a job?" I ask, as I remove the coin purse which was still tied at my waist. I take out a copper coin and place it in front of Lumpy. "Can you take this to Hero, please?" I glance over to Hero beside me, so that Lumpy knows who I'm talking about. Lumpy picks the coin up in his mouth and carries it across my leg and onto Hero's, while I tuck the purse into a knothole behind me – I'm not going to need it to break into The Keep.

Hero stiffens as Lumpy climbs onto her, but once he's dropped the coin in her lap and crawled off again, she relaxes. "Thank you, Lumpy," she says, picking up the coin and looking at the symbol of unity on it – the alkonost and the human holding each other tight. Her eyes dampen as she glances over to me, and once again I feel her thoughts. This time they're of our friendship, lost and found.

Echo rises to her feet and takes a deep breath. "Shall we set off?" she asks, looking around at us all. Everyone has finished eating and the evening air is cool and fresh.

Emotions rush through me like a flock of birds taking flight. I'm scared, but also filled with hope – not only that we'll free Nightingale, but that we'll do something incredible that will help all of us, and everyone on Morovia, reclaim some of the happiness of the past.

As I rise to my feet, another happy memory fills my mind – of one of my last days in Spark before *Joy* sank – of the day that my mother and I walked beyond the lemon grove…

The Day My Mother and I Walked Beyond the Lemon Grove

Three years ago, on the day before the Day of Union, my mother and I went on an adventure. We did this every year, and it had become a tradition that I found as exciting as the Day of Union itself.

We left early in the morning, at the same time as Nightingale, so that we could walk together along the beach, then through the town to the hospital on the ripward side. There we said goodbye to Nightingale, who was going to work, the same way we always did, by pressing our foreheads together. Once Nightingale had left, my mother turned to me with her eyes sparkling.

"Where are we going?" I asked, my feathers lifting in excitement. Even though we'd always lived in Spark, somehow on these days my mother would find somewhere to take us that I'd never been before.

The previous year, my mother had persuaded the librarian in Spark library to take us into the basement, where the oldest, most precious, dustiest, broken and torn books were kept, and we spent hours looking through ancient music scores together. I knew how to read music – my mother taught me before I could read words – and we sat and hummed tunes to each other, sang lines of lyrics we liked, and my mother jotted down her favourites in a notebook.

The year before the library visit, we walked highward along the beach until we reached a tiny crack of a cave, about half my height and just wide enough for my mother and me to squeeze through. After about twenty paces it became clear that the cave was actually a tunnel, and we emerged from the other end into a small, hidden, crescent-shaped cove, with a pebble beach and high cliffs striped with layers of grey and golden rocks. We spent all day there, sifting through the pebbles and picking out what my mother called "Fate's claws", which were finger-sized rocks that looked like curved claws. Really, they were fossil shells, an ancient ancestor of oysters. I put my favourite one on my bedroom windowsill at home, and the rest I lined up, all in a row, near the lavender plants in our roof garden.

I looked up at my mother, wondering if our adventure today would be indoors or outdoors. "It's a surprise," my mother said, taking my hand in hers. "Come on."

We walked highward, through narrow streets lined with square homes in a rainbow of colours. It was a warm and sunny day and the air was filled with the scent of lemons. When we took a small, overgrown footpath between two houses I realized why – my mother had brought me to a lemon grove, containing about thirty trees, each of them bright with ripe yellow fruit. "Are we picking lemons today?" I asked excitedly, but my mother laughed and shook her head and led me across the grove.

At the far edge of the grove there was a wide, shallow stream bubbling over small pebbles. We followed it into a woodland that sloped gently uphill. The river narrowed and became louder as it rushed over large, pale-grey boulders. Occasionally there were small, calm pools between the boulders, where dragonflies darted and tiny fish swam in shimmering shoals.

After about an hour of walking, I became aware of a continuous *shushing* sound that became louder and louder. My feathers tingled. "What's that noise?" I asked, but my mother only smiled and walked faster.

Soon I saw it – a small but beautiful waterfall. White foam cascaded down a fern-clad cliff about twice my height, and crashed into a deep, round plunge pool with three steep sides.

My mother put her bag on the grassy ground at the edge of the pool. "Would you like to come for a swim with me?" she asked.

"Of course!" I nodded, and my mother pulled two felt blankets out of her bag and laid them on the grass in the sunshine. We stripped off most of our clothes and waded into the water. My head feathers pulled tight against my scalp and the long feathers on my mother's arms overlapped and drew close to her skin. It was so cold our muscles tensed and our shoulders lifted to our ears as we walked tentatively forwards, until our bodies got used to the temperature.

When we were finally submerged, my mother nodded towards the rushing waterfall. "Come and see," she said and we swam together around the edge of the pool, until we were approaching the waterfall from the side.

The noise of the plunging water was deafening now and spray filled the air, coating our faces and head feathers with glistening drops. My mother grabbed hold of a lip of rock to the left of the waterfall with one hand and pulled me close with the other, so I was wedged between her and the smooth rock walls. Then, together, holding onto the rock lip, we shimmied along the wall behind the waterfall.

When we were completely behind the waterfall, my mother lifted me up and placed me onto a ledge that was just wide enough to sit on, then she pulled herself up beside me.

It was breathtaking. A curtain of water rushed down in front of us and crashed into the pool below our dangling feet. The rock seat we were sitting on felt like it had been smoothly carved especially for us. The noise of the waterfall meant we couldn't hear each other, so we sat, unspeaking, side by side, watching the water tumbling down. I held my mother tight, my arms around her chest, part scared, part excited and part amazed by the wonder of it all.

I'm not sure how long we stayed there. I think when wonderful things happen time stretches and sways, so you can never grasp its length. All too soon, my mother

slipped back into the water, lifted me down beside her, then we shimmied back to the calm of the plunge pool and out onto the grassy bank.

We lay on our sun-warmed blankets, our feathers now lifted to dry in the warm air, and we laughed at the sky. "How do you know about this place?" I asked.

"My own mother used to bring me here," my mother replied.

"I wish I'd met her." I sighed. "And that we could all have done this together."

"Ah, but we are all doing it together, Linnet." My mother turned onto her side to look at me and the blue and yellow hues in her skin glowed in the sunlight. "We carry those we love in our hearts, always." She turned away again and closed her eyes. "I feel her with me all the time. Especially when I sing. Do you remember the lullaby I used to sing when you were very young?"

I nodded. "You told me your mother sang it to you too."

My mother laughed again. "I'm sorry, I've probably told you many times."

"You can tell me as many times as you like." I smiled.

"When I sing that lullaby, it feels like my mother is at my side." My mother sat up, opened her bag and pulled out a flask, two wooden cups and a paper parcel. "And when I eat walnut cookies made from her recipe, I feel her too."

"Walnut cookies!" I sat up.

We ate the cookies and drank the milk in the flask, which was cooled with ice and creamy-thick. Then we dressed and wandered slowly back to Spark, hand in hand.

We stopped in the market, as we always did, to choose dresses for the Day of Union. Everyone always wore beautiful silk clothes for the celebrations, often borrowed from the clothes-swap stall that appeared once a year. My mother had brought our dresses from the previous year in her bag, and we left them at the stall. My mother chose a long, orange dress instead, while I chose a knee-length red one that perfectly matched my red head feathers.

Afterwards, we walked to the beach, but instead of heading home we wandered ripward, following the setting sun. When the air cooled, we sat together on the sand, gazing at the colours that bloomed like flowers on the horizon as the sun dipped into the sea. I snuggled close to my mother and she wrapped her warm, feathered arms around me and sang the lullaby that we had talked about earlier.

The sweetest music
tender hearted and wild
a soulful of songbirds
in the breath of my child
on feathered shoulders
divine dreams afloat
cradled in purest love
sigh a golden note.

My heart rejoices
when yours beats near
your lips in the softest smile
bring a mountain of cheer
your heart-deep laughter
that came before words
heavenly harmonies
the purest I've heard.

The sweetest music
I've found in you
the heart-song we share
everlasting and new.

"I'll miss you tomorrow," I whispered when my mother finished singing. I knew I'd see her in the afternoon when she got back from her short voyage on the ship *Joy*, but I always missed her when she wasn't there for the celebrations on the beach in the morning.

My mother pressed her forehead against my own. "We carry those we love in our hearts always, remember," she whispered back. I smiled and held my mother close until the sun disappeared and darkness cloaked the beach. Then we walked home together, hand in hand.

CHAPTER 18

COLD-FEET CANYON

We leave Echo's hideout at sunset and swim across the calm pool and channel until we reach the bank. Fleur floats her satchel across using Echo's raft to keep the powders dry, and I carry the rope ladder I made, strung over my chest.

As we climb out of the water, fear creeps over me. Echo can't use her magic to keep us hidden in the swamp, as she needs it for the golden feather, and the nervousness of discovery thrums around us like the insects buzzing in the twilight. But everyone's faces are set with determination as we follow a shadowy trail highward.

Whiskers walks at my heels, Lumpy perched high on her head, and I sense their unease too. We've never been away from Nightingale for this long. It's been two days, and I think, as well as missing Nightingale,

Whiskers and Lumpy are missing the steady rhythm of our lives. I know I am. And I miss the feeling of my father being close; the way he made little noises so I knew where he was, and the small hand gestures he made to safely guide my movements.

The last of the light is swallowed by growing shadows and for hours we walk in almost total darkness; feeling our way forwards with hands outstretched, ducking beneath low limbs of giant trees, and balancing on roots that snake across black waters so rich with larval life they churn.

Finally, the swamp thins and moonlight falls through the canopy, gilding everything in silver. Kestrel's, Jay's and Echo's head feathers shimmer as they walk ahead of me. Hero, behind me, is helping guide Fleur and Silver to the best spots to place their feet. I glance back to check they're all right, and fill with warmth for Hero. She is how I remember her now – her strong hands quick to help, her piercing gaze noticing what's needed. She moves branches aside for Fleur and Silver, and tests boggy ground is safe with her staff before they step into it. Hero sees me looking at her and smiles. I smile back and walk on in silence, feeling like one of the missing pieces of my life has clicked back into place.

Echo, Jay and Kestrel pause at the high-side edge of the swamp. Ahead of us lies a small grassy meadow that stretches to Cold-Feet Canyon – the steep-sided gorge that separates the Mournful Swamp from the Rippling Marsh.

The canyon is a wide, deep scar, so filled with black shadow and white mist that it looks like a strip of night has laid down on the ground to rest. Beyond the canyon lies the marsh, veined with silver streams. The marsh is very different to the swamp. It's a wide-open space, with no trees to block the light. Tall reeds sway beneath a huge, starry sky – as wide as the skies over the sparkling sea. A wave of nostalgia crashes over me as I think of sitting with my parents on our balcony in Spark, spotting constellations and shooting stars together.

"The bridge to cross the canyon is leeward of here," I whisper, leading the way into the meadow, but staying in the shadow of the swamp. The landscape is more open now, and the danger of being seen is making my feathers pull tight against my head. Whiskers draws close to me and Lumpy's eyes narrow at the change in scenery.

Silence falls over us like a blanket. The droning of insects that surrounded us in the swamp is fainter now, and everyone's footfalls are quieter on the soft mossy grass. My breathing feels too loud and I try to calm it.

Cold-Feet Canyon begins to curve highward, and we're forced to follow it away from the cover of the swamp. I feel vulnerable, the way I do when I think about not having singing magic. My gaze darts around as I look for bogatyrs. All is still, but I feel like a group of them could step out of the darkness at any moment.

When the bridge appears, I sigh with relief – once across the canyon, it will be easier to find somewhere to hide amongst the tall reeds of the marsh – but my heart pounds with fear for what comes next. We're going to have to cross the suspension bridge over Cold-Feet Canyon; a place known for bone-chilling mists and mysterious disappearances.

Once, on the Melancholy Mudflats, someone told a story about an icy fountain that sprayed up from the river in the bottom of the canyon so powerfully that it knocked someone off the bridge. They said the waters were so cold they must have come from deep beneath the roots of the island and been forced up through a crack in Morovia itself.

None of us mentioned these things when we made our plan, I think because we didn't want to admit they might be anything more than scary stories. But right now, as I peer along the bridge, these thoughts are loud in my mind and my stomach knots with worry.

The bridge stretches into darkness, hovering over the endless blackness in the canyon below. Pale grey mist shrouds the far side the bridge, so I can't be sure where it ends. Coldness seeps into the vanes of my feathers as I think about walking over that abyss. One slip, one fall, and…

I try to swallow back my fears and focus on the task ahead. The bridge is made simply, from planks of wood and rope. It's just wide enough for us to walk single file, holding onto the rope rails. "Should we cross one at a time?" I whisper, worrying about the strength of the bridge.

"I think we should stay together," Hero says. "I know bogatyrs built the bridge to be strong enough for several people at once, and we can help each other if—"

Hero is interrupted by a loud, sudden splash that echoes upwards from deep within the canyon. Water droplets spray into the air and Jay jumps back in fright, his feathers pulled tight and his eyes wide. Whiskers whimpers and Lumpy lifts his sword-leg so high he nearly topples backwards. I lean down and scoop them into my arms.

"What was that?" Kestrel asks, his voice wavering.

We all stare at each other, fear in our eyes. It must have been something big – very big – in the river below. Echo opens her mouth to say something, but no words come out.

"Have you heard the stories about people disappearing here?" Jay looks up at Fleur, his blue skin as pale as a night jellyfish.

Fleur wraps an arm around him. "Stories like those are made up to frighten people. Don't think about them now, Jay."

I want to say something comforting too, but danger is buzzing in my ears and I think if I speak everyone will hear the fear in my voice.

"Be brave, Jay." Hero looks down at him sternly. "And if you can't be brave, then pretend to be. Because really, that's the same thing." Hero slides her staff out of its pouch on her back. "I'll go first and make sure it's safe." She steps onto the bridge before anyone can disagree with her.

The bridge creaks and sways as Hero walks slowly forwards over the planks. She holds the rope rail with one hand and her staff with the other. After a few steps, she turns back to us and smiles reassuringly. "It's safe. Come on."

Echo nudges Jay and Kestrel to follow Hero, and she stays close behind them.

"You go next, with Whiskers and Lumpy, and my mother and I will go last," Silver says.

"All right." I hold Whiskers and Lumpy close to my chest with one arm and grip the rope rail with my free hand. I step onto the first plank and my stomach lurches at the bridge's movement, but I pull my shoulders back and take a few more steps, looking straight ahead.

With each step my bare feet get colder. The planks are damp and icy, coated in a thick frost, and I curl my toes around their edges to stop my feet from slipping.

My stomach lurches again when Fleur and Silver step behind me, making the bridge wobble even more. I hold Whiskers and Lumpy tighter, and feel Whiskers shivering and Lumpy frantically tapping her head in a signal to retreat. I breathe slowly, trying to remain calm as we take step after step, until we're completely enveloped by and suspended over darkness. The planks beneath my feet shift and tilt worryingly and my feathers tighten against my scalp so much my head aches.

My gaze drifts downwards and my heart pounds louder. Below my feet, swirling slowly in the blackness, are long wisps of icy, white mist. Another sudden, loud splash booms upwards and freezing droplets spray around us. Lumpy squeaks in fright and Whiskers lets out a high-pitched whine as she squashes against my chest. Everyone stops still.

"Keep moving," Hero calls from ahead. "I can see the other side now. We're over halfway across."

I take a breath and another step. Then stop still again as something swoops out of the darkness to my right. My heart accelerates as the thing speeds straight towards me. I duck down, thinking it's about to hit me, but then it turns and glides away at the last moment and I realize it's an owl – a huge one, with a wingspan as wide as my outstretched arms. I stare after it, my brow furrowed as I try to work out what's on its back – it looks like a small creature is riding the owl, the same way that Lumpy rides Whiskers.

"Did you see that?" Jay asks, his eyes shining with nervous excitement.

"Yes. Let's keep moving." Kestrel nudges Jay gently onwards.

We walk on a few more steps. My toes are now

aching with the cold, apart from
my littlest toes, which have
gone completely numb.

Suddenly, the owl
swoops back again, this
time from my left. It
flies so close, a few of
my head feathers part
and lift. Then the owl
turns full circle and flies
under the bridge. Looking
down through the planks, I see
the creature on its back is small and golden-
furred, with a long, slender body. It's holding onto one
of the owl's tousled ear tufts and squeaking loudly.

"What on Morovia?" Fleur whispers behind me.
"Is that a weasel riding an owl?"

"Yes!" Jay exclaims excitedly. "She's called
Rabbitsnatcher, and the owl is Blakiston. My father has
used his singing magic to speak to them a few times.
They're from Fixed Land, but they visit the island
when it drifts close, to hunt for fish together."

The weasel – Rabbitsnatcher – lets out a mighty cry
for a creature so small, and the owl swoops up and

away from the canyon. I stare after them in shock. Rabbitsnatcher turns, stares back at me and squeals again, so urgently that, with a rush of fear, I feel like she's trying to warn us of something.

A moment later there's a splash as loud as thunder that makes every muscle in my body tense. A freezing wind shoots up from below, so strong that our feathers, hair and clothes are all drawn upwards. Then a pillar of gushing icy water explodes beside us, completely soaking us. I shudder at the cold and gasp for breath, then my mouth drops wide open when I spot *something* huge and dark on top of the foaming water.

We all lean away from the thing as it surges upwards, which makes the bridge tilt. Terror grips me so tight I stop breathing. Whiskers curls herself up into a shivering ball in my arms, and Lumpy turns his back on the thing rising up on the fountain of water and squashes himself against my neck.

The thing is a massive creature – twice as big and twice as broad as any of us – with a mouth gaping so wide that it could swallow any one of us whole. Its dark grey skin shines with wetness, and rushing water blasts up all around it, spraying us with freezing drops.

I blink water away from my eyes and watch in

horror as the creature hurtles towards us. Two large pectoral fins either side of its huge body flap like wings, and a tall grey tail fin smacks back and forth frantically, spraying even more water into the air as it flies closer. It's a fish – the biggest, giantest giant catfish I've ever seen. And it's riding on the water fountain to reach us.

My eyes widen as I stare into the catfish's enormous incoming face. Long, thick barbels trail from its cavernous mouth, and its wide-set silver eyes are like two winter moons. The eyes flash and the mouth opens so wide

that I see into its fleshy throat and gills. My head draws back away from the catfish, but there's nowhere for me or any of us to escape to. We're trapped here on this wobbly bridge, being drenched with freezing water, and the catfish is about to strike.

Hero lifts her staff to defend us, but she can't reach the catfish, who is heading straight for the middle of our group. Jay gasps and Kestrel turns to shield him. The catfish flaps and twists at the top of the fountain, locks eyes on Echo, then lunges for her, its gaping mouth reaching for her head. Echo pales in fright.

My heart drums in panic. I keep hold of Whiskers and Lumpy with one arm but let go of the rope rail so I can try to pull Echo down with my other hand. But Echo is frozen with fear, and the catfish's mouth is so close to her head I scream.

I yank Echo again and yell her name. But still she doesn't move. Then Hero suddenly grabs the rope rail and, with one swift movement, swings over the rail so her body is flying across the blackness below. The bridge lurches and everyone wobbles. Hero sweeps through the water-filled air, holding her staff with one hand and the rope rail with the other, a deathly plummet beneath her. She's risking her life, for Echo.

The catfish flaps a pectoral fin, trying to hit Hero, but Hero is too fast. She whirls her staff at the catfish and blocks it with a wet *thwack*. The catfish flinches but remains on course – its mouth still heading straight for Echo. With a groan of effort, Hero reaches up as her body swoops down, and she hits the catfish again, this time on its underbelly. The catfish twists away from Echo, but manages to smack Hero's head with one of its fins. Hero cries out in pain and almost loses her grip on the bridge.

I rush to put my hand over Hero's and squeeze tight, trying to hold her safe as she dangles from the bridge by one hand. A trickle of blood runs down Hero's cheek and I realize with horror that the catfish must have spines on its fins. With another grunt of effort, Hero swings her legs up and kicks the catfish's side. Finally, the catfish closes its mouth and begins to fall from the fountain. But it writhes as it falls and its tail fin flaps towards the bridge.

"Hold tight to the rope rails!" I yell, moving my hand off Hero's, now that she is more secure, and so that I have a better grip on the bridge myself. I draw Whiskers and Lumpy even closer to me with my other arm as the huge tail smacks the planks beneath my feet. My body shakes and rocks as the bridge creaks and swings violently.

I look around the swaying scene, desperately trying to see if all my friends are secure, and hear a *snap* that sends dread through my veins. "One of the ropes has broken!" I shout, at the same moment that the bridge tears apart and we zoom through the air. I clutch the rope tight with one hand and hold Whiskers and Lumpy with the other. I hear my friends screaming, above and below me, as the half of the bridge that we're holding onto swings down towards the canyon wall.

For a moment the giant catfish is falling through the air beside me, still surrounded by glistening, foaming water. Its gaping mouth lunges for my trailing legs and I pull them towards my body in panic. Then we're whipped away from the catfish and the fountain by the swinging bridge and smack hard into the rocky canyon wall. The air is punched out of my lungs, and my arm that was shielding Whiskers and Lumpy throbs painfully.

"*Ow!*" Fleur yells below me.

"Is everyone still here?" I call when my breath returns. I look above me and try to make out the dangling shapes. Hero is holding onto the rope rail with one hand, like me, and her feet find the planks as my gaze darts to the shapes above her. Echo, Jay and Kestrel are all there, their hands and feet gripping the floor planks, which now rise vertically up the canyon wall like a ladder.

I look below me and see Fleur and Silver, also gripping the planks. I scramble to get my own feet onto a plank and exhale once I do, as the weight on my one hand is reduced. Whiskers whimpers and Lumpy turns and stares up at me with his eyes bulging rounder than I've ever seen them.

I'd like to feel relieved that we're all still here and not plummeting into the blackness below. But we're soaked in icy water and must now climb this broken bridge somehow. And, I realize with a shudder, the giant catfish might leap for one of us again at any moment, carried upwards on another freezing fountain.

I clutch Whiskers and Lumpy, terrified that I'm going to drop them. I've been so worried that our plan to break into The Keep might go wrong and we might end up imprisoned there, that I never considered that we might not get to The Keep at all. I certainly never imagined that we'd end up here, in danger of falling into Cold-Feet Canyon, or being swallowed by a giant catfish, and never seeing Nightingale – or anyone on Morovia – ever again.

CHAPTER 19

THE RIPPLING MARSH

The rope rail of the broken bridge burns my hand as I cling onto it tight, and my toes ache as they struggle to grip the narrow edge of the planks. Whiskers is shivering in my other arm and Lumpy is stiff with fear. I'm soaked through with freezing water and terrified we're going to fall into the canyon below.

The darkness is so thick I can barely see anything but wisps of white, icy mist swirling around my friends and me, as we focus on climbing out of here, one plank at a time.

"Can you manage with Whiskers and Lumpy?" Hero calls from above.

"I think so." I try to sound confident. I've climbed with Whiskers and Lumpy plenty of times before, but not like this. I feel like my toes might lose their grip on the wet planks, and the thought of the plummet below is making blood pound in my ears. "Jay, can you sing magic to keep the catfish away?"

"I can try." Jay begins singing a high-pitched whistling song that includes the slow fluctuating chirps of an osprey.

I pull my body tighter to the bridge, cling on with my toes, then quickly move my hand from the rope to a plank. For a tiny moment my fingers slip, and I let out a cry of panic as I think I might fall, but then I'm holding on again, my heart racing.

"Stay still. I have an idea." Hero slides her staff into the pouch on her back and, slowly and carefully, manages to take her deerskin tunic off by wriggling one arm out, then the other. She's wearing a thin linen tunic beneath it, and she climbs down to me before easing the outer deerskin one over her head. Then, while clinging onto the planks beside me with one hand, she wraps the deerskin tunic around Whiskers and Lumpy, over my shoulder and behind my back. She ties a knot in it using her teeth along with one hand, and when she lets go Whiskers and Lumpy are secure in a sling against my chest.

I slowly move my hand away from them, double-checking they're secure before I let go completely.

"That's perfect, thank you." I grip a plank with my now free hand, relieved to feel the extra security of another hold.

Hero and I climb up the bridge side by side. We keep checking on Fleur and Silver below us, but they're doing fine, and the catfish doesn't leap again. When we reach the top of the bridge and collapse onto grassy ground, everyone lies down, gasping to catch their breath.

Once my heartbeat calms, I sit up and look around. The sun is peeping over the marsh ahead, throwing golden light over the landscape and over my friends. I look at Hero lying beside me, and every doubt I had about her dissolves in the dawn, because she just risked her life to save Echo and all of us. Unity on Morovia feels closer than ever. But it's too dangerous to walk over the exposed marsh and break into The Keep in the light of day, so we can't move forwards until darkness falls again.

"Let's find somewhere safe to rest and prepare for what's next." I look ahead to where the grass merges with the marsh. There's a winterberry thicket between the two, with densely packed, glossy leaves. "We could hide in there."

Everyone murmurs in agreement and we rise to our feet and walk on, water dripping from our shivering bodies. In the distance, highward across the marsh, the Magicless Mountains rise up, bright white. And there's something else being illuminated by the rising sun: a long white wall with crenulations along the top of it.

My heart accelerates again, because that must be the wall to The Keep. Behind it lies my father, and all our hopes for the future. And tonight, we'll be climbing over it.

The sun's heat soon dries our clothes and warms our bodies. Fleur treats the cut on Hero's cheek, and all our bumps and bruises, with a lotion from her satchel. We share the last of the bread from Spark, and go over our plan again and again, until I feel like I could do it in my sleep. I can't rest though, because as each hour passes, I know I'm closer to seeing Nightingale again.

The heat is intense, and the silence overwhelming. There's no breeze to rustle the reeds of the marsh, and the long-legged marsh birds are too hot to flap their wings or sing. Even the midges are suspended, almost still, as if they're too heat-stricken to dance through the heavy air. It's an uncomfortable silence, which makes my ears strain for the sound of bogatyrs.

Occasionally Whiskers dips into a narrow stream the other side of the thicket and emerges with a root to eat. Every time she moves, I'm on edge, thinking that bogatyrs might hear or see her, and that would lead them to us.

After she disturbs a family of marsh ducks, who clatter loudly out of the water, I ask Whiskers to stay close, because her movements are making me so nervous. She lies on my foot and dozes, her fur steaming in the heat. Lumpy half-buries himself in a small patch of mud nearby and eats the worms and spiders who, dazed by heatstroke, almost crawl right into his mouth.

As the afternoon turns to evening, anticipation builds inside me, and by the time the sun sets I'm fidgeting with energy. The others are too. Hero stands at the edge of the thicket, staring at the wall in the distance and moving her staff from hand to hand. Silver sits on the ground, fiddling with his locksmith tools. Fleur measures small quantities of powders into tiny, straw-webbed glass vials. Kestrel quietly helps Jay practise his singing magic. And Echo sits cross-legged, eyes closed, her chin lowered as she sings more magic into the golden feather around her neck.

I wish I had my own magic that I could use to help her. Silver moves closer to me, and I remember how he made me feel better on the day I discovered I was the only alkonost in my class without singing magic, by taking me to Uncle Clay's workshop.

"Are you all right?" I ask Silver, thinking about Uncle Clay again, and Silver nods. "I haven't thanked you for everything you're doing, Silver."

"Morovia is our home," Silver whispers. "We can't keep letting Captain Ilya tear it apart. This is our chance to change everything for the better."

"I'm worried that one of us, or all of us, will get hurt or imprisoned," I say quietly.

"I'm worried too." Silver nudges my arm. "But we need the worry, to help keep us safe."

I nod and flex my fingers and toes, thinking about the first part of our plan, which is to climb The Keep walls. I look nervously at Whiskers and Lumpy. Part of me would like to leave them here, in relative safety, but Whiskers would only follow me with Lumpy on her head. And Hero has let me keep her deerskin tunic to use as a sling to carry them if I need to.

Finally, the last rays of sunlight dissolve into the marsh and I lift the rope ladder I made over my shoulder. Whiskers, realizing we're about to leave, lowers herself to the ground beside Lumpy so that he can climb onto her. Then we set off in silence. Stars appear in the darkening sky, and because the moon hasn't risen yet the stars seem to glow bolder and brighter than ever.

We follow the bank of the narrow stream that Whiskers kept dipping into, and it widens into a deep, dark river that reflects the sky as it cuts through the marsh. Water flows easily here, instead of swirling and stagnating, like it does in the swamp. The ground grows softer and squelchier, until we're ankle-deep in its wetness and reeds are rising over our heads.

The wall of The Keep looms closer, shining through the darkness, and worries tighten inside me with each step. I try to empty my mind and focus on listening for bogatyrs and looking for the best spots to place my feet. Where the ground is matted with roots, I don't sink so deep.

The river beside us is broadening and spilling out over the marsh. We walk close together, so if one of us slips into deeper water we have an arm to grab. Hero and I are side by side at the front with Lumpy and Whiskers between us. Echo, Jay and Kestrel are behind us, and Fleur and Silver behind them. Despite the danger all around, I feel a swell of gratitude that I'm surrounded by friends.

I glance at Hero and wonder whether to give her necklace back, the one tucked in the tiny bag around my neck. Then she would know how much her friendship has meant to me for the years we've been apart. It might give her strength tonight. If we both wore our necklaces, it might give both of us strength. But Hero's face is stiff and stony again, like it was when we first reunited, although now I realize it's because she's focused on the plan ahead.

"Do you see the sluice gate?" Hero whispers and I peer through the darkness to the wall in front of us. It's less than a hundred paces away now, and is almost as tall as our last home-tree. Where the stream hits the wall there's a thick wooden panel, at least three times taller than me, which must be the sluice gate.

Chains, as wide as my arm, rise out of the water either side of the gate and up to a platform at the very top of the wall. From there, the bogatyrs must be able to raise the sluice gate to release water from the moat when it gets too full. As Hero predicted, the gate is closed because the heatwave has made the water levels low, but Hero hoped that she and I could climb it.

"Will you be able to climb one of those chains?" Hero asks and I nod. Climbing chains can't be that different to climbing ropes, and I've done plenty of that in the swamp.

"What about you?" I ask, and Hero nods back. "Race you up?" I raise my feather-eyebrows in a challenge, thinking about the times Hero and I would race along Spark beach.

Hero raises her eyebrows back at me. "You think now is the time for games?" she says with a stern look, but there's a familiar warmth in her eyes that makes me smile.

"We have to wait until the patrol passes," I whisper, remembering our plan, and Hero nods again. Our friends gather together and hide in the reeds. I scoop Whiskers and Lumpy up and secure them into their sling.

Then we stare at the top of The Keep wall until finally the silhouettes of two bogatyrs appear. I hold my breath, my heart beating loud and fast. The bogatyrs walk slowly ripward. I can only see their torsos and heads, so they must be following a walkway sunken between parapets on the top of the wall. The bogatyrs cross over the sluice-gate platform and my heart drums up into my throat.

In a few moments, once the bogatyrs have walked a little further into the darkness, Hero and I will climb the wall. This is the point of no turning back. We'll either escape with Nightingale or get caught.

My gaze drifts up, over the bogatyrs, to The Keep beyond. I can't see what lies inside it, but I can see the white cliffs of the Magicless Mountains pushing up into the night sky, and a memory pushes its way into my mind of the one and only time that I've been here before...

The Night My Father and I Camped in the Magicless Mountains

Five years ago, when I was eight years old, on a Swoopday in late summer, my father and I set off for an adventure in the Magicless Mountains. My mother was working, singing in the theatre in back-to-back shows for two days, so my father and I had decided to go camping together – just the two of us.

We took a cart ride highward until we reached the big stone bridge that crossed onto the rip side of the island. From there we travelled on foot, each wearing a big backpack stuffed with supplies and carrying long driftwood sticks the sea had washed up, to use as walking poles on the rough terrain.

Back then, The Keep didn't exist. The Magicless Mountains were an undulating place cut by pure white cliffs, dotted with birds' nests and tangled shrubs, with grass and wild-flower meadows in the valleys between peaks. Buzzards and red kites soared through the blue sky, and fluffy clouds clung to the mountaintops, like sea foam clings to rocks on the beach.

Nightingale and I wandered along well-trodden paths near the bridge, where people from the island often came to picnic and bird-watch. I asked my father hundreds of questions as we walked. I wanted to know the names of brightly coloured flowers and butterflies dancing in the breeze; which peaks had been climbed and which hadn't; why singing magic didn't work here; and if there was any truth in the old mountain tales of sky creatures made of light and cave-dwelling animals with colour-changing fur. Nightingale listened to all my questions and answered them as best as he could, and when he didn't know the answers he said that we'd find out together. In those days, before *Joy* sank, I always felt that he was with me completely, giving me all of his attention and listening to my every word.

Slowly, we walked beyond the known paths into wilderness, unexplored and wild. We climbed a peak that had no name and made camp as the sun set on the high-rip side of the island. The sun had risen in almost exactly the same place that morning, and I remember thinking how amazing it was that Morovia must have rotated a half-turn as it floated across the ocean that day, without me even noticing its movement.

Nightingale had carried our small blue tent here, along with our grey felt blankets and some fire logs, which Aunty Fleur had soaked in one of her potions to make them burn warm and bright for hours. I had carried fresh water and iced milk in flasks, and treats that my mother had baked: bread flavoured with wild garlic, a jar of soft lemon cheese, and a big round seed cake sweetened with raisins.

We made a fire and cuddled up together beneath the blankets, toasting the garlic bread on sticks, then melting the soft lemon cheese on top. Nightingale even warmed the seed cake, by wrapping it in hazel leaves and sitting it on a hot stone by the fire.

The stars appeared, one by one, until the sky shone as brightly as the sea in Spark Bay when the glowing algae bloomed. Nightingale had brought his treasured guitar, the sunset-red one with twelve shiny gold strings, and after we'd eaten he sang song after song that drifted up to the stars and seemed to make them dance and shine brighter.

I asked Nightingale what it was like, after a lifetime of singing magic, to come to a place where your magic didn't work. I wondered if it made him feel powerless, like I did because I had no magic yet. But Nightingale said it didn't make him feel any different. He said all the things that he was most proud of in life he'd achieved without magic, and that our greatest power is always deep inside us and not in our magic at all.

As the night drew on, a half-moon rose and a sweet scent drifted around us, crisp and clean, like the air around our roof garden after a rain. The scent grew so strong, I asked Nightingale what it was. He lifted me up, still wrapped in my blanket, and carried me away from the fire to a huge leafy shrub, taller and wider than Nightingale's height.

White star-shaped flowers shone through the darkness, and pale grey moths fluttered all around them, as if the shrub itself was singing magic like my mother's.

"It's night-blooming jasmine," my father said. "It only flowers in moonlight, releasing this lovely scent, and moths come to drink its nectar. Sometimes bats and small birds, too. When your mother and I were younger, we used to camp in these mountains, always near one of these shrubs, because they're your mother's favourite."

"It's beautiful," I said, as Nightingale lowered me to the floor so that I could step closer to the jasmine, and be surrounded by its scent and the fluttering moths.

Nightingale began singing one of the old songs of the island, in the ancient bird-people's language that sounds like birdsong, sea winds and rolling waves all at once. He put his arms around me and we danced right there with the moths, my small feet between his long, clawed ones and our head feathers raised so that the scented air tingled against their vanes. We stepped and swayed and Nightingale spun me round so fast my feet lifted off the floor and I felt like I was flying through the star-filled sky.

I don't remember when we stopped dancing, so I think I must have fallen asleep in his arms, beside the flowers, under the stars. But I remember waking in the night, my head on his chest and the sound of his heartbeat beneath my ear. The felt blankets were tucked around us, and the stars were so bright that

I could see them shining down on the white cliffs even through the fabric of our tent.

Tonight, as I look up to those same white cliffs pushing into the night sky, all I want is my father back; to be able to pull him so close that I hear his heartbeat again, and to tell him that I've missed him – not just for these last three days, but for these last three years.

CHAPTER 20

OVER THE WALL

I hold my breath as the bogatyrs continue walking along the top of the wall. From the silence, I think all my friends must be doing the same. Even Whiskers and Lumpy, tucked into their sling against my chest, are quiet and still.

As soon as the bogatyrs disappear into the darkness of the night, Hero turns to me and nods. *It's time.* Suddenly I feel strangely calm. Focusing on making our plan a reality is easier than worrying about it. We have about ten minutes until the bogatyr patrol returns, so we need to move fast.

Hero and I slip silently into the stream beside us. The water is still warm from the heat of the day, even though the sun set hours ago, and we swim smoothly, side by side, until we reach the sluice gate. Whiskers keeps her snout raised, just below my chin, and I can feel Lumpy's delicate skin against my neck.

When we reach the gate we split up. Hero grabs the chain on one side and I grab the chain on the other, and we start to climb. Each of the chain's links is as wide as a bracelet, but made of cold metal as thick as my thumb. It's easy to grip the links with my fingers and toes and I quickly and silently lift my body upwards.

Hero, on the other side of the gate, has a different climbing style. She grips the whole chain in her strong hands and uses her upper body strength to pull herself up, while hooking her ankles around the chain below. We reach the top of the wall at the same time though, climb over the parapet and crouch on the walkway to catch our breath.

The sound of dripping water echoes around us, as it falls from Hero's deerskin trousers and linen tunic, and the deerskin sling I'm now wearing over my worn-thin clothes. Every drop sounds too loud and makes my nerves stretch and my feathers pull tight against my scalp with the fear of being caught.

There's another noise coming from the other side of the inner wall, too. I strain my ears and make out the clack and clatter of thick shells knocking against each other. My heart races as I peep over the parapet. It's the giant crabs.

The space below is over two hundred paces wide. A huge wall rises on the other side of it, even higher than this one. Between the two walls is a deep, dark moat. The side closest to us is filled with still, black water, but on the other side there's a bank full of huge shadowy shapes, low and smooth like the hummocks of the marsh.

I stare at the giant crabs in awe. They shift with rasps and creaks, and as they come into focus I feel wobbly. Each crab is bigger than a person – if I stood on the ground beside them, I would be able to look straight into their stalked eyes. And I could lie across their backs with space to spare. Their pincers could open and close around my waist... I push the thought away with a shudder.

Hero taps my shoulder and I duck down again behind the parapet. She points in the direction the bogatyrs patrolled, then creeps after them. I remain where I am, because our plan is for Hero to use Fleur's sleepbane on the bogatyrs while I send the rope ladder down for our friends.

Whiskers is whimpering and shaking against my chest, and I know it's because she's sensed the crabs below and is scared of them. "Shhhh," I say as quietly as I can. "I'll keep you safe, Whiskers." My voice falters though, because if Jay's singing magic doesn't work to drive away the crabs, I have no idea how we could defend ourselves from so many huge creatures.

I lift the rope ladder over my head, loop it around a solid section of the crenulated parapet and lower it slowly and quietly down the other side. One by one, Echo, Jay, Kestrel, Fleur and Silver climb up, until we're all silently huddled together on the walkway.

As I pull the ladder back up, Hero returns. "The bogatyrs on this wall are asleep," she whispers. I'd like to breathe a sigh of relief, but worries about the next stage of our plan are now unfurling inside me. I keep glancing at Jay nervously as I secure the rope ladder to the opposite parapet and lower it down. The bottom of the ladder splashes softly into the water of the moat and I wince at the noise.

"I'm going to sing some magic," Echo whispers. "To create silence around us, so any bogatyrs nearby won't hear Jay singing."

"Are you sure?" I frown. This wasn't part of our plan, because Echo needs to save her magic for the golden feather.

"I'm worried bogatyrs on the far wall will hear us if

I don't." Echo begins singing a slow, soothing tune. At first her voice sounds like the ocean, gently washing onto a damp, silty shore. Then it softens into the sound of a sea breeze, swirling over sand dunes and weaving through tufts of marram grass. I feel her magic filling the air, echoing out thoughts of silence and stillness that overpower all the night-time noises, until all I can hear is the faint whisper of her song.

I turn to Jay. "Have you seen the size of the crabs?" I ask quietly, even though I know my voice won't travel beyond Echo's magic now.

Jay smiles his missing-tooth smile. "Crabs always run away from my singing magic. Their size won't matter." He stands and begins to climb over the second parapet, but Kestrel stops him.

"Maybe you should try using your magic from here," Kestrel suggests.

"You know I need to be closer to the crabs for it to work." Jay shakes his head. "And I need to be on the same level or my magic will drift over them."

Kestrel nods reluctantly. "Promise you won't let go of the ladder."

"You're all worrying for nothing." Jay smiles again and climbs down the ladder.

We peer after him, silent apart from Echo's whispering song. The crabs must sense Jay approaching, because they move as one, standing with a clatter and scuttling towards the moat.

I hold my breath as Jay starts singing, softly and quietly at first, but then louder when the crabs don't respond. They're still heading towards him, some of them swimming through the water now. A few of them are nearly halfway across the moat already.

"His magic isn't working," I whisper urgently, "pull him up."

Kestrel, Silver and Fleur all start pulling on the ladder, but Jay keeps climbing down it, singing louder. I know that he desperately wants his magic to work, the same way I want my magic to come so I can help. When he runs out of ladder, Jay slips into the water and lets go of it, despite the crabs still swimming towards him. He treads water and tries singing a different tune.

Kestrel leans over the parapet, lowers the ladder again and calls Jay with an urgent whisper, but Jay only sings louder. I glance at the wall opposite, worried that, despite Echo's magic, Jay's singing is going to draw the attention of bogatyrs patrolling the other side of the moat…but there's no sign of anyone yet. I look back down at the crabs still advancing on Jay and panic surges through me.

Both Kestrel and I rise at the same time, I think with the same idea – to leap over the parapet to help Jay – but Whiskers surges out of her sling and blocks us both. Her claws scramble against my neck, then she clambers over Kestrel, barging him out of the way. I try to grab her, but she's caught in Jay's magic. Jay's song isn't working on the crabs, but it's working on Whiskers and she's fighting to get to him. I yell in alarm when Whiskers dives into the moat below, with Lumpy croaking angrily on her head.

Whiskers and Lumpy land next to Jay with a splash. My eyes widen in horror as a massive crab closes in on all three of them, its claws clacking together.

"Please stay here to help pull us up," I say to Kestrel as I grab the top of the rope ladder, swing over the parapet and climb down as fast as I can. I must get Jay, Whiskers and Lumpy out of the water before the crab reaches them. All three of them are here because of me – I can't let them get hurt.

I glance down, my heart racing. Jay is still singing, trying different pitches and tunes, but nothing is working. The crab stretches one of its front arms and reaches forwards. Its claw opens, dangerously close to Jay and Whiskers, so I jump off the ladder, aiming my feet right at the crab's head.

CHAPTER 21

GIANT CRAB ATTACK

I jump onto the crab's head and its whole body dips beneath the surface. I skid off its slippery shell and splash into the water, between the crab and Jay. The water is so cold I gasp for breath and the darkness here in the bottom of the moat is so disorientating that my heart races in panic.

"Climb back up the ladder," I call urgently to Jay, who is still singing. "We need to figure out why your magic isn't working." I look around for Whiskers in the darkness and spot her flailing in panic to the side of me. Lumpy is clutching onto one of her ears with three limbs, and waving his sword-leg at the crabs rapidly approaching us. I reach out, grab Whiskers and pull her tight against my chest.

The giant crab I landed on surges upwards again, breaking the surface less than my body's-length away.

Its huge yellowish eyes glare at me from the ends of their stalks, and it lifts its claws towards me. I lean back and kick my legs, frantically trying to get away from the crab and reach the rope ladder.

One of the crab's claws reaches for my ankle. I kick it, but the claw is as solid as rock and doesn't budge. I kick it again and my foot slips onto the sharp edge of the claw, grazing the skin on my heel. I stifle a cry of pain and thrash my legs even faster.

Jay grabs my shoulder and tries to pull me away from the crab, but he barely makes a difference. My feet are still right in front of the creature, and one of its claws is about to clamp down on my left ankle. I inhale a deep breath, thinking my only chance of escape might be to dive under the black water, but Whiskers suddenly wriggles free and surges towards the crab's head, grunting fiercely.

Whiskers's long teeth flash as they snap down over one of the crab's eye stalks. The crab jerks backwards in shock, then turns its claws on Whiskers. I try to grab her, to pull her to safety, but she's out of reach. A crab claw closes around her and a silent scream swells in my throat.

Then a high, clear note cuts through the night. It's coming from the ladder behind us, and from the corner of my eye I make out the silhouette of Kestrel, climbing down while singing. His song rises in pitch and my eyes widen as Whiskers swells in the water and the crab draws its claw away from her in confusion. I remember Kestrel saying his singing magic made animals bigger and I realize he's focusing it on Whiskers!

Within a second, Whiskers is bigger than a horse, and she keeps on growing. The huge mound of her body almost blocks my view of the crabs in front of us. I gaze at her, amazed by the power of Kestrel's magic.

Whiskers snaps her jaw and the crab she was holding by the eye stalk is now dangling from her mouth. Then Whiskers flicks her head and the crab goes flying into the shadows on the bank opposite, where it lands with a crunch and scuttles away in terror.

The other crabs stop still. Scores of eye stalks turn towards Whiskers, and the yellowish eyes on the ends of them glimmer with fear. Whiskers stares back, her half-smile widening over her massive cheek, then she charges towards them, water splashing all around her like shooting stars glistening through the darkness.

I stare after Whiskers in shock. She's now as big as the orca I once saw hunting near Fisher's Flock, and the crabs are swimming away from her, clambering over each other in their rush to escape. In one great mass, the crabs roll onto the bank and fall into shadow as they press themselves up against the far wall, their shells clattering together.

"Report!" A deep voice booms from the top of the wall opposite and I freeze in panic. Two bogatyrs appear, each one holding a long, burning torch. The flames reflect on their armour, making them glow orange. Some of the noise we've been making must have escaped Echo's magic.

Whiskers sinks low into the water, disappearing like a bark beetle into a furrowed trunk. I hold my breath and become aware of Jay and Kestrel softly splashing as they tread water beside me. *Fate, please don't let them see us.* The thought repeats over and over inside my head, even though I'm sure it's too dark and the bogatyrs are too high up to see what's going on here in the very bottom of the moat.

Echo stops singing so that Hero's voice, as strong and deep as the bogatyr's, can carry across the moat in reply: "All clear!" she shouts. "The crabs are fighting over a swamp-rat."

The bogatyrs on the opposite wall grunt in response and move on. Echo begins to sing again, and I sigh with relief as I swim towards Whiskers. She rises out of the water, sits down on the bank and scratches her head with a back foot that is now longer than I am tall. I shake my head in disbelief as I move alongside her. "I can't believe you did this," I whisper to Kestrel as he and Jay step beside me.

"Me neither." Kestrel grins. "It's been so long since I last used my magic, I wasn't sure it would work."

I reach up and pat Whiskers's shoulder while holding my breath, because her musky smell has swelled along with her size. "Are you up there, Lumpy?" I whisper, peering up at Whiskers's ear. I hear a faint croak and see a tiny flicker of movement. "Your magic doesn't work on toads then?" I ask Kestrel.

"It only works on one animal at a time. If I focused on Lumpy it might work on him, but I thought making Whiskers bigger would be more useful, because she was already attacking the crab," Kestrel replies.

"Thank you. And thank you too." I turn to Jay.

"But my magic didn't work." Jay frowns.

"You tried everything you could," I say, "and you pulled me away from that crab too."

Jay's frown relaxes a little. "I guess I did."

Echo, having climbed down the ladder and swum across the moat, emerges from the black water. She's followed by Silver, Fleur and Hero.

"This way," Hero whispers and we follow her ripward along the bank, while remaining close to Whiskers's enormous side. The crabs stare after us, but none of them dares even inch forwards.

Whiskers skips confidently along and I smile as I realize she's finally faced her fear of crabs and overcome it. I reach up and pat her leg again when we draw close to a huge waterwheel jutting out of the wall. "Stop here," I whisper, looking up at the wheel, which is almost as big as Whiskers. The next stage of our plan is to climb onto the thick axle that runs through the middle of the wheel, and slide along it through a hole in the wall and into the iron forge the other side. Then we'll actually be inside The Keep.

The thought of being so close to Nightingale is making my heart skip with anticipation. I can almost feel his forehead against my own as I imagine us falling into a hug.

"I'll go first and check the forge is empty," Hero whispers as she steps onto one of the wheel's thick spokes. The wheel creaks slightly but doesn't move, and Hero swings herself smoothly up onto the axle, which is as wide as a thick tree branch. Within moments

Hero has wriggled along the axle, through the hole in the wall and disappeared.

I stare after her, my ears straining for any sound of bogatyrs in the forge on the other side, but it's silent. Hero sticks her head back out of the hole and nods to show us it's safe. Fleur climbs up next, followed by Silver, Echo and Jay.

"Can you make Whiskers small again?" I ask Kestrel and he nods and stares at Whiskers. This time the pitch of his song falls and as it does Whiskers shrinks, her nose twitching rapidly. Within seconds she's back to her usual size and I scoop her into my arms, scratch the top of her head and give Lumpy – who looks rather stunned by Whiskers's changing size – a wink. Kestrel clambers up onto the wheel axle and I secure Whiskers and Lumpy into their sling before climbing up last.

I crawl through the hole in the wall and step onto a cold stone floor. It takes my eyes a moment to adjust to the darkness. The forge is an enormous room, with a high vaulted ceiling.

Just ahead of me is a huge wooden hammer that must be powered by the movement of the waterwheel, and beyond it is a wide raised fireplace surrounded by all kind of tools and the biggest set of bellows I've ever seen. The rest of the room is empty and has an echoey feel. There's a wide set of double doors on the opposite side of the room, but everyone is crowded around a narrow door in the wall nearest to us.

Silver is on his knees, pushing one of his locksmith tools into the lock. The lock makes a clicking sound and Silver turns the handle and pushes the door, but it doesn't budge. "It must be bolted from the other side," Silver whispers.

Hero's shoulders fall. "I forgot about the bolts. Both this door and the double doors are always bolted from the outside, too."

"Is there another way out?" I look around the forge again, but there are no other exits, apart from the way we came in.

Hero shakes her head and frowns, but Fleur lifts her satchel over her head and smiles. "I'll have to start the explosions earlier than planned then."

CHAPTER 22

EXPLOSIONS

"I can make a small explosion to open the door." Fleur glances at the raised fireplace behind us. "And I could set up a larger explosion in that fireplace to go off immediately afterwards. When bogatyrs come to investigate, they'll have to deal with the fireplace before anything else, which should give us enough time to move away from here unseen."

I put my arm around Whiskers and Lumpy, who are still tucked into their sling, and look around the room for a place to shelter, because I don't want them to be scared by explosions. There's a small alcove in a corner near the double doors and I move towards it. Everyone apart from Fleur follows me, and we huddle together as Fleur fiddles with vials from her satchel. She sprinkles a line of powder along the base of the narrow door, then moves to the fireplace.

Fleur pokes at the thick ashes until a few glowing embers are revealed. She sprinkles an orange-coloured powder on them that immediately starts to smoke. Then she lights a wooden splint, returns to the door and ignites the dark powder. Bright sparks spit into the air and Fleur rushes over to us. "Cover your ears!" she says as she ducks low, and I curl over Whiskers and Lumpy.

A huge bang echoes around the room and the air fills with smoke. "Hurry!" Fleur runs to the door and we follow her. The smoke rising from the fireplace is now thick and orange, and there's an ominous hissing sound coming from the embers. Whiskers trembles in the sling, and I lower my chin and try to whisper reassurances to her and Lumpy. Guilt for bringing them both here is twisting my stomach, but I try to ignore it and get them away from the smoke and noise as quickly as possible.

The door has been blasted completely off its hinges and is lying on the ground several paces away. We all step into the night and look around cautiously. Ahead of us are two long rows of cylindrical towers, taller than the houses in Spark. They're black in the darkness, but with wide, curved holes in their bases that glow a bright, fiery orange, and pale grey smoke rises from their open tops. They must be the bloomeries, where the quarried rocks are smelted into iron. This is where we split up. Fleur, Jay and Kestrel are going to make more explosions in the bloomeries, and Hero, Silver, Echo and I are going to find Nightingale.

The shouts of bogatyrs rise not far away, and the thump of heavy bootsteps echoes over the rocky ground. "We'll meet near the bridge," I whisper as I glance over to Fleur, Jay and Kestrel. Our plan is to escape over the stone bridge on the lee side of The Keep once we have Nightingale, and leave Echo here to use her magic to convince Vasha to release everyone in the quarry.

Jay and Kestrel nod, and Fleur grabs my hand and squeezes it. "Good luck," she whispers, before beckoning Jay and Kestrel to follow her. I turn to Hero, who is going to lead Echo, Silver and me to Nightingale. Thinking about seeing him again is making excitement fizz inside me, and I keep picturing the surprise and joy on his face when we come to free him.

"This way." Hero tilts her head and we follow as she weaves between the bloomeries, then takes a narrow path that dips steeply down into a dark valley between pale chalk cliffs that smell of the sea and sulphur. It's strange to think that this is one of the places that Hero has been spending her time, while Nightingale and I have been hiding in the swamp. Both of our lives changed so much after *Joy* sank.

A massive boom sounds behind us, making the cliffs and ground vibrate. Whiskers tries to wriggle out of her sling in panic and I stop to calm her down and check she and Lumpy are all right, but Silver nudges us on. "That's the explosion in the forge going off. There'll be more soon, noisy and distracting for the bogatyrs, but my mother will keep them controlled so that no one is hurt."

Hero glances back at us. "Come on," she urges.

I catch up with her, and my gaze is drawn to a narrow path branching off to our left. "Does that lead to the quarry?" I whisper, thinking of all the people who have been sentenced to live and work there, Kestrel and Jay's parents among them. Hero nods and I make a silent wish that our plan will succeed and everyone will soon be free.

Silver stops and follows my gaze, and his face pales. I regret my question immediately and reach out to grab his hand. "I'm sorry, Silver," I whisper, knowing he will be thinking about his father now, and how this is the place where he died. Silver squeezes my hand and blinks back tears.

"Come on." Silver pulls me onwards and we jog to catch up with Hero, still holding hands. The path we're on curves, then slopes back upwards. The sight of a low stone building ahead makes my heartbeat quicken. The map Hero drew on the floor of Echo's home is still firmly in my mind, so I know this building is where the holding cells are – and where Nightingale will be. My hand tightens around Silver's with nervousness. I hope Nightingale is all right, and that we can get him out of here safely.

Hero beckons us to the side of the building, which has an ironclad door. Silver lets go of my hand, kneels in front of it and takes out his locksmith tools. I press myself against the wall next to him and put an arm around Whiskers and Lumpy. Echo is at my side and Hero stands a little way off, keeping watch.

Another boom comes from the direction of the bloomeries, along with the shouts of bogatyrs. Flames are roaring and sparks shooting into the sky, so I think the bogatyrs are being kept busy by Fleur's explosions, as planned.

It doesn't take Silver long to pick the lock, and he smiles as he rises to his feet and pushes the door open. I expect Hero to go in first, but after peering inside to check for bogatyrs she holds out her arm, inviting me to go through. I rush inside, the thought of seeing Nightingale making my feathers lift so high they catch the air around them.

Beyond the door, a corridor runs between rows of small cells with iron bars. I move swiftly along, looking for Nightingale. But all the cells are empty. "Where is he?" I whisper.

"Keep going," Hero calls from behind Silver and Echo. "Through the gate ahead."

The iron gate ahead of us is locked so I wait for Silver to pick it. Even though it only takes him moments, I'm fidgeting with impatience. Finally, the gate swings open and I rush along another corridor between rows of more iron-barred, empty cells.

My heart is thumping and a cold dread is rising in my chest. "Something's wrong." I stop and turn around, my feathers falling and tightening against my scalp. Silver and Echo are behind me, but Hero isn't with us any more. She's remained by the iron gate at the other end of the corridor, and she's now closing it.

"What are you doing?" I yell as I rush back towards her.

She doesn't look at me as she swings the gate shut and clamps a huge iron padlock through the hasp.

"Hero!" I reach the gate, grab the iron bars and stare into her face with complete disbelief. "What are you doing?" I repeat.

Hero's face is lowered, but she glances up at me briefly. Her eyes are solemn, watery pools. "I'm sorry, Linnet. But this has to be done, for the safety of all the islanders." And then she turns and walks away, leaving us imprisoned and alone.

CHAPTER 23

THE CELLS

"Hero!" I call desperately, but she disappears into a group of armoured bogatyrs walking towards us. She pauses for a moment to speak to the one in front. It's Captain Ilya. A swell of bitterness makes me frown and step backwards. He's wearing his iron helmet with the metal feather on top and the band of chain mail that always covers his neck.

"Step into separate cells." Captain Ilya glares at me, Echo and Silver, his iron-grey eyes narrowed with distrust.

My gaze shifts from Captain Ilya to the bogatyrs behind him. There are eight of them, each one of them huge, heavily armoured and wearing the full iron helmets that protect them from singing magic. The sight of them makes me feel like I'm trapped in deep, sucking mud with the tide rolling in. Hero has betrayed me, betrayed all of us. And there's nothing we can do to get out of this.

Echo moves first. She calmly walks into the cell nearest to her and stands as tall as she can with her chin raised proudly. But her eyes are full of sadness. The cells seem to spin around me. I want to think of something, anything, one of us could do to stop this happening, but I can't.

"Walk into a cell," Captain Ilya repeats, louder, "or I will put you in one."

An image of Captain Ilya pushing Nightingale so roughly he fell onto the dirt road fills my mind and my eyes burn. I glare at Captain Ilya in anger, but slowly back into the cell behind me. I nod to Silver, who is standing with his fists clenched, trying to signal him to do the same before he's pushed by a bogatyr. I have no idea how we're going to get out of this, but I know it will be more difficult if any of us are injured.

Captain Ilya unlocks the gate and steps through with bogatyrs either side of him. All squashed together, with their armour gleaming, they look like a pack of reef sharks hunting in a narrow channel.

Captain Ilya walks to within a few paces of Echo and glares down at her. "Take the golden feather from your neck and place it on the floor."

Echo stares back at him defiantly.

Captain Ilya takes another step forward. He towers over Echo. Then he reaches for the feather. His hands are covered by chain-mail gloves. My heart plummets as Captain Ilya tears the golden feather from Echo's neck, drops it to the floor and crushes it beneath an ironclad boot. Echo's eyes burn as she continues to stare at Captain Ilya.

Captain Ilya looks away from Echo and takes a step back. "Search them all," he barks. The bogatyrs split up, and two enter each of our cells.

I put my arms protectively around Whiskers and Lumpy, who are still in their sling, as a bogatyr steps in front of me. "It will be easier if you take them out yourself," the bogatyr leans towards me and says with a gentle voice. I stare at the bogatyr in shock, wondering how someone with even a little kindness could work for Captain Ilya. But I lift Whiskers, with Lumpy clutching her ear, out of their sling and place them gently on the floor beside me.

"They won't hurt anyone," I say. "And I'm not carrying anything else." I lift the sling over my head and pass it to the bogatyr, and turn the pockets of my shorts inside out to prove it. The copper coin Hero gave me falls to the floor and I frown at the symbol of unity.

The bogatyr ignores the coin, checks the sling and passes it back to me. I continue staring at the symbol of unity, thinking how our friendship, and unity on Morovia, must be worth so little to Hero.

The other bogatyr in the cell leans forwards suddenly and grabs the tiny leather bag I wear around my neck and I flinch in shock and anger. The cord snaps and the bogatyr fumbles to open the bag and empty its contents. My mother's yellow feather drifts to the floor as my and Hero's necklaces spill onto the bogatyr's gloved hand.

"They're my personal things," I say between gritted teeth as I grab back the necklaces and crouch down to retrieve my mother's feather.

"She has nothing dangerous." The first bogatyr steps between me and the bogatyr who tore my tiny necklace-bag off.

"What about the swamp-rat and the toad?" the other bogatyr asks in a gruff voice, and my heart thunders with dread at the thought that Whiskers and Lumpy might be taken away.

"They pose no threat." The first bogatyr turns and signals the other to leave. They both step out of my cell and lock it. I crouch down beside Whiskers and Lumpy, relieved they're still with me, but burning with outrage that we're all trapped in here.

"We've taken the boy's lockpicks." The bogatyr who searched Silver steps out of his cell and locks it, while another bogatyr locks Echo's cell.

A wave of hopelessness crashes over me. Hero betrayed us. The shock of what has happened is making my chest so tight and tender that it hurts to breathe. We failed to find Nightingale. The golden feather that might have brought unity to Morovia is crushed into dust. And we're locked in The Keep. I look at a small barred window above Silver's head. The black night sky beyond is tinged orange from the glow of Fleur's explosions.

I wonder where Fleur, Jay and Kestrel are. Hero knows our whole plan, so she's probably leading bogatyrs to them right now. Anger and frustration surge through me. How could Hero do this? *Why* would she do this? I thought we were friends. She rescued us in Spark, saved our lives at Cold-Feet Canyon and helped us to get here. But it must have all been lies, all part of some awful plan to lock us up here. And I was too foolish to see it. A groan rises in my throat and I swallow it back.

Captain Ilya turns and walks away and the other bogatyrs trail behind him. "Last two stay on guard." Captain Ilya waves his hand as he disappears down the corridor.

The last bogatyr swings the iron gate shut and locks it, then remains standing on the other side with another bogatyr, both with their backs to us.

I stroke the top of Whiskers's head. She nuzzles into me and Lumpy croaks mournfully. "How could Hero do this?" I whisper, aloud this time, as I pour my and Hero's necklaces back into my tiny leather bag, carefully place my mother's feather on top, then tie the broken cord and fix the bag back around my neck.

"I thought you were best friends." Silver lowers himself to the floor in the cell opposite me and leans his head back against the stone wall on the far side.

An image of Hero and me lying on Spark beach side by side, our cheeks pressed together, rises in my mind, so clear and strong that I can feel the warmth of her skin against mine. "I thought we were too," I whisper. A tear spills down my cheek. Whiskers grunts softly and pushes her whiskery face between my chin and shoulder to comfort me.

"This isn't about your and Hero's friendship."

Echo looks around her cell, her gaze flitting from the barred window to the barred gate like a trapped bird. "Hero was acting on what she felt was right, rather than friendship. Which is admirable when you think about it."

I remember Hero's last words to me: *This has to be done, for the safety of all the islanders,* and I frown. "But we were friends. She should have trusted me."

"Trusting anyone comes with a risk." Echo sighs. "And maybe trusting friends is the greatest risk of all, because we give them our hearts, our hopes and our dreams."

"I should never have trusted Hero." I collapse around Whiskers and rest my face on her neck, beside Lumpy.

"What I don't understand is why Hero saved us from bogatyrs back in Spark." Silver furrows his brow. "She helped us escape. Why would she do that, just to imprison us all when we got here?"

"Because of me," Echo says simply. "Hero must have wanted you to lead her to me."

My chest tightens as I think how Hero must have been deceiving us right from that first moment when she defended me from bogatyrs in Fleur and Silver's kitchen. Perhaps she even followed me to Fleur and Silver's home, after she saw me in the trees when Nightingale was being taken away in the wagon.

I thought Hero was acting out of friendship, but it was a lie, and everything since has been a lie too. "This whole time, Hero has wanted to get you into The Keep?" I look at Echo and she nods.

"I'm leader of the Unity Movement, and my singing magic allows me to conceal myself. Captain Ilya has wanted me in The Keep for years, but has been unable to find me. He and Hero must have come up with this plan to capture me by using you."

"But she could have let the catfish take you in Cold-Feet Canyon," Silver says, his brow still furrowed.

"Wanting someone imprisoned is quite different from wanting them to be swallowed by a giant catfish," Echo says.

"Hero *used* me," I grumble bitterly, but my words are drowned out by heavy footsteps. A group of bogatyrs is approaching and trapped amongst them are Fleur, Jay and Kestrel.

"Oh no," I murmur as the last tiny flame of hope – that our friends might have somehow rescued us – flickers out inside me. I bury my face in Whiskers's fur, unable to look at my friends as the bogatyrs search them, then lock them in cells beside us.

"Hero did this..." Silver begins to explain to the others, after all but two of the bogatyrs have left, but I hum into Whiskers's fur, not wanting to hear his words.

Even though Echo said this isn't about my and Hero's friendship, it still feels like it is. It feels like everything that is happening to us here in these cells, and everything that is happening on Morovia, is a reflection of what has happened between me and Hero. Because if there is no trust between us, and if there is no hope of our friendship being healed, then I don't see how there is hope for any alkonosts and humans to ever live in unity.

I pick up the copper coin and stare at the symbol of unity with tears in my eyes. The future of Morovia seems as cold and bleak as the cells around us, and I realize I haven't felt this much despair since the days after *Joy* sank...

The Days After Joy Sank

Three years ago, on the Day of Union, I was standing on the beach, bathed in afternoon sunshine and surrounded by the sweet smell of sea-kale flowers. Nightingale had his arm around my shoulders and Fleur was holding my hand. The beach was filled with alkonosts and humans, their arms linked, their smiling faces upturned to the blue sky and their voices joined in song.

Two hearts sincere
Our voices loud and clear
Singing as one
Beneath a golden sun...

My heart ached with pride and there were tears of joy in my eyes as I sang along. I felt part of something beautiful.

But then the air darkened and cooled so rapidly that Nightingale drew me close against his chest. I looked up and the sun was gone. The sky was covered with a thick sheet of bruise-purple cloud, which looked heavy, as if it might fall upon us.

Everyone stopped singing and silence engulfed the beach. Then the wind started. A cold breeze that swirled around us, ruffling feathers and whipping up hair. Fleur's hand tightened around my own.

"The sea," someone murmured and everyone turned as one towards the shore. I couldn't see, because I was so much shorter than everyone else, but I somehow sensed how the sea had pulled away from us. I couldn't hear its rhythmic roll onto the sand any more, and I couldn't feel its salty spray. Fear crept over me, colder than the wind, and goosebumps rose on my skin.

Panicked whispers rushed through the crowd, and I heard snippets of sentences that made my heart pound.

"There…on the horizon…"

"It's *Joy*."

"Beyond *Joy*… The line of white… That's a wave."

"But it's enormous…"

I pulled away from Fleur and Nightingale and ran out of the crowd, towards the sea. But it was far, far away, further back than the lowest spring tide. I stopped still, beyond the edge of the crowd, and stared at the horizon.

There was *Joy*, tiny in the distance, her bright red sails billowing. Without thinking, I held up my hand to wave – we always did when we saw the ship sail past. I imagined my mother standing on the deck in her new orange dress, her blue and yellow wings outstretched and the orchestra around her.

But then I saw the wall of white behind the ship and I frowned in confusion. It couldn't be a wave. It was higher than the ship and it was growing larger with each passing moment.

People were shouting now, calling out names and orders to run into the houses that lined the beach.

"Linnet!" I heard Nightingale's voice and turned my head towards it.

"I'm here!" I shouted, and he pushed out of the crowd and lifted me into his arms as if I was a toddler again. "What's going on?" My voice was muffled against his shoulder and he didn't answer. He began running, with his fast and jerky run, up the beach towards our home. I heard his breath flying in and out of his lungs like wings. And behind us I heard the long slow inhale of the ocean. The air seemed to stretch, and the bruise-purple cloud lowered around us like a strange fog. I didn't want to look at it, so I squeezed my eyes shut and held tight to Nightingale.

I felt Nightingale run up the steps to our home and heard him call to people nearby. "You can come in here! Hurry! Everyone needs to get indoors, upstairs! Quickly!" Nightingale lowered me to the floor beside our door and told me that he'd return in a moment. I opened my eyes again. Our home was filled with people. Fleur grabbed my hand, pulled me into my parents' bedroom and told me to sit with Silver on the floor against the bed. There were at least ten children squeezed into the room, all looking as confused as I felt. Then Fleur disappeared again.

"What's going on?" I asked Silver.

"I think it's a tidal wave," Silver whispered, and several of the children's faces turned towards him, their eyes widening with fear. Silver tried to calm them, saying it would be fine, that the island would ride the wave, and that we'd be safe here, in an upstairs home.

I snuck away. I wove between the people crammed

into our living room until I reached our balcony. Someone had shut the glass doors and covered them with a huge piece of wood that I think might have been part of our downstairs neighbour's shed. I knew then that something must be very wrong. We never shut our balcony doors in summer, not even when it was stormy. We would sit and watch the rain clouds move across the sea and along the shore.

I peered through a knothole in the wood and saw the wall of white rolling closer. I held my breath and my body froze as I watched *Joy* disappear into the wave without a sound. The ship was there one moment, then she was gone. I kept blinking, expecting *Joy* to reappear, higher up or lower down on the wave. But I didn't see her again.

The wave grew higher to the rip side of the island, which made the horizon tilt, and I suddenly felt like the whole of Morovia was tilting too. Perhaps it was.

Time seemed to speed up. I tensed in fear as the wave rushed towards us, impossibly tall and wide. I clutched the edge of the wood covering our balcony doors, unable to move or look away.

The wave smashed onto the shore and the beach itself lurched upwards. I knew then that the island was definitely moving, bobbing up and over the wave, to protect us. The white foam that hit the beach turned brown with sand. There was a roaring sound as the wave rushed towards us, but the angle of the beach and the way the water spread out diminished the wave's power. As it grew slower and smaller, some of my fear ebbed away. By the time the water hit the buildings, it sloshed calmly against the walls of our downstairs neighbour's – Lark's – home.

I remember thinking that Lark's home must be flooding, but I'd seen him here, in our living room, holding a bowl with his pet angelfish in it, so I knew he was safe. I looked up and down the flooded beach, as much as I could through the hole in the wood, and it was empty of people. Everyone must have got indoors. And we were safe in here. But there was no sigh of relief.

Someone moved the wood that was covering our balcony and opened the glass doors. Everyone stared out to sea, unblinking, scanning the now calm waters.

"Where's *Joy*?" I asked, after what seemed like an eternity. I still hadn't seen the ship reappear, but I thought – I hoped – that somebody would see something I'd missed.

Nightingale appeared at my side and lifted me into his arms. "Where's *Joy*?" I asked again. But Nightingale didn't reply. He collapsed into a chair and held me close. My mind raced with possibilities of where my mother and all the people on *Joy* might be. Perhaps the ship had been carried further away from the island, and now it needed to sail back. Maybe we couldn't see it because the bright red sails had ripped off, and now they needed to be mended.

If *Joy* herself had broken or sunk, then everybody would be in lifeboats now, rowing back to shore. I knew *Joy* had lots of lifeboats. I'd seen them in rows along the side of the ship. I stared out to sea as Nightingale held me close, and I strained my eyes to spot one of the tiny boats.

I stayed there for hours as our home slowly emptied. People's faces were lined with worry. I wanted to tell them all that it would be fine. *Joy* was a strong ship. And there were plenty of lifeboats. It was only a matter of time before everyone on board returned to shore...

But evening came and there was still no sign of *Joy*, or any lifeboats. Only Fleur, Clay and Silver remained in our home. Clay was chopping vegetables to make soup, and Fleur and Silver were tidying up. Nightingale was staring out to sea, his eyes huge and his russet skin paler than I'd ever seen it.

"She will come home," I whispered, but as I said

the words I remembered seeing *Joy* disappearing into the wave. My heart stopped beating and tears welled in my eyes. "Halcyon will be fine," I said, trying my hardest to believe it.

Nightingale didn't answer, and we carried on sitting together, staring out to sea.

That night and the following days passed in a blur. Fleur, Clay and Silver stayed with Nightingale and me, but all I remember anyone doing was staring out to sea. Hero came to see me, but she wouldn't come into our home. She stood on the doorstep, her face hot and covered with tears. She shouted things I didn't understand, then threw her necklace to the floor and left. I picked it up and tried to run after her, but Fleur stopped me. She said I should stay with Nightingale, and Clay went to check that Hero was all right.

When he returned, Clay said that Hero was upset about *Joy* being missing, but that he had made sure she was on a wagon, safely on her way home. So I carried on staring out to sea. I needed to spot the lifeboats, or maybe even people swimming. If everyone came home, then everything would be all right again.

I'm not sure how many more days passed before we heard the news. It was Uncle Clay who brought it. I think everyone must have been talking in hushed whispers until that point. Because when Clay spoke, his voice was so loud and clear it echoed around the room.

"They found *Joy*," he said. His face was pale grey and deeply lined. He looked old and, as I turned to Nightingale, I remember thinking that he looked much older too and frail, as if he might crumble in the gentlest breeze.

"Is everyone all right?" I asked. My stomach was cramped up so tight I felt like hunching over, but I sat up, stiff-straight, and looked into Clay's eyes. He looked away from me, blinked and shook his head.

Fleur drew close and wrapped an arm around me. My mouth opened but no words would form. I wanted to say there must have been some mistake. There were lifeboats. But the world seemed to fold around me and finally I gave in to my cramping stomach and hunched over and over, until I was a tiny ball on the floor, and Clay lifted me up and carried me to my bed.

CHAPTER 24

THE TRIAL

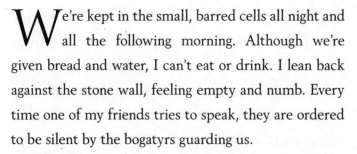

We're kept in the small, barred cells all night and all the following morning. Although we're given bread and water, I can't eat or drink. I lean back against the stone wall, feeling empty and numb. Every time one of my friends tries to speak, they are ordered to be silent by the bogatyrs guarding us.

Whiskers sighs sadly on my lap and Lumpy croaks gloomily. I think about Nightingale – where he is and whether I'll see him today, if his trial is going ahead, and if any of us will ever figure out a way to escape from here now.

Finally, at some point during the scorching, stifling afternoon, a group of armoured bogatyrs stomp down the corridor towards us. "On your feet!" one of them says gruffly.

I wobble as I rise, stiff from the long hours sitting

on the floor. The bogatyrs wade into our cells, clanging and banging their armour. They must be so hot – a brief flush of sympathy for them runs through me. But then they surround us like an inescapable moving cage of iron, and I go back to resenting them.

The bogatyrs lead us all outside, even Whiskers and Lumpy, who stay at my heels. The sun is gleaming down on a huge courtyard, making it glow. In the darkness last night, I didn't realize how white everything here is. The ground, all the loose rocks and all the dust in the air is made of white chalk, dazzlingly bright in the light. I shade my eyes with a hand, but still need to squint.

Slowly, Captain Ilya comes into focus. He's standing in the centre of the courtyard, the golden feather on his helmet shining like a sunbeam. Several bogatyrs are by his side, and a group of courtiers too, dressed in pale blue silks with golden jewellery dripping from their necks, wrists and ankles.

One of the courtiers is younger than the rest and is wearing a narrow golden crown on top of a shiny, coiled black plait. There are several small golden feathers sticking up from the crown. This must be Crown Heir Vasha. I huff out a hot, angry breath, thinking of the golden feather containing Echo's magic that could have brought unity being crushed under Captain Ilya's boot. Golden feathers are a symbol of kindness on Morovia, after the kindness the ancient bird-people showed the humans who were shipwrecked here. So for Captain Ilya and Vasha to be wearing them when they have treated people so cruelly is hypocritical and wrong.

I look around for Nightingale, but he's not here, and worry for him twists in my stomach. The bogatyrs arrange my friends and me in a line in front of Vasha and I frown as my eyes adjust to the light. I've never seen the Heir before today and I tilt my head in curiosity because their posture is familiar: straight-backed, with strong hands poised for action. I look up into their face.

It's a girl, with golden-brown eyes and a piercing gaze that is looking beyond me, as if she can't bear to look at me.

"It can't be," I whisper, blinking to try to refocus the scene in a different way. Maybe Crown Heir Vasha simply resembles Hero. They can't be the same person, because that would mean Hero has lied to me from the very first day we met, six years ago. But no matter how much I blink, it only confirms the truth. Hero, my ex-best friend, is the Crown Heir of Morovia.

"The Crown Heir will be judging and sentencing you today." Captain Ilya's voice thumps across the courtyard like a hammer striking rock. He proceeds to name us, one by one, and list our crimes. His words disappear behind memories of my and Hero's friendship. The day I met her in the market when we were seven years old. She was wearing the blue silk tunic of a courtier and the deerskin trousers of a bogatyr, and she was quick to help anyone and everyone.

"...using, or being complicit in the use of singing magic..." Captain Ilya's voice bangs on as I picture Hero sitting with my parents and me, all of us singing together, and my mother's magic making butterflies dance around us. Hero laughed and held out her hands, hoping a butterfly would land on her fingers.

"...plotting to destroy Crown property...being an enemy to safety..." Captain Ilya goes on and I shake my head in disbelief.

"Why?" I shout suddenly, staring right into Hero's eyes. "Why didn't you tell me you were Crown Heir?"

Captain Ilya ignores me and continues speaking, but Hero holds up her hand. Captain Ilya frowns and stops talking. Hero walks towards me, pauses a few paces away and finally returns my gaze.

"Six years ago, I was a child who wanted friendship away from the palace and my royal duties." Hero looks away from me again. "But that's a lifetime ago and doesn't matter any more. I'm the Crown Heir, and it's my duty to keep everyone on Morovia safe."

"We aren't dangerous." I look along the line of my friends, then turn back to Hero. "You know that. We only wanted to rescue Nightingale and—"

"Nightingale used his singing magic to hypnotize people and steal from them," Hero interrupts. "The humans and alkonosts of Morovia have a right to live without magic being used on them. What Nightingale did was wrong, and there are many more alkonosts who can, and do, use their magic in dishonest and dangerous ways." Hero looks at Echo and frowns. "You all planned to have Echo use her magic on me to influence my thoughts and decisions. You would have let her alter my mind without my consent. You must see how wrong that is."

"We were trying to make Morovia a better place," I protest. "We want to put an end to Captain Ilya's awful rules that divide us, and we want alkonosts and humans to live in unity."

Hero holds up her hand to silence me, like she did to Captain Ilya, but I carry on talking, louder and faster. "Alkonosts are not allowed to sing! And we've had *everything* taken away from us. This island is our home and we have a right to live here freely."

"Everyone on this island has a right to live here *safely*," Hero responds so fiercely I step back. "Singing magic is dangerous in a thousand ways. It sank the ship *Joy*. My parents—" Hero stops abruptly. Her eyes blaze and fill with tears. She looks like she did three years ago, when she threw her necklace to the floor. My heart sinks in despair. Even after all these years, Hero still blames alkonosts for her parents' death. Hero's mother, I now realize, must have been the human queen of Morovia. Maybe her father was a bogatyr like Hero said he was, or maybe not. But either way, her parents were on *Joy* together. And seeing Hero glaring at me now, I think she hates me and all alkonosts for what happened to the ship.

"For all we know, it might have been singing magic that shipwrecked humans on Morovia thousands of years ago." Captain Ilya spits out his words and anger flares inside me.

"Why would you suggest something so horrible?" I yell at Captain Ilya. "Alkonosts saved the lives of many of the humans who were shipwrecked here and offered them a home!" But as I'm speaking, I think how I don't know what caused that shipwreck, and I don't know what caused the tidal wave that sank *Joy* either. Doubts swirl inside me and I glare at Captain Ilya, realizing that this is what he does – he takes the little doubts that people carry inside them like quiet, unhatched eggs, and he pokes them until they crack, then feeds what's inside, making it grow into suspicion and hate.

Captain Ilya sneers as he turns away from me and I realize this is all his fault. Hero is just a child, like me, and after she lost her parents she needed comfort. But all she had was Captain Ilya, whispering in her ear, telling her that *Joy* sinking was the fault of alkonosts and that we were dangerous. No wonder Hero has acted this way. Captain Ilya has influenced her more than any singing magic ever could.

I wish I had chased after Hero that day she came to see me, after *Joy* sank. If I had, then maybe I could have stopped everything that has happened since. Maybe I could have helped Hero through some of her grief and pain, and stopped hatred for alkonosts from swelling inside her.

"Nobody knows for sure what caused the tidal wave," I say. "It's wrong to blame and punish all alkonosts for it. Captain Ilya has divided this whole island. Can't you see how awful life has become here, for everyone – alkonosts and humans?"

"We're doing what's needed to keep everyone safe." Hero's face hardens and she straightens her back. "It's my duty as Crown Heir. And, as Crown Heir, I sentence you all to assist in the quarry. It's essential work, as more iron is needed to protect all Morovians from singing magic. When we have enough iron to keep everyone safe, then we can relax the new rules and give alkonosts more freedom." Hero turns her back on us and walks away, towards Captain Ilya.

"Hero, please," I say. I want her to turn around and

see me as she used to. "I'm your friend." Whiskers whines and Lumpy croaks.

"I'm not Hero," she says without turning around. "And we're not friends any more."

The tiny leather bag around my neck that contains my and Hero's necklaces suddenly feels too heavy, like the parcel I stole that contained a treacherous rock instead of golden treasures. I want to tear the bag off and throw our necklaces to the ground, like Hero did. For all these years I've carried them round pointlessly, thinking our friendship meant something. But it was a lie right from the start. Hero has used me: first to escape the palace and her royal duties, then to have someone to blame for *Joy* sinking, and now to lead her to Echo. If there was ever anything good about our friendship, then it sank with the ship *Joy* and is lost for ever. And there's nothing I can do about it.

CHAPTER 25

THE QUARRY

Bogatyrs lead us away from the courtyard and down the path I recognize from last night that leads to the quarry. I blink back hot, angry tears and try to focus on the one thought that is bringing me some comfort – that I will soon be with Nightingale.

The white chalk cliffs rise around us, dazzlingly bright in the afternoon sunlight. I feel dizzy from lack of sleep, food and water as we're funnelled into a narrow chasm that dips steeply downwards. The chasm ends with an iron gate, at least four times taller than me and guarded by seven bogatyrs. One of them unlocks the gate and we're led through.

Beyond the gate, a vast white landscape extends out, almost as big and busy as the town of Spark. The quarry is a deep, oval pit, ringed by layers of flat, open terraces that are as wide as streets. All along the terraces are hundreds of tents, so covered with chalk dust that I can barely make out their colours.

Around the tents hundreds of people, mostly alkonosts but some humans too, are working – kneeling down and digging into the ground and the cliff walls with small wooden tools. Nearly everyone is an adult, but there a few children my age or older, too. Some are lifting dark nodules from the chalk, which range from palm-sized to the size of a kickball, and carrying them to hand-drawn wooden carts. The sounds of tools scraping and people grunting with effort echoes all around the quarry. My gaze roams the terraces, desperately searching for Nightingale.

One of the bogatyrs points to a large wooden shed at the edge of the quarry. "You'll find tents, blankets, water pouches, hand tools and carts in there. Outhouses are behind the shed. Food and water are brought twice daily, and the iron nodules you dig out are collected at the same time."

"What about Kestrel and Jay? They're too young for this kind of work," I say.

The bogatyr glances down at Kestrel and Jay. "Do what you can to help," he says gruffly, before turning and walking away.

Silver puts his hand over his eyes to shield them from the dazzling white scene. "No one said how long we'd be kept here."

"I need to look for Nightingale," I say, unable to think of anything but finding him. Jay and Kestrel murmur an agreement – they want to look for their parents too.

"Silver, Echo and I will set up a camp over there." Fleur points to a fairly empty space nearby. "You three can go and search for your parents and come back whenever you're ready."

I nod, hope and worry churning inside me as I walk towards the quarry. I stop on the top terrace and stare, searching again for any sign of Nightingale: his long, reddish-brown head feathers, his bird feet, his jerky walk. I can't see him, but the quarry is huge so he could be out of sight. I decide to walk clockwise along the top terrace and work my way down to the lower terraces, calling his name as I go. Jay and Kestrel scramble down to the terrace below and set off in the same direction, calling for their own parents.

As I walk, I stop to ask people if they've seen Nightingale. I describe his feathers and feet, but I'm met with blank stares and apologetic head-shakes.

My hope curdles into despair the further I walk and the more people I ask. Nightingale's feet are so distinctive, I'm sure that if he were here someone would remember him. Panicked thoughts race through my mind that something terrible might have happened to him here, but if that were true, surely someone would know about it?

Cries rise from the terrace below and I look down to see Jay and Kestrel engulfed in a feathery hug. They must have found their parents. I rush on, even more determined to find Nightingale.

Whiskers, struggling in the heat, is barely able to keep up with me, so I slow down a little and shout as I run. "Nightingale! Has anyone seen Nightingale?" I call, but only murmurs of *"No"* and *"Sorry"* rise from tired, hot faces. The thought that he isn't here, and that maybe Hero is keeping us apart on purpose, fills me with anger.

After several loops of the quarry, along upper, middle and lower terraces, I still haven't found him. I'm exhausted and Whiskers is so tired she's dragging her paws. Lumpy, who is still clutching Whiskers's ear, looks half asleep. I lift Whiskers into my arms and climb back up the sloping paths cut into the cliff face until I reach the camp that Fleur, Silver and Echo have set up. They've pitched two simple tents and are sitting in front of one, looking downcast and exhausted.

Fleur pats the ground next to her as I approach, and I collapse beside her. Whiskers flops out of my arms onto the ground, panting. I rub her neck. "You're going to have to find a way back to the swamp," I say quietly. "You too, Lumpy. I should never have brought you both here." But Lumpy narrows his eyes and croaks defiantly, and Whiskers nuzzles closer to my side.

"You didn't find Nightingale," Silver says, his face lined with worry.

"I don't understand why he's not here." I rub my forehead. It's aching from the bright light. "I'm worried about him."

Jay, Kestrel and their parents walk towards us, carrying their tent and tools all bundled up in a small hand-drawn cart. "We thought we'd join you." Jay smiles.

"I'm Plover, Jay and Kestrel's father," the man holding Jay's hand says with a kind, tired smile. He's tall and thin, with black and white head feathers and pale, blue-grey skin streaked with chalk dust.

"And I'm Osprey, the boys' mother," the lady with her arm around Kestrel says. She's also tall, with brown feathers on her head, neck and shoulders, and white skin. Like Plover, she's covered in chalk dust and looks tired. "Are you hungry or thirsty? We have food and water we can share."

"That's kind of you." Fleur smiles. "I'm Fleur and this is my son Silver."

Echo nods a greeting. "It's good to see you again, Osprey, Plover."

"Do you know each other?" I look from Echo to Osprey and Plover.

"Plover and Osprey have both worked with the Unity Movement," Echo explains.

Plover crouches beside Whiskers and gives her a stroke. "I can talk to animals with my singing magic." He looks around at the white cliffs. "Well, I can when I'm not here in the Magicless Mountains. I used my magic to deliver messages from the Unity Movement in the swamp to allies in Pero Palace Complex, by giving written notes to birds and telling them who to deliver them to. But I was caught."

"Is that why you're here too?" I ask Osprey.

"I was caught helping Plover." Osprey nods. "But I myself don't have any singing magic."

My heart skips a beat. I've never met an adult

alkonost without singing magic before. "I'm Linnet," I say. "And this is Lumpy and Whiskers. I don't have any magic either." It feels strange to say it out loud in front of everyone, without adding something about how it will soon come.

"Everyone has magic." Osprey winks. "It's just not always singing magic."

"I'm looking for my father, Nightingale," I say. "I know he was captured and sent to The Keep, but he isn't here in the quarry. Do you know where else he might be?"

"There are some holding cells and also a small infirmary for the sick or injured. Perhaps he's there?" Osprey suggests, lifting a water pouch from her cart.

I remember how Captain Ilya pushed my father to the ground. "He could be in the infirmary," I say. "One of his feet was hurt when he was captured."

"If that's the case, they'll heal him before putting him on trial." Osprey opens her water pouch, and I'm wondering whether it would be rude to ask for some for Whiskers and Lumpy when Osprey pours a little into her hand and offers it to Whiskers herself. Whiskers smiles her half-smile and laps it up as Osprey coos softly into her ear. I lean forwards, dab my fingers into the water and drip some beside Lumpy so that he can crawl into it and drink through his skin, like all toads do.

"Has anyone ever escaped from here?" Fleur asks, looking beyond the terraces to the high white cliffs.

Plover shakes his head. "The cliffs on the high side and rip side are sheer, and plummet down onto a rocky shore far below. And on the low side and lee side they border The Keep, which is always full of bogatyrs. The only way out is through the iron gate, and that's kept locked and guarded at all times."

I put my head in my hands and groan. "So this is it?" I murmur. "We're trapped here with no chance of escape."

Fleur wraps an arm around me. "Don't give up hope, Linnet."

"I don't want to." I frown. "But what can we do?"

Echo rises to her feet. "We work, we eat, we drink, and all the while we watch closely and we think, until the way forwards becomes clear."

"We've learned that the best way to survive this place is one day at a time," Plover says. "It's difficult, but everyone here is kind. We help each other, keep each other company and give each other hope."

Osprey nods in agreement. "Come on, I'll help set up a tent for you, Lumpy and Whiskers." Osprey smiles as she offers Whiskers another palmful of water, and I give her a small smile back as her kindness wraps around me.

The sun slowly sinks as we set up more tents. Plover gives each of us a piece of bread and Osprey fills water pouches for us all. Even though the afternoon is turning to evening, the quarry is still filled with the scratching and scraping of tools against chalk.

Every so often someone frees a dark round nodule and places it in their wooden cart. Most are small and seem easy to carry, but the larger ones look heavy, as sometimes two or even three people struggle to carry them. These nodules must be the rocks that contain the iron that Hero and the bogatyrs want so badly, to protect themselves from singing magic.

Once my tent is set up and Whiskers and Lumpy are dozing inside, I pick up a small wooden trowel and go to look for a nodule myself. Not because I think anyone needs protecting from singing magic, and not because it's what Hero sentenced me to do, but because the bogatyrs at the gate keep scowling at us, and Plover says they often separate people who aren't working and place them on the far edges of the cliffs to work alone.

I kneel at the back of the terrace and begin scraping the rock. The chalk is harder than I thought it would be, and it takes me a while to even make a small hollow. Plover walks over and gives me some useful advice – how to scrape along faint lines of weakness in the rock, how to hold the trowel so it won't give me blisters, and how to look for the pale orange stains that signal a nodule might be close.

My friends all come to listen to the advice, then kneel and work alongside me. We continue long into the dusk, complaining about the hardness of the chalk and the weakness of the wooden tools, and about Hero's treachery. But we cheer when we find nodules, even though they're all small – no bigger than my hand. They're heavy for their size; rounded, bulbous, orange-tinted things that smell of iron and sulphur. Digging them out is a job none of us want to be doing, but I feel grateful that we're doing it together.

When it finally gets too dark to see, we return to our tents. I say goodnight to everyone, wrap a rough woollen blanket around myself and curl up next to

Whiskers and Lumpy, exhausted but unable to sleep. I can't believe I'm still not with Nightingale, and that Hero's betrayal has left us trapped here.

I stare out of my tent at the stars twinkling over the dark shadows in the quarry, and I start humming the tune to the Song of Unity, like I used to do when I couldn't sleep in Spark. My quiet music drifts into the vast night and tears well in my eyes, because the song is all about kindness and unity – things that Captain Ilya, Hero and the bogatyrs have torn apart. But I carry on singing anyway, because somehow the song brings me comfort too. Perhaps because it reminds me that alkonosts and humans worked together for unity once – and if that happened once, then it could happen again.

Hope trickles into me as I sing the lyrics. Then I remember another song that I heard after *Joy* sank, which also brought me strength during a terrible time…

The Song My Mother Left Me

Three years ago, some days afer *Joy* sank, I woke in the middle of the night. I'd been dreaming about my mother singing to me on the beach, her warm, feathered arms around my shoulders. I closed my eyes and tried to get back to sleep, to recapture the dream, but I couldn't.

I went to our balcony. Nightingale was there, having fallen asleep in his chair while staring out to sea. The air was calm but cold and I got an extra blanket from my parents' room and tucked it around him. Then I gazed at the starry sky over the silvered sea. The distant outlines of both Eldovia and Buyan were visible, and I felt somehow comforted that they were floating close to Morovia that night.

Faint music was drifting from the high-side edge of the beach and I craned my neck and peered into the darkness. I saw tiny lights all in a row, flickering like candle flames. Curiosity overwhelmed me. I picked up a shawl and crept out of the house.

It felt good to be outside, with the soft sand against my bare feet and the tingle of salty air and starlight on my skin. My head feathers lifted as I approached the music and the lights. They sensed that something magical was happening.

The outline of a house rose out of the darkness, where I knew there had been no house before. It was wooden, old and crooked, and it was sitting on the beach with its windows glowing golden as they looked out to sea. All around the house was a rickety white fence with strange glowing orbs balanced on top.

Fast-paced dancing music was bouncing out of the house's windows, and the house's eaves were bobbing up and down to the beat. At least two balalaikas were being played, along with an accordion. Feet were stamping and voices were raised in whoops of delight. The joy and excitement of the scene made my heartbeat quicken as I drew closer, but then I stopped still when I realized the fence was made of bones. And the glowing orbs were skulls. Candlelight was shining out of their eye sockets like sunbeams.

I frowned in confusion. The sounds from the house were happy, yet the fence spoke of death. I stood, transfixed by the strangeness of it all, until the music and voices dwindled into silence, and the cold night air crept so deep into my body that I began to shiver.

The house lifted slightly and my mouth opened in shock as I glimpsed two legs beneath it, with huge chicken feet that were bigger than my whole body. The front door turned towards me and one of the windows next to it winked.

"Hello?" I felt like I was asking the house if it was alive. Or if it was real. Maybe this was all a dream.

The door swung open and a lady stepped out onto the porch. She was short and round, with a big warty nose, wrinkled white skin and thinning white hair floating out from under a headscarf decorated with skulls and flowers.

"Greetings, Linnet!" she sang as she danced towards the bone gate in the fence. She stopped beside it and beckoned me closer.

My legs wobbled as I walked towards her. "How do you know my name?" I asked.

"I have guided many souls to the stars this evening, and your mother was one of them. I saw her memories. I saw you." The lady smiled, revealing crooked teeth. "You can call me Baba."

"Baba," I repeated, looking at a bundle strapped to her chest with a bright green fabric wrap. "Is that a baby?" I asked curiously.

Baba moved the wrap slightly and I saw soft red curls of hair. "Yes, this is baby Marinka. She isn't really meant to be here," Baba whispered with a wink. "But she is stubborn. In fact, she is proof that almost anything can be achieved with stubbornness." Baba kissed the top of Marinka's head and tucked her back into the wrap. "Now, what are you doing here, Linnet? A Yaga House is no place for the living."

"I heard the music and the dancing...what do you mean, you guided my mother?" I pulled my shawl tighter around my shoulders.

"Your mother died when *Joy* sank, along with many others. We've had the most wonderful party tonight to celebrate their lives." Baba let out a cackling laugh as she did a little twirl. "There was food and dancing and the sharing of beautiful memories, and now all the dead are making their journey to the stars."

"My mother is gone?" I remembered Clay shaking his head when he said they'd found *Joy*, my father looking like he might crumble and Fleur wrapping her arms around me. I swayed, feeling dizzy and cold, like I was swirling in a whirlpool.

Baba pushed the bone gate open, wrapped an arm around me and ushered me onto the porch steps. "Sit here a moment. It's not technically allowed, but..." Baba glanced up at the house's eaves and grinned. "You don't mind, do you, House?"

The balustrade of the porch steps curved around me in a strange, wooden hug and tiny white blossoms erupted on the spindles beside me.

"What..." My voice drifted away as I stared at the flowers. Baba disappeared through the front door and the house seemed to shuffle down, to sit more comfortably on the sand. "House?" I asked again.

The eaves nodded, two windows blinked and a friendly sigh escaped from the chimney. More flowers, this time tiny blue ones, grew from the steps I was sitting on. Baba returned with a steaming mug and placed it in my hands. "Cocoa," she said.

I wrapped my fingers around the mug and took a sip of the hot drink.

"Not many living souls find their way here." Baba sat down next to me. One of her arms was wrapped protectively around baby Marinka, snuggled against her chest. "This is a Yaga House, where dead souls come to celebrate their lives and say goodbye to this world before they move on."

"So my mother is gone," I repeated in a whisper.

"Your mother has moved on to the stars, yes." Baba nodded.

"I'll miss her." My eyes filled with tears and my throat thickened. The house's balustrade wrapped around me even closer.

"Of course you will, child." Baba reached into a pocket and pulled out a small paper bag. "Sugared almond?"

I peered into the bag and took one of the smooth, pastel-coloured ovals. It bled a creamy sweetness onto my tongue.

"Remember, you have the power to call your mother whenever you need her." Baba popped a sugared almond into her own mouth and smiled.

"What do you mean?" I asked.

"We can write the people we miss back into our lives at a moment's notice. Close your eyes," Baba ordered and I did as she said. "Now, think of your mother."

I pictured my mother sitting beside me on the beach, her warm, feathered arms around my shoulders, protecting me from the cool air. Behind my eyelids I saw the colours of the setting sun blooming on the horizon. I felt my mother's warmth and I heard her song around me.

...on feathered shoulders
divine dreams afloat
cradled in purest love
sigh a golden note...

"Memories are stubborn," Baba said, "like baby Marinka." Baba cackled again and I opened my eyes to see her kissing the top of Marinka's head once more. "Your mother touched the world, and she touched you, and those touches persist. You can use them to bring her close whenever you need her. You can *think* your mother close. You can *sing* her close." Baba leaned towards me and whispered, her eyes glittering as if she was telling me a treasured secret. "When your mother passed through The Gate she was singing, and her song was stubborn. It wouldn't leave this world. I believe your mother left that song here especially for you. Do you hear it?"

I closed my eyes again, and I heard my mother's lullaby once more.

The sweetest music
I've found in you
the heart-song we share
everlasting and new.

"Your mother left that song here for you," Baba whispered again. "It's there whenever you need it. It's a hug that lasts a lifetime."

I felt my mother's forehead pressed against my own, and a tear escaped from the corner of my eye. "I hear her." I nodded. "I feel her."

"And you always will. Your mother is part of the great cycle, as are we all. We are here, we are there, in each other's thoughts, in the world, in the stars. Round and round we go." Baba chuckled. "Would you like another almond?"

I opened my eyes again and took another sweet, and another sip of cocoa. "Thank you." I leaned back against the warmth of the hugging, flowering balustrade. "And thank you, House," I added, looking up at the crooked, gently puffing chimney.

"You have one more question." Baba tilted her head to me and I looked at her in confusion. "About your father, Nightingale," Baba said.

"Nightingale," I whispered, more tears welling in my eyes. It was the first time I'd called him Nightingale instead of Father, and it seemed to fit, seeing as how I had to take care of him now. "How can I help him?" I asked. "He hasn't spoken since *Joy* sank."

"Nightingale wears his grief like a cloak pulled tight against him. He can't see out and no one can see in. Keep talking to him. Be stubborn. And one day, he will poke his head out from the cloak and reply." Baba lifted the empty mug from my hands. "Remember, almost anything can be achieved with stubbornness. You can use it to fight for what is important. Now go, and don't come back for a long, long time." Baba smiled and disappeared into the house. The door swung shut and the lights in the skulls all blinked out.

I rose to my feet and looked up at the house once

more before I left. Its eaves curved into a soft smile and it poked a long, clawed toe out and waved. I waved goodbye too, then wandered back along the beach, through the darkness of night. I was alone again, but I could feel my mother's hand around my own, and I could hear her lullaby warming the cold night air around me.

...the heart-song we share
everlasting and new...

CHAPTER 26

REACHING OUT

I'm woken by the sound of wooden wheels creaking and scraping across chalky ground. Despair falls over me as I remember where I am. Whiskers and Lumpy are both staring at me expectantly, and I know they're wondering when we'll return to the swamp. My mouth is dry and my hands and knees sore from scraping the cliffs yesterday evening. I pull Whiskers close, and whisper to her and Lumpy that we'll find a way out of here soon.

The sun is already dazzlingly bright, even through my tent. I must have slept beyond dawn. I crawl out and see everyone in the quarry dragging their hand-drawn carts loaded with iron nodules towards the wooden shed, where a long line of people are gathering.

"Good morning." Osprey is standing nearby. "The bogatyrs will be here soon. Come on."

We drag our carts towards the shed. Whiskers stays at my heels, with Lumpy frowning on her head. Even though it's early, heat waves shimmer in the dust-filled air. I watch everything closely, like Echo suggested, hoping that an idea for an escape plan will reveal itself.

I spot my friends close to the front of the line and realize, with a twinge of guilt, that Osprey must have stayed behind to wait for me while I slept in. Everyone looks exhausted, but when I catch their eyes they give me reassuring smiles. It makes me think how they must be pulling at hidden depths to be kind and strong, so that we can be each other's refuge from the awfulness of being imprisoned here. Some of the lyrics to the Song of Unity that I sang last night, alone in my tent, flow through my mind:

Kindness, the fireside warm
The refuge from the storm
My hands, your feathers strong
Our futures filled with song.

A group of bogatyrs clatter down the path towards the gate, shattering my thoughts. They're rolling two huge iron wagons, a smaller wooden one and another loaded with water barrels. The gate is unlocked, the wagons are rolled through, then the gate is locked again.

Near the shed, the bogatyrs begin emptying the carts full of nodules into the large iron wagons with a loud clanging that echoes around the quarry. Water pouches are filled and loaves of bread and pieces of fruit are given out.

It must take almost an hour for Osprey and me to reach the front of the line. There are two bogatyrs distributing water, and I step close to one whose dark, mournful eyes remind me a little of Nightingale's. While the bogatyr is filling my water pouch I ask quietly, "Please, I'm looking for my father. I know he's in The Keep, but he's not in the quarry. He has long reddish-brown head feathers and clawed feet. I only want to know if he's safe."

The bogatyr glances at the other bogatyrs before whispering, "He's in the infirmary. His trial is in three days – on Songsday."

"Is he all right?" I ask, too loudly in my eagerness, and the bogatyr knocks the water barrel and grumbles something, I think to disguise our conversation. Then he passes back my water pouch and gives me a small nod. I mouth a thank you. I'm relieved to know where

Nightingale is, but worries about how badly he's injured tighten in my stomach.

Three days, I think, as I walk with Osprey back to our camp. My empty cart feels heavier than when it was full. Thousands of minutes stretch painfully ahead of me, full of worry for Nightingale, and the drudging work scraping nodules out of the cliff.

But as I look around at the people who have been imprisoned here for many moons or even years, my impatience turns to determination. I will use this time to watch and think, so that when Nightingale arrives, we can plan an escape.

By the end of Swoopday – the evening before Nightingale's trial – I feel like I've lived in the quarry for a thousand years, but I still haven't come up with a single idea for how we might break free.

I'm sitting outside my tent, watching the sun sink behind the cliffs with Whiskers and Lumpy at my side. Jay, Kestrel and their parents are already asleep in their tent. Silver and Fleur are sweeping chalk dust out of theirs. And Echo is on one of the lower terraces, talking to an old friend from the Unity Movement.

I feel defeated. I wanted to have a plan by now, something I could tell Nightingale when we're reunited, to ease the pain of him finding me here. But even though I've snuck to every edge of the quarry, and spent every moment watching and thinking, I've found no chance of escape. *What if there is no way out?*

"Are you all right, Linnet?" Echo asks as she sits beside me. I was so lost in my thoughts I didn't even see her returning.

I shake my head, too scared to speak, because if I do I think too much will come out all at once. Echo puts an arm around me and begins gently humming a tune I don't know. Her feathers are soft against my skin, and the song vibrating in her chest is soothing.

Singing has been one of the few things that's brought me comfort over the last two days. Whenever I've felt despair, I've sung the Song of Unity. A few times my friends have joined in, and when our voices rose together, my feathers lifted with hope and I felt full, deep inside – like I do when the tide washes into the swamp.

Strangely perhaps, thoughts of the swamp have brought me comfort too. I've daydreamed of pushing my toes into wet mud to search for tubers; of fishing with Whiskers and Lumpy in clear streams; and of foraging for scallops and seaweed on the mudflats while a sea wind blows through my feathers. And I've thought about the wooden hut that Nightingale built for us the first year we lived on the swamp edge, with the rope swing outside and the carved driftwood animals. I ache to see Nightingale again, and to escape from here together.

Silver and Fleur walk over and sit beside Echo and me. Fleur drinks a sip of water, then pours a little into her hand. She offers some to Whiskers, and drips some gently beside Lumpy. A smile creeps over my face. I love how everyone shares their food and water here, even with Whiskers and Lumpy.

Whiskers has been wandering around the terraces in the cooler mornings and evenings, stopping to be stroked and scratched by people who smile at her warmly and offer her scraps of bread or fruit.

Collecting food for Lumpy has become almost like a team sport in the quarry. If someone spots a spider or a beetle, everyone nearby drops their tools and scrambles around to catch it. A cheer rises when finally the tiny creature is cupped into someone's hands, then they rush up the terraces to bring it to Lumpy.

The offering is always left inside my tent, and people watch excitedly as Lumpy hunts it down, or pushes it with his sword-leg into what has become known as his larder-corner, where he guards a collection of spiders and beetles for later meals.

All this has meant that after only two days, I've met almost everyone in the quarry. After leaving Lumpy's offerings, people stay to talk. Sometimes they talk about when and why they were captured, but mostly people prefer to share their happy memories. They talk about where they lived on Morovia, what their old jobs were, who their friends were and how they liked to spend their time.

People sometimes talk about what they plan to do when they're free again. Those separated from loved ones want to find them. Most people want to return to their old homes and lives, but a few people, having lost everything, want to leave the island and make a fresh start somewhere else – like Nightingale suggested we do that last night I was with him.

When I think back to how one of my biggest reasons for wanting to stay on Morovia was my and Hero's friendship, bitterness swells inside me.

"I've been such a fool," I say suddenly, unable to

keep my thoughts inside any longer. Echo stops humming and looks at me, her feather-eyebrows raised in a question. "For trusting Hero," I explain. "I thought she was my friend, but she never has been. In all the years we were close, she didn't even tell me that she's Crown Heir."

"She said she wanted friendship away from the palace and her royal duties," Fleur says gently and I frown. "I'm not making excuses for her," Fleur adds quickly. "I'm just trying to understand why she kept that secret from you. I often watched you two playing together, and I believe that you truly were the best of friends, despite that secret."

"She betrayed me and imprisoned us all in here." Anger burns in my chest and a hot tear escapes from my eye. I want to shout at Hero, and run away from her, and ask her why, all at once. I want to know what was real and what wasn't. But it doesn't even matter any more. I wipe the tear from my cheek. Silver looks at me with concern and I shake my head in resignation. "My and Hero's friendship is like one of those broken watches we used to play with, Silver. It can't be fixed."

"I don't believe a watch is ever truly broken." Silver nudges my arm. "It might need a great deal of care and attention, and perhaps some new parts. You just have to decide whether it's worth the effort. Maybe it's the same with friendships."

I shake my head. "Even if there was a way that I could try to fix our friendship, I don't see how it could ever be the same. Not after her lies and betrayal."

Silver frowns in thought. "Sometimes a watch needs so much work, and so many new parts, that instead of fixing it I use it to build something completely different."

I think about Silver's words, and my and Hero's broken friendship, and the division all over Morovia. "Everything is so awful, I don't think it can be fixed. If we could pull it all apart and build something new, that might work. But how can we do that when we're imprisoned here?"

"I don't know." Silver sighs.

Echo hugs me tighter. "I don't know either, but we must keep trying to figure this out. Sometimes answers come when you least expect them." She starts humming again. This time, the tune to the Song of Unity.

The sun disappears behind the cliffs and cool shadows stretch over the quarry. Whiskers nuzzles closer to my leg, and Lumpy – disturbed by Whiskers's movement – lets out an indignant *"Phoot"*.

I start singing the words to the song and, as usual, they comfort me. Fleur smiles. "Do you remember when you sang this dressed as Gamayun? Your parents were so proud."

I nod, thinking about the picture that Nightingale painted of me wearing the feathered costume. I think about Gamayun too, and why she first sang the Song of Unity thousands of years ago. Back then, alkonosts and humans weren't friends at all. They were suspicious of each other.

Gamayun's song brought everyone together – but not as friends at first. Friendship took time and came later. In the beginning, alkonosts and humans simply came together to work for the same thing – unity.

Maybe it doesn't matter that my and Hero's friendship is broken, and that many alkonosts and humans aren't friends. We don't need to be friends to work for unity – we just need to want the same thing.

I pull the coin Hero gave me out of my shorts pocket and look at the symbol of unity: the alkonost and the human, holding each other tight. Maybe, to build unity, all we need to do is reach out and close the distance between us. When Hero gave me this coin, she said that we want the same thing, but that we've been fighting for it in different ways. If that's true, and if enough Morovians want the same thing, then surely we could join together and bring change for us all. So I just need to think of a way to bring us closer together…

Something sparks inside me, like one of Fleur's explosions. *I have a plan!*

I bite my lip as I wonder how and if I could make it work. Different thoughts edge into my mind and I push them all together, like Lumpy pushing small creatures into his larder-corner. I need to teach everyone a song – an old song, but it needs a new verse, too. I crawl into my tent and begin humming and singing and playing with words. Excitement fizzes inside me.

Thousands of years ago, Gamayun sang a vision of a kind and united future, which changed people's minds. Maybe, if I pick the right words, the right verse and the right song, then I could sing a vision of a better future too. And if enough voices rise with mine, then together we might have the power to change Morovia for ever.

My plan feels as delicate as a spiderweb. It needs many threads to grow strong, and if Hero doesn't reach back when I reach out, then it won't work at all. But just the tiniest chance of success makes it worth trying, for all of us.

CHAPTER 27

SINGING MAGIC

I wake with the first light of dawn and start on my plan immediately. I walk around the quarry with Whiskers and Lumpy, talk to every person who is awake, sing them my song and ask them to pass it on to others.

After about an hour the sun has crept over the cliffs and I've done a full lap of the upper terrace. I consider doing another lap, but my song is already being passed from person to person, around and down the terraces, so it won't be long before everyone has heard it.

I don't know what time Nightingale's trial is or if Hero will be judging him – and Hero being there is an essential part of my plan – but hope is skipping in my heart like Whiskers skipping at my heels.

By the time I return to our camp, my friends are awake. I tell them about my plan and my song and their eyes light up with excitement. There's a bounce in everyone's step as we drag our carts over to the shed to give our rocks to the bogatyrs and collect food and water.

As we wait in line, my song whispers from person to person like a butterfly dancing. Smiles pass between everyone and I think, even if this plan doesn't work, at least it's bringing some happiness into the quarry today.

When the bogatyrs arrive, I ask the one with the dark, mournful eyes what time Nightingale's trial is, but he shrugs. He gives me an orange with my food ration, though, and remembering the orange that Hero and I shared on the day we met, I take it as a good omen from Fate, and immediately share it with everyone around me. Even though it's old and wrinkled, it tastes almost as delicious as the one I shared with Hero six years ago. Perhaps because, like back then, the orange is sweetened with hopes and dreams.

My friends and I return to our camp and start digging in the back wall of the terrace, all in a row. But I'm itching to move on to the next stage of my plan, and the thought of missing Nightingale's trial is like a chaffinch's alarm call inside my head.

I go into my tent, where Lumpy is diligently guarding three beetles and a spider, and I pull my and

Hero's necklaces out of their tiny bag. I stare at them with a mixture of sadness and hope.

Hero's betrayal has changed our friendship for ever and I don't know if I'll be able to trust her again. But I need to remember some of the good times we had together and the bond we shared, and I need Hero to remember, too. Then our hearts might fill with enough love to reach out to each other, and if that helps Hero realize how happy and united Morovia could be, then it might make a difference to everyone on this island.

My plan has three parts. I need to get Hero's necklace back to her. And I need her to hear my song. The third part I have no control over: I need Hero to listen, really listen, and then choose to think and act differently. Because ultimately, she's the one who holds the most power to create change. My fingers tremble with apprehension as I coil Hero's necklace up into a little ball and tie it so that it doesn't unravel.

"Are you ready?" I whisper to Lumpy, holding up the necklace-ball. "Can you take this to Hero?"

Lumpy croaks, takes the necklace in his mouth and begins crawling out of the tent and along the shady back edge of the terrace, towards the iron gate. He must remember the last place we saw Hero was the courtyard of The Keep, and I breathe a sigh of relief. I didn't want to carry Lumpy any closer to the gate, in case the bogatyrs noticed when I put him down. I follow though, so I can distract the bogatyrs at the gate while Lumpy sneaks past. Whiskers follows too, with the slightly lost look she always has when Lumpy isn't on her head.

"What do you want?" one of the bogatyrs asks as we approach the gate.

"I wondered what time the trial is today?" I stare at all the bogatyrs with my chin raised. They stare back at me, which is perfect because it means they don't notice Lumpy crawling through the bars and away past their feet.

"Get back to work," the bogatyr dismisses me gruffly.

"Please, my father is on trial and—"

"Get back to work," the bogatyr repeats firmly.

"All right," I mumble, risking a glance at Lumpy. He's almost hidden in shadow, making his way past the last of the bogatyrs. "One more thing," I say, wanting to distract the bogatyrs for a few more seconds. "It's my swamp-rat, Whiskers. She really needs a bath and I wondered—"

"Get back to work!" the bogatyr shouts so angrily I jump back.

"Fine." I turn and walk away, worry for Lumpy knotting up inside me. I know he'll stay at the edge of the path, but at some point, when he sees Hero – *if* he sees Hero – he'll end up crawling over the exposed ground of the courtyard. Guilt for putting him in danger squeezes my chest. Maybe the song would have been enough without the necklace. I push the thought away because it's too late for regrets now.

I walk back to our camp and tell my friends what I plan to do next. Although their faces crease with worry, they nod in agreement and say they'll try to cover for me if the bogatyrs notice I'm missing. I ask Whiskers to stay in our tent, but she only moves closer to me so I tuck her into her sling. Then I sneak away to the lee side of the quarry and, when I'm out of sight of the bogatyrs, I begin climbing the sheer chalk cliff.

Where there are no handholds, I use my little wooden trowel to scrape small holes just big enough to push my fingers and toes into. It must take over an hour, and the sun beating down on me is so hot that my feathers lift to almost vertical. But finally I reach the top of the cliff and peep my head over to see the view.

The Keep is laid out below me like the map that Hero drew on the floor of Echo's hideout. The square courtyard is surrounded by cliffs and walls. I can see the wide, rushing river beyond the lee-side wall, and the moat beyond the forge on the low side. The holding cells are directly below me, and beyond them is a small building that must be the infirmary, where Nightingale is.

A large group of bogatyrs are gathered outside a building near the forge, which I think must be where they eat and rest, and a few smaller groups are patrolling the edges of the courtyard, but there's no sign of Hero or any trial yet. I crawl onto a small ledge, try to get as comfortable as possible, and wait.

Finally, when the sun is blazing directly overhead and the smell of Whiskers is making my eyes water, I hear the clip-clop of hooves approaching. Four horses, with courtiers riding them, cross the bridge into The Keep.

The courtiers are wearing blue silk tunics and deerskin trousers. Hero is one of them, and she doesn't look happy. She's frowning, perhaps from the bright light and heat, and she looks as tired as those of us who scrape for iron nodules in the quarry all day.

When she dismounts, Hero doesn't stand as straight-backed as usual and her eyes seem filled with sorrow. I feel torn, deep inside. I'm still angry with Hero for her betrayal and her part in all this cruelty. But my heart also aches to see her pain and wants to help her. I decide to listen to that part of me, push away my anger and choose kindness. But I can only help Hero, and all of us, if she chooses kindness too. I hope my song will help her realize that; I hope it holds the power to create change.

"It *must*," I whisper to myself, trying to think of a bargain that I could make with Fate. But nothing seems a fair offering compared to getting my father back and freedom for us all.

One of the courtiers fusses with Hero's long plait, pinning it up in a circle. When her crown is secured on top, it seems to weigh Hero down. It's strange to see her like this and think that she has always been Crown Heir. Sadness that she never felt able to tell me wells up inside.

Hero is led over to the large group of bogatyrs, where she's offered fruit and water. Captain Ilya appears and steps beside her. The sight of him makes outrage burn inside me, but instead of pushing the feeling away I use it to make me even more determined – to fight for change and to end all the injustice and suffering that he's caused.

I scan the courtyard, looking for Lumpy, and spot him at the edge of one of the bloomeries, resting in the shade. When Hero, the courtiers and the bogatyrs gather in the centre of the courtyard, he begins crawling slowly towards them.

My heartbeat quickens. I turn, look down at everyone trapped in the quarry and wave my hands. It doesn't take long for one of them to spot me, then a few more. They reply with small nods, not wanting to alert the bogatyrs at the gate that I've climbed up here. Then they keep a covert watch, waiting for the signal to sing.

Lumpy draws closer to Hero, but she hasn't noticed him yet. Nobody has. The door to the infirmary opens and a bogatyr steps out with Nightingale. My eyes fill with tears of concern and relief.

He's walking with the help of a stick and one of his feet is bandaged. He looks exhausted and defeated, but he's alive, and finally so close that I can see him. I bite my lip to stop myself from shouting out to him, because every fibre of my being wants to tell him I'm here.

I watch as Nightingale is led to the centre of the

courtyard and stood in front of Hero. Nightingale's eyes are narrowed against the dazzling light. I don't think he recognizes Hero. His gaze roams around and settles on Lumpy, who is such an obvious green-brown splodge against the bright white ground that I'm surprised no one else has noticed him.

Lumpy must see or sense Nightingale, because he changes direction and picks up speed as he moves towards my father. I frown, because I wanted Lumpy to deliver Hero's necklace to her, but he's been distracted by Nightingale. I bite my lip harder, hoping it won't matter and that somehow the necklace will find its way to Hero anyway.

Hero notices Nightingale staring in confusion at Lumpy and her eyebrows draw together. She moves towards Lumpy, leans down and holds out the lower fabric of her tunic. Lumpy climbs onto it and Hero stands, lifting Lumpy with her. Then Hero calls a courtier to her side, and gently pours Lumpy into their tunic. My heartbeat drums up into my throat as Hero speaks to the courtier without noticing the necklace.

But then Hero stops abruptly and peers down at Lumpy. My spirit soars as she reaches out to him, takes her necklace and holds it up. It unravels in the light and

Hero's eyes shine with tears as she stares, open-mouthed, at the half a golden heart.

I turn to everyone in the quarry and raise my palm high, which is the signal to begin. A deep rumbling hum sounds that rises in volume and pitch, and my skin and feathers tingle as it swells into a tune.

Harmonies and melodies lift on hundreds of voices, singing my and Hero's song – the song we made up together, six years ago, on the beach.

We built a castle on the shore
flower flags and shells for doors
a seaweed garden to explore
in our castle on the shore, on the shore.

My heart flutters and I find I'm too nervous to look at Hero to see her reaction. So I climb back down the cliff instead, as fast as I safely can. The song echoes all around the terraces and, when I reach the ground, I feel it thrumming inside me. My voice joins the others as I run to my friends while singing.

The tide rushed in, wave by wave
flooding moat, towers cave
falling shells, a flower grave
as the tide roared in, wave by wave.

The noise of bogatyrs, their heavy iron armour clanging, approaches the quarry gate and I tremble as everyone sings the verses again. Will Hero be with the bogatyrs? What is she feeling? Is her heart swelling and aching like mine? Or is she still as angry and upset as before?

The iron gate creaks open and bogatyrs walk through, Captain Ilya amongst them, a deep scowl on his face. "Silence!" he shouts.

But we all sing louder.

Then Hero walks into the quarry. Her eyes scan the terraces, and I will her to see me as I lead all of our voices into the final verse – the new verse that I wrote last night, especially for today, especially for her.

The castle we built washed away
flowers lost, shells astray
but fresh sand shifts into the bay
we could build anew today.

Hero's eyes find mine and I hold up my own necklace high. The half-heart sparkles like the one dangling from Hero's hands and I look into her eyes and sing.

Fresh sand shifts into the bay
we could build anew today.

Hero's hands are trembling like mine, and her eyes are filled with tears. I realize something that I should have realized long before now. Hero isn't full of hate. She's full of fear. Ever since *Joy* sank, she's been scared, and she's scared now.

I understand something of Hero's fear, because I've felt powerless and vulnerable too. But I could show Hero how fear can be overcome by togetherness instead of division.

I walk towards her, and as I do my voice rises above the rest and reaches the clear and perfect note that begins the Song of Unity. One by one, other voices rise to reach the note too, and our song swells and fills the quarry, carrying its story of how alkonosts and humans worked together to build unity after a tragedy and created a beautiful home for us all.

Shipwrecked on golden sands
Surf cloaking outstretched hands
Light souls fly over waves
Lift hearts from ocean graves.

Hundreds of voices unite with mine and soar up into the sky.

Kindness, the bird in flight
The star map in the night
Your hands, my feathers strong
Our futures filled with song.

Captain Ilya glares at me, his eyes aflame, but I keep walking towards Hero and sing louder.

Hold onto me
We float on salted seas
Swim side by side
Climb into clear blue skies.

"Crown Heir." Captain Ilya steps towards Hero, his voice taut with anger. "They must be silenced. If their magic overpowers the iron—"

"Let them be," Hero says. "They aren't singing magic."

But as I continue walking towards Hero, my voice lifting with so many others, our song echoing around the quarry and rising into the bright blue sky, I realize we are. Not the kind of magic that Captain Ilya believes can cause tidal waves and sink ships. We're singing a different kind of storm, one that could change the landscape of this island for the better.

New worlds on ancient lands
New friendships proudly stand
Dual fruits of trees entwined
Two joyful songs combined.

At this moment, I feel like our song is more powerful than anything on Morovia – more powerful than Captain Ilya, the bogatyrs and all the fear, suspicion and hate that has divided the people of this island. Voices, singing together, surround me, until I feel like I'm floating upwards with our song.

Kindness, the fireside warm
The refuge from the storm
My hands, your feathers strong
Our futures filled with song.

Hero moves towards me and we stop an arm's-length away from each other.

You hold me near
Protect from tides of fear
Stand side by side
Float into vernal skies.

I smile and watch Hero's fear begin to ebb away. She holds out her hands, and I hold out mine, and we fall into a stiff and awkward hug. But then she softens, and I feel her cheek resting comfortably against mine. It's warm, as it was on the day we lay on the shore, side by side, building a sandcastle.

Two hearts sincere
Our voices loud and clear
Singing as one
Beneath a golden sun.

CHAPTER 28

THE RAIN

Hero and I hold each other tight as the Song of Unity rises and falls around us. Part of me wants to stay in this moment for ever. But another part of me wants to rush forwards in time and ask if Hero will free Nightingale, and all of us, and let us return to our old homes and lives.

"Crown Heir Vasha," Captain Ilya says firmly. "You aren't safe here. None of us are. The alkonosts are singing. What if together their magic is stronger than the iron?"

Hero moves her head so that she can whisper in my ear. "Linnet, I'm scared," she says. "I don't want to be, but I am. Because of what happened to *Joy*. I'm scared of singing magic and of not being in control of what happens on Morovia."

"I understand you're scared," I whisper back, still

holding her close. "But this division isn't going to take away your fears. It's cruel and wrong and it's tearing our island apart more than the tidal wave ever did."

Hero shudders as a sob rises inside her. "I never meant things to get like this, Linnet. I just wanted to keep people safe, but everything has spiralled and got so awful and now I don't know what to do—"

"You must use your power to stop this," I say firmly. "Then, together, we can begin to change everything for the better."

"Crown Heir Vasha," Captain Ilya repeats. "We must stop the singing. We must keep everyone safe."

I turn to Captain Ilya and try to keep my voice steady, even though his sharp gaze makes me tremble inside. "No one here wants to harm anyone. We only want our freedom. We've done nothing wrong and you have no right to keep us imprisoned here."

"Singing magic caused the tidal wave—" Captain Ilya begins but I interrupt him loudly.

"You have no proof that anyone here caused the tidal wave. Do you?"

Captain Ilya's mouth is still open, but no words come out. His face reddens and his eyes flicker with frustration.

Hero looks from me to Captain Ilya and pulls her shoulders back. "Linnet is right. We have no proof that anyone here caused the tragedy. What we're doing is wrong. I should never have let this happen." She frowns at Captain Ilya. "I should never have let you lead me and Morovia down this path. If my parents had been here..." Hero's jaw clenches and she takes a slow breath in. "They wouldn't have wanted this. And they would have protected me from your influence." Her voice wavers and she pauses before continuing. "But I shouldn't have let myself be swayed by you. I should have listened to more voices than just yours. And I should have been stronger, and kinder." Hero glances round at everyone in the quarry. "I'm sorry," she says. "I've treated you all so cruelly." She looks at me and a tear rolls down her cheek. "Yet you've responded to me with kindness and song. And a reminder of the power of unity." Hero turns back to Captain Ilya. "We must stop this right now, and free everyone here."

Captain Ilya shakes his head. "I can't do that."

The last hums of the Song of Unity fade into silence.

Hero stares at Captain Ilya, her gaze more piercing than ever. "Free everyone here," she repeats.

Captain Ilya stands firm. "I can't do that. The safety of the islanders is my responsibility. You are still just a child and—"

"Where are the keys to the gate?" Hero interrupts, looking from Captain Ilya to the nearest bogatyr. The bogatyr glances at Captain Ilya nervously, then shakes his head and backs away. Hero asks another bogatyr, but they do the same thing.

Hero lifts her chin and looks at all the bogatyrs standing behind Captain Ilya. "I am Crown Heir of Morovia and I order everyone imprisoned here to be freed." A murmur rushes around the terraces and a few people cheer. The bogatyrs shift uncomfortably. Some of them raise their staffs.

"These people are not a threat to the safety of Morovia," Hero says loudly. "We are the threat – all of us who have let our fears lead us to cruelty. We've imprisoned innocent people and torn our island apart. This is wrong and we must stop it."

"No!" Captain Ilya shouts. "This must be done, for everyone's safety. Singing magic is dangerous!" He turns to me. His voice has changed. It has a strange desperate edge, like he's upset and pleading with me to understand him. It takes me so much by surprise that my mouth drops open.

Captain Ilya removes his helmet with the chain-mail scarf. His skin is flushed red and his grey eyes are stormy. "Singing magic is dangerous because it's uncontrollable," he says. "And I *know* it's uncontrollable, because the only way I can stop my magic from doing harm is with iron." He looks down at his helmet and chain-mail scarf. They're trembling in his hands.

"You have singing magic?" I stare at Captain Ilya in confusion. "Are you an alkonost?" My gaze searches his head, but there isn't a single feather amongst his pale-yellow hair.

"No, I'm not," Captain Ilya snaps. "I'm human, so I shouldn't have magic at all. That in itself is proof of how little we understand singing magic." Captain Ilya looks at Hero, his face twisted in anguish. "I didn't know I had magic until three years ago, on the Day of Union. I was in the palace, keeping you safe – because you hadn't gone with your parents on the voyage around the island."

Hero glances over to me. "I stopped going on the Day of Union voyages when we became friends, because I was worried Halcyon might recognize me," she whispers. "I didn't want you to find out that I'd been lying to you."

"I went to the balconies to watch *Joy* sail past," Captain Ilya continues. "The day was so calm I could hear music and singing drifting from the ship's deck." His eyes fill with tears and his shoulders crumple. "I hummed the tune that I heard…and then…"

I lower my face and cover my eyes with my hands, as if that might hide the image forming in my mind. "The sky darkened," I murmur. A cold dread is filling me, both at the memory and at what I think Captain Ilya is about to confess.

"A wave grew," Captain Ilya says weakly. "It was

huge. It rose behind *Joy* like a mountain. I stopped humming immediately, but the wave kept growing…" Captain Ilya pinches the bridge of his nose and squeezes his eyes shut. "It was my fault. I sang magic and it caused the tidal wave."

My stomach cramps, like it did on the day I found out that *Joy* had sunk with no survivors. *Captain Ilya caused my mother's death.* I stare at him in shock, not knowing how to stem the anger that has flared up inside me.

"How can you be sure it was you?" Hero whispers, her face paling.

Captain Ilya opens his eyes again and takes a deep breath. "The moment I hummed, I *felt* the magic. It was like nothing I'd ever felt before. There were vibrations in my throat that rolled out to sea, connecting me with the wave, and I couldn't control them. I can't explain it, but I know I caused the tidal wave that sunk *Joy*. I didn't mean to, I didn't want to, but I did." Captain Ilya lifts his helmet high and shakes it. "That's why we need iron to protect us from singing magic." His voice rises fiercely. "You must all keep working until we have enough of it to protect everyone on Morovia. And until we do, nobody must be allowed to sing."

"No, wait…" I step in front of Captain Ilya without thinking and hold up my hands. I want to stop him from continuing down this path, in which he keeps us all imprisoned. But how can I convince him of anything? How can I even talk to him when just the sight of his face makes me feel so angry. He caused *Joy* to sink, then he tore our island apart.

Hatred suddenly rises from my stomach, hot and bitter, and I remember Nightingale saying that hate can shadow the goodness inside us. I don't want that to happen to me. I want to help make things better, for wus all.

I take a deep breath, lower my hands and look into Captain Ilya's pain-filled eyes. And I realize that to find a way forwards, just like I had to do for me and Hero, I am going to have to choose love over hate and kindness over anger.

"What happened with your magic and *Joy* was a terrible accident," I say slowly, trying hard to let go of the blame I feel towards him, so that we can reach an understanding. "I agree we need to build a safer future for us all. But there must be another way to stop an accident like that from happening again – a way that doesn't involve dividing us and imprisoning innocent people."

Captain Ilya frowns at me and I notice his fingers are still trembling. I realize he's scared, like Hero. And he's let his fear grow into so much anger and hate that it's spilling out and poisoning all of Morovia.

I don't know how to take his fear away or calm his anger or stop his hate. But I think maybe, like Hero, Captain Ilya needs to feel someone reach out to him with kindness. And if he reaches back, that could be the first step towards change. So I move closer to Captain Ilya and offer him my hand. "We could figure this out, together. We could help each other to learn and heal, and make things right for everyone on Morovia." I hold my breath as I wait for him to respond.

Captain Ilya stares at my hand, his jaw clenched and his frown deepening. I think I understand something of the battle going on inside him. So I try to hold my hand steady and look into his eyes calmly, even though grief for all he has done is still aching inside me. "I am choosing kindness over everything else," I say, to myself as much as Captain Ilya. "But to move forwards from here, you must too. I know it's not easy. But I believe it's worth it, for *everyone* on Morovia to live freely and safely. We can only make that happen if we're willing to listen to each other and work together."

Echo steps beside me, frowning solemnly. Tears well in my eyes because I know Echo's brother, Tern, was on *Joy*. I glance up at Fleur, Silver and Hero, knowing that Captain Ilya caused the deaths of their loved ones too. I would understand if they couldn't offer him kindness now. But Echo reaches out her hand to Captain Ilya, and she's followed by Fleur and Silver, Jay and Kestrel, Osprey and Plover...and finally Hero too. All of our hands reach out to Captain Ilya, and I think of the matted roots in the marsh and how they stopped us from sinking.

"I could help," Echo whispers, stepping so close to Captain Ilya that he's only a hand's-breadth away from her. "I could help you learn to control your magic, if you'll let me."

A tear spills from Captain Ilya's eye. He looks into Echo's kind, round face, and he takes her hand. Relief washes over me as Captain Ilya collapses into Echo's soft, feathered arms and a cheer rises around the quarry.

Hero's gaze drifts around the terraces. She has a sad smile on her face. "People of Morovia..." She speaks loud enough for everyone to hear. "I've let suspicion, lies and fear divide us. Many wrongs have been done; by me, by Captain Ilya and by others here. We're going to have to find a way to face them, make them right where we can, and make sure they don't happen again. I understand today hasn't solved all of our problems, but I hope it's a turning point. And the first step to building unity must be to free everyone here. Then we must find a way to build a better future, together."

At Hero's words, I sigh with relief – a sigh so long it's like the song of the tide when it rushes into the swamp. A breeze swirls, fresh and cool, cutting through the stifling, blazing heat of the sun. The breeze spins around the quarry, kicking up dust. Bogatyrs lay down their staffs and take off their helmets.

"Can you unlock the gate and fetch Nightingale, please?" Hero asks the nearest bogatyr. My heart leaps, and as the bogatyr unlocks and opens the iron gate, my sigh rises into a hum of excitement, like the night-song that rises in the swamp when the sun sets. A raindrop falls onto my cheek, wet and cold.

I look up into the sky and hum louder with satisfaction, and another raindrop hits my face, then another. My hum builds into a song that flows from my heart, and rain begins pouring down. It bounces off the bogatyrs' armour and the chalk ground and the carts full of iron nodules. Everyone's feathers and hair dampen in the rain and stick to their heads, framing their smiling faces. Happiness shivers through me and goosebumps rise on my skin.

Whiskers wriggles excitedly and I lift her out of her sling so she can splash in a brand-new puddle, a wide half-smile on her whiskery face. A courtier brings Lumpy over, and he flops onto Whiskers's head, croaking happily. Then Nightingale appears at the gate and I rush towards him, a smile beaming on my face. He holds out his arms to me and laughs. I collide with him and pull him so close that I hear his heartbeat.

"I love you, Father," I whisper, and he squeezes me tight and tells me that he loves me too. We're together again. The spring rain has finally come. And the landscape of our island is going to change, this time gently and carefully, for the better.

EPILOGUE

The Island of Morovia is shaped like two halves of a heart that fit together to make a whole – like the necklaces that my friend Hero and I wear.

I know now that Hero's real name is Vasha, but I've always called her Hero, and when I asked if I could keep calling her that, she said yes. Our friendship is not the same as it was three years ago though. It's something new, and each day it grows and changes, just like Morovia is growing and changing too.

Hero isn't Crown Heir any more. In fact, there is no human queen and no alkonost queen either. The people of Morovia decided, together, that ruling the island is too much responsibility for any one or two people, and that in fact it's dangerous to have so much power in so few hands. So now Morovia is ruled by a group called the Golden Flock.

Over fifty people – alkonosts and humans in equal measure – are part of the Golden Flock, and they have each sworn, on a seabird feather dipped in gold, to be guided by kindness and fairness above all else. The Flock meets in Pero Palace Complex almost every day to discuss the running of the island and make decisions together. Fleur and Echo are both part of the Golden Flock.

Fleur travels to the meetings from her and Silver's home in Spark. And when Fleur is not in meetings, she still loves working in her apothecary shop. Silver is continuing with his apprenticeship at Circadian, while saving to open his own watchmaker's.

Echo spends most of her time at the palace working with the Flock, but she's also teaching Ilya – who is no longer a captain – how to control his magic. She believes the Island of Morovia must have gifted Ilya his powerful magic for a reason, and that maybe one day he could even use it for good, perhaps to steer the island away from dangers. Echo visits the Magicless Mountains twice a week to give Ilya his lessons, because it's safer for him to practise surrounded by iron-filled rocks, and also because Ilya, along with many of the ex-bogatyrs, have been sentenced to work in The Keep for their wrongs during the last three years. They don't work scraping nodules out of chalk cliffs though – they're dismantling the holding cells, pulling down The Keep's high walls, filling in the quarry and restoring the landscape.

The Golden Flock plans to turn The Keep into a haven for wildlife, with a pool where the giant crabs can live safely, cliffs for birds to nest on, and a grass and wild-flower meadow for butterflies and bees to dance over. When it's ready, Nightingale and I plan to go there and plant some night-blooming jasmine together.

Echo said the last time she visited The Keep, Ilya and the other ex-bogatyrs there had renamed it The Refuge. She smiled as she described how both the landscape and the people were being healed. Many alkonosts and humans have been volunteering to help with the work there, and as they do, the last vestiges of suspicion and fear are dwindling away and are being replaced by respect, appreciation and friendship.

Even Ilya is making alkonost friends. Echo says that he's deeply remorseful for the things he's done and understands how he let his fears twist into hate. But as he's learning how to manage his singing magic, he's also learning how to manage his fears instead of being led by them. He talks about his fears with Echo, and that stops them from growing out of control. And because this has helped Ilya, the Golden Flock have invited everyone on Morovia to talk with them about their doubts, fears and suspicions too, because once they're out in the open – instead of growing inside us like unhatched eggs – we can face them, together, and help them fly away.

Hero has returned to her old home. I asked her if she wanted to live with Nightingale and me, but she preferred to stay in the palace so that she can continue with her studies at her old school, and watch the meetings of the Golden Flock. She wants to be part of the Flock when she's older, so that she can help and protect the people of Morovia. I know Echo keeps a close eye on her, so I don't worry about her too much.

When we first left the quarry, Nightingale and I went back to our old home in Spark. We sat on our balcony, and I heard my mother's songs on the breeze. I'm not sure if Nightingale heard them too, because he pulled his cloak of grief tight against him again.

I walked to where my mother and I sat on the beach on our last day together, and I felt her wings around me. I realized then that I've been carrying my mother's songs and the feel of her all this time. My memories of her weren't in Spark, they were always in me.

After a few days, Nightingale poked his head out of his cloak of grief. But we didn't talk about my mother. We talked about the swamp, and how we missed its sights, sounds and smells; its beauty and its calming rhythms. And we talked about Lumpy and Whiskers, who had followed us to Spark, and how it was clear they weren't happy in the town. Lumpy *phoot*ed at the dry, sandy beach at least twenty times a day and Whiskers grunted angrily every time the tide washed a crab onto the shore.

Nightingale and I packed up some of our most precious things – my mother's songbooks, Nightingale's sunset-red guitar, the clay bowl I made my parents as a midwinter gift, my favourite drawings and some of the treasures from my windowsill – and we wandered down to the hut that Nightingale built on the mudflats at the edge of the swamp. It was still there, along with the rope ladder and swing, the mobiles made of seabird feathers and shells, and all the animals carved from driftwood.

Several alkonosts had moved back into the huts on

the mudflats, including my friends from school, Dunnock and Brambling, and their mother, Robin. We did the same. Whiskers and Lumpy dug burrows behind our hut and were much happier. And Nightingale and I were happier too.

Such a lovely community formed that other people – alkonosts and humans – moved to the mudflats too, in search of new beginnings. Plover, Osprey, Jay and Kestrel built a hut near ours, so we see them every day. And our old downstairs neighbour Lark moved right next to us. I love hearing him talk softly to his pet angelfish late at night.

The Golden Flock organized a wagon service to carry those of us living on the mudflats to Spark every day, so that the children could go to school and the adults could go to work. So most mornings I say goodbye to Whiskers and Lumpy and they play in the swamp while I go to school, and Nightingale goes to his job at the hospital.

After school, I walk to Fleur and Silver's home and chat to them while I wait for Nightingale to finish work, so that we can travel back to the mudflats together. Fleur and Silver come to visit Nightingale and me on the mudflats too, and so do Echo and Hero.

Every Songsday, my friends arrive early in the morning and we spend the whole day together. Silver, Hero and I love to play kickball with Jay, Kestrel and our other friends, and beachcomb for shells, seabird feathers and driftwood to carve things out of. And we often explore the swamp with Whiskers and Lumpy; climbing trees, swimming, making dens, or just sitting and talking for hours.

In the evenings everyone who visits the mudflats and everyone who lives here gathers around a bonfire and we share a meal and sing songs. Our voices join together and drift over the tidal inlet and out to sea, maybe even all the way to Eldovia and Buyan, which seem to float much closer to Morovia these days. Nightingale plays his old, treasured guitar, and both grief and joy fill the air, and a smile spreads over his face that is happy and sad all at once.

Not long after we moved back here, I woke in the middle of the night and found Nightingale staring out to sea with a lost look in his eyes. I told him, for the first time, about Baba and the House with Chicken Legs, and how my mother had left her song in this world so that I could sing her close whenever I needed her. I sang Nightingale the lullaby, and finally, with tears rolling down his cheeks, he talked about his feelings with me. We held each other until the sun rose again, and all the time I could feel my mother by our side.

Since that night, Nightingale and I have spent many evenings sitting together, sharing memories of my mother. We've fallen into the past together, then climbed out together, and it's helped us both. By bringing Halcyon close, it's made us closer, and I no longer feel like Nightingale is drifting far away.

My singing might not be like other alkonosts. I can't call butterflies with my songs or mesmerize people or talk to animals or make flames brighter or make lightning strike the ground. I've been having lessons with Echo again though, just for fun, and last week, after our lesson was cut short by a heavy rain, Echo said that I do have singing magic, but she won't tell me what it is. She says I will figure it out for myself when the time is right.

To be honest though, at the moment singing magic doesn't feel so important. Because the songs we now sing together on Morovia are of family and friendship, of kindness and unity, and that makes them the most powerful songs of all.

Author's Note

Dear Reader,

The Thief who Sang Storms, like all my books, has been inspired by a mixture of Slavic folklore and my personal experiences.

This time, I reimagined the Russian folk poem *Nightingale the Robber*. Nightingale had bird-like features and a powerful, dangerous whistle. He was cast as a villain in the poem, but of course we know the villain of one tale might be the hero of another.

The hero of this story is Linnet, a young girl with feathers. Linnet is sure that if she could just learn her singing magic – the magical gift of her people, the alkonosts – then she would be able to unite her island home.

This theme of unity grew from my perceptions of the world at the time of writing. Sadly, I saw conflict everywhere; people with opposing views, passionately fighting for their causes, each of them convinced they were the hero, not listening to those they had cast as villains. I felt lost and unsure of how I – or anyone – could help move us forwards.

Linnet became everything I wanted to be – hopeful, determined, and completely sure that she will be able to help make her world a kinder, better place for everyone. Despite her own personal struggles and obstacles that seem impossible to overcome, Linnet holds on to her belief that the people of her island can unite.

For three years Linnet's home, the floating island of Morovia, has been torn apart by tragedy, lies and prejudice. The people of Morovia have been literally divided, with the alkonosts like Linnet banished to the swamp on one side of the island, and the humans living separately on the other side. Frustratingly, the power to bring change appears to lie in the hands of those who do not want to listen or act.

So how can Linnet create a new beginning for the people of her island? And how can any of us be brave when storms take hold?

I can't promise this book contains a magic solution to end all conflict and bring people together. But stories do hold power; to spark imaginations, to stimulate new ways of thinking, and to fire discussions where we listen to each other and share our hopes and fears. Only then can we work to close the distance between us.

I hope this story of a young girl with feathers who dreams of unity encourages readers to believe that working together is the way to change our world. That together, we can sing magic.

Sophie A.

Sophie Anderson, March 2022

Acknowledgements

The Thief who Sang Storms hatched, fledged, and flew into the world with the help and support of many people. Heartfelt love and gratitude to:

My husband Nick, our children Nicky Belle, Alec, Sammy, and Eartha, and our collie Star, for endless love and light. And to all our loved ones and friends, with an extra hug for the Birschels, Les and John Cole, Gillian, Lorraine, and Anti Racist Cumbria, for all you do.

My amazing agent Gemma Cooper, and all at The Bent Agency. You keep on making my dreams come true!

My brilliant, wise and kind editors, Rebecca Hill and Becky Walker. Creating stories with you is an absolute joy.

Designers Katharine Millichope and Sarah Cronin, and illustrator Joanna Lisowiec, for making this book so utterly gorgeous.

All at Usborne; Sarah Stewart for the copyedit; Gareth Collinson and Alice Moloney for the proofread; Katarina Jovanovic, Stevie Hopwood, and Hannah Reardon Steward for publicity and marketing; Penelope Mazza for production design; Christian Herisson, Arfana Islam, Boyd Denton, Lesley Preston, Jo Caulkin, and Angela Williams for championing my stories and getting them into so many bookshops; Sylvia Gaitas for production control; Jacob Dow and Jessica Feichtlbauer for managing pre-order packages; and the whole publishing and sales team. I am proud and thankful to be part of your flock.

The many wonderful writers and illustrators who have inspired, educated and lifted me, with an extra golden feather for James Mayhew, Antonio Reche-Martinez, Nadine Aisha Jassat, Kiran Millwood Hargrave, Cerrie Burnell, Yaba Badoe, Galina Varese, Manjeet Mann, Clara Vulliamy and the Trans Cis Collective, Jo Clarke, Abiola Bello, Nicola Davies, Jackie Morris, Darren Chetty, Adam Ferner, Nenna Chuku, and everyone in the Writer's Hour Group.

All the booksellers, book reviewers, librarians and teachers, whose passion and dedication help my books reach readers; Fiona Noble, Charlotte Eyre, Gavin Hetherington, Alison Brumwell, Jake Hope, Zoey Dixon, Steph Elliott, Mathew Tobin, Ed Finch, Tom Griffiths, Kate Heap, all at Waterstones, Will Smith and Sam Read Bookseller, Tamsin Rosewell and Kenilworth Books, A New Chapter Books, and so many more. I am in awe of the work you do, and deeply grateful for each and every one of you.

Above all, thanks to my readers. Together, we sing magic.